TAINTED

The Nadine Swift Story

REGENIA BOWENS

NEWMAN SPRINGS PUBLISHING
320 Broad Street
Red Bank, NJ 07701

First originally published by Newman Springs Publishing 2023

ISBN 979-8-88763-343-5 (Paperback)
ISBN 979-8-88763-344-2 (Digital)

Printed in the United States of America

Red Flags

STARING AT THE picturesque landscape from the balcony of her bedroom, Nadine contemplated nothing but an anxiety-inducing experience. She was not looking forward to this upcoming excursion to—for lack of a better word—a dreaded flea market. Everything was as it should be, she decided, glancing in the full-size mirror in the foyer. She slid designer shades upon her face with a smirk of satisfaction. Having never frequented such a place of her own free will, she had promised a coworker that she would at the very least look, on the promise that there were great finds waiting to be discovered. With a sigh of resignation, she waited until the top of her convertible was in place before pulling out of the curved driveway.

Some may call her house a mansion. But to Nadine, the three-level; 4,500-square-feet; Mediterranean-style house was simply home. The home she felt she deserved. It was perfect. Like everything in her life, it had to be. A quick shake of the head and blinking of her eyes forced memories of her childhood to vanish before they could creep in fully. The image she had created for herself was who Nadine Swift was now, not that depressing childhood that she had no choice but to endure. There were positives from her upbringing that strengthened her as a woman, but those were the only things she chose to hang on to.

With agitation slowly creeping in, Nadine circled the parking lot for a third time.

With a small amount of satisfaction, this would be the perfect excuse to avoid this dreadful endeavor, she thought silently.

Just as she was about to give up, wouldn't you know it—a parking space. With resignation, she pulled into the space with the full intention of walking through swiftly and exiting just as swiftly. After

1

a thorough check of her appearance, a click of the alarm on the fob, and a glance around the parking lot at the numerous inexpensive cars and trucks, Nadine rolled her eyes and began to stroll, barely paying attention to the items the vendors were selling.

"How are you doing today, lovely lady?" came a voice that broke her determined stride.

"I'm fine. Thank you for asking," she replied.

"Looking for anything specific?" the gentleman asked.

Turning, she was met by the friendly dimpled smile of a handsome man. A quick perusal was all it took to conclude that he *definitely* wasn't her type at all. Gold chain with a large enough medallion, earrings in both ears, and a handsome face confirmed this was a ladies' man.

Be cordial, she reminded herself. "No, just looking," she stated dismissively, sliding her shades atop her head as she glanced over the merchandise he had on display.

Her intentional attempt to display distaste wasn't lost on Wesley.

Bougie is what came to mind as he took in the sight of the woman standing before him. With a keen eye for spotting quality, he determined without her noticing, designer everything from head to toe.

"Everything I sell is legit. Brand new," he assured, finally securing her attention.

"Is that a fact?" Nadine questioned, eyeing him with obvious doubt.

"I have a few antiques as well if that interest you," he added with a dialect and accent that was a mixture of both Northern and Southern.

"Old is not my thing," she stated with a quick unfriendly smirk that disappeared just as fast. "That is, unless it holds true fiscal value," she added, looking directly into dark-brown eyes for longer than intended.

Her scrutiny wasn't missed. With smile remaining in place, he allowed her the freedom peruse his face.

Miss High and Mighty checking me out, he thought, before a noticeable, yet slight shake of her head brought her back to reality.

"Honestly, I'm just looking to see if anything catches my eye."

"Beautiful lady! I have handbags and perfumes that are perfect for you!" came the voice of another vender.

Without warning, a counterfeit Dooney and Bourke was forced upon her arm. Not one for being touched without permission, Nadine snatched her arm from the accosting vender.

"What are you doing!" she asked incredulously.

"Check this out, beautiful lady," he stated, attempting to spray a sample of a cologne on her wrist. "You are going to love this."

With a shove stronger than expected from a woman, the irritating man stumbled backward, disturbing a few items in Wesley's display.

"Sir! I do not like to be handled, and I'm allergic to certain fragrances, namely the cheap kind!" she stated through gritted teeth, shoving the fake handbag into his chest as she spoke.

The two stared at each other with mutual disdain. With a mask of contempt, the man slowly gathered himself, never taking his eyes from Nadine. He turned to walk away. Uttering the word *bitch* just loud enough for Nadine to hear. His attempt to bait a response from her was unsuccessful.

A deep sigh helped in regaining her composure. She plastered a broad smile on her face, deciding to allow a glimpse of the type of "bitch" she really was to come out.

"Let's take a look at what you have," she stated to Wesley.

"Are you okay?" he asked with a concerned look upon his face. "Some of these venders can be too pushy trying to get a sale."

"Pushy? I can think of a better word. How about *asshole*?"

The use of profanity was a telltale sign that Nadine's anger was growing.

"I can agree with you on that." He laughed.

Selecting several framed art pieces, vases, an iPad, even an antique train set—what the hell was she going to do with that—she handed over a several hundred dollars to Wesley, never attempting to haggle about the prices.

The vendors on either side silently watched, listening to the exchange.

"I must say, lovely lady, that you have been my best customer this morning. And it's truly appreciated."

"Well, you've assisted me as well," she replied kindly.

"Wesley. Wesley Johnson," he said, extending a hand to introduce himself.

Staring at the extended hand, Nadine hesitated before accepting it with a reply, "Nadine Swift."

The rough palm of a working man's hand gripped hers.

"I'm here every other Saturday with my merchandise. If there's something specific that you need just give me a call, and I'll do my best to locate it for you and give you a fair price."

This must be one of his many approaches to snagging women, she silently thought.

Not wanting to give a wrong impression and refusing to be one of his many conquered women, Nadine simply replied cordially. "That's very kind of you."

She accepted his offer to help load her flea-market finds. The convertible Audi R8 confirmed his earlier assessment of her.

"Definitely bougie," he repeated to himself. He refrained from commenting on her car, knowing that doing so would be a turn off to this woman.

"Thank you so much for your help," she said, repositioning the shades to conceal her eyes.

"Not a problem. Thank you for your business," he said, holding out his business card.

With a quizzical expression, Nadine accepted the card.

"I look forward to hearing from you," he added.

"Yeah," she said after a short pause.

She was relieved that he hadn't started rattling on and on about the car. That had become such a bore to her. Such actions were viewed as red flags that said, "Guess what! I'm not use to nice things." Admire in silence was more her style. She had learned this early in her career by observing during business gatherings and inadvertently listening to the comments of those that considered themselves as the haves of society.

Wesley eyed the attractive woman. She amused him. Her attempts at aloofness made him smile. He knew right away that she was attracted to him. He also knew that she had standards that she felt he didn't fit into. These facts didn't irritate him at all. In fact, her purchases allowed him a few extra hours to chill before getting dressed and heading out for a few beers. Besides, one of his hit-or-miss chicks had been bugging him lately about hooking up.

Yes, Wesley Johnson was a ladies' man. *Why settle for one when you can have many?* was his motto.

Glancing over his shoulder at the exiting Audi, he thought, *She might be worth pursuing.*

*****

Driving along, basking in the satisfaction of her flea market finds, Nadine's mind momentarily reverted to the self-confident vendor, Wesley. Yes, he was attractive in a different kind of way. His style was completely urban when compared to hers.

He was nice, she thought. But then he had to be; she was a customer after all. Unnerved by her thought of this vendor, she turned on Sirius music and began singing along with an R & B oldie as she contemplated the placement of each purchased item.

*****

On the edge of downtown, in a luxurious condo, Andrew Noah struggled with the urge to contact Nadine. The two of them had agreed upon an arrangement that after a year and a half he had grown tired of. Having seen her soon after moving into his condo, he was immediately attracted to her. After numerous attempts, he was able to convince her to go on a couple of dates.

She was a little standoffish, direct, and guarded at first. It had surprised him when she invited him over for drinks. It was then that she presented him with a proposition no man in his right mind would refuse.

"Nice decorating style," he had said upon entering.

"Thank you," she responded from across the room where she poured two glasses of wine.

"Please have a seat," she said, moving to a glass serving cart.

He selected the sofa, which allowed him to admire her from behind. He could tell that she wore thongs.

"I have a proposition for you," she had said, handing him the glass, then sitting in a chair.

"Okay," he had said, noticing her passive expression.

"I'd like for the two of us to enter into an agreement. A private agreement, of course."

"Go on," he had said, eyeing her curiously.

"I would like to propose that the two of us come together, maybe once a month, for the purpose of satisfying our most basic urges," she had said.

He sat silent, staring at her in disbelief for a few moments, wondering why a beautiful woman would feel the need to make such a proposal.

"May I ask why?" he had said cautiously.

"Well," she began, "I'm not dating anyone right now. I'm attracted to you, and I get the impression that you find me attractive as well. I'm not looking to interfere with any relationship that you are already involved in. And naturally, I would require that you use protection."

He stared at her. She sat with her eyes downcast, chewing on her bottom lip, waiting for his response.

"I'm not dating anyone either," he said.

She didn't look at him. "Okay," was all she had said.

"Once a month is not regular enough," he countered. "Every other week works better for me."

"Things may get complicated if we meet that often," she said, now looking at him directly.

"Every two weeks," he repeated.

"So do I call you or how do you think we should do this?" she asked nervously.

"Since neither of us are seeing anyone right now, let's agree that regardless of who calls, we make it happen," he suggested.

"No strings attached?" she asked.

"If you call, I'll come because I know you need me to," he had said.

After a moment of thought, she said, "Okay. I guess I can do that."

"It's Saturday. Want to start right now?" he had asked.

Her eyes widened as she looked at him.

She's scared. He chuckled to himself.

"I think I'm going to need another glass of wine," she said nervously.

"Let's both have another," he had suggested with a smile.

That was almost two years ago. They were both more comfortable with each other, and neither of them were dating anyone else. But now he wanted more. He wanted her heart.

*****

Having mastered the curve of the driveway, she parked in a three-car attached garage. This house was Nadine's second personal real estate investment. She had chosen to leave her previous furniture in her downtown high-rise condo. Coincidentally, it was the same building where Andrew lived. Recently leasing it for double what she'd paid in monthly mortgage payments had been a great business strategy. That place was close to the firm that helped with the long hours of work and lack of social life she had endured. It reflected her personality at that time. Now the desire to spread out and enjoy life had driven her to seek out the edge of the suburbs.

There were neighbors but not on the other side of the walls. She had entered a different phase in her life. It wasn't kids, marriage, and the white picket fence that she was after. It was simply companionship. Not the hang-out-at-the-clubs or bootie-call type of companionship, but rather a committed relationship with good communication, mutual respect, and shared ideas and interests without the fake strings of marriage. She didn't need a man to take care of or rescue her from loneliness. Financially, she was secure. A date with the opposite sex wasn't an issue either. Most importantly, she didn't want anyone prying to discover or judging her for a childhood she had no control over.

The echo of her footsteps could be heard as she walked through the house. She wanted to take her time to decorate each room with care. Because of this, many rooms were unfurnished months after moving in. Displaying her personality was an absolute must in not only her home, but in everything she owned.

After climbing the staircase, she opened double doors that led to the master bedroom, the single completed room. It was spacious with a king-sized four-poster bed in the center of the sleeping area with the view of an eighty-five-inch television mounted over a gas fireplace with sconces on either side. Overhead was a tray ceiling and crown molding. Two dressers and chests were necessary to accommodate her foldable clothes. Abstract artwork adorned the wall above the headboard. She had heated wood flooring installed, rejecting carpet. Her love of plants was evident by the perfectly placed greenery.

An equally spacious adjacent seating area was furnished with a plush sofa and two matching chairs with ottomans. Ceramic lamps sat atop mahogany side tables. Matching glass bookshelves filled with books were separated by a credenza that hid a retractable television and discrete refrigerator. Large floor vases sat upon plush carpet. The area was encased on two sides by a wall of windows that led to a large balcony that provided a complete view of the neighborhood and beyond. This is where Nadine relaxed, planned, dreamed, and cried.

She had risen the corporate ladder against all odds. Hard work, determination, and refusing the easy climb that most beautiful woman chose made success more valuable for Nadine. She was division vice president of her firm. Her ability to make decisions in board meetings was strengthened by her decision to begin purchasing small amounts of stock in her company as soon as she was hired. At that time, the endeavor caused her to live paycheck to paycheck. Now she was the current holder of two-thirds of the company's stock.

She knew the lyrics of her life well. She had made the executive decisions. Now she was going to enjoy the results. Removing a bottle of wine from the discrete fridge and pouring herself a glass, Nadine sat back and basked in the thought of having nothing to do before clicking on the television to watch a Western flick. Nadine was a loner. She socialized but was perfectly comfortable with entertaining herself.

*****

Across town, in his two-bedroom apartment, Wesley took another sip of his beer before continuing his stroll through social media. Like most people, he didn't view himself as being addicted to the electronic platform. To him, he was merely looking at the antics of the populace and searching for items he could resell. He viewed himself as a loner, intentionally private. He knew lots of people but only socialized with a few. Like Nadine, image was everything to Wesley.

Sitting, Wesley pressed the Call button of a saved number in his phone. Reclining, he waited for the answer he knew would come.

"Hello," a female voice said, answering the phone.

"What's going on, lovely lady?" Wesley asked.

"Hey, Wess," the woman responded.

"What are you up to this evening?" he asked.

"I'm about to hop in the shower. You want to come over and help?" she asked.

"I just might do that," he responded. "What do you have on?"

"When you get here, the answer will be nothing," she said.

"That's not the answer I want to hear," he said.

"Tell me what's the correct answer," she encouraged.

"Can you make it happen?" he asked.

"I always do," she said. "What's the answer?"

"Meet me at the door, with nothing," he instructed.

"Consider it done," she said.

"I'm on my way," responded Wesley, ending the call with a smile.

His apartment, although small, was uniquely decorated in the hues of brown, dark mahogany, burgundy, and green. Female clean and manly comfortable would be a perfect description. The finishing touch and his pride and joy was the too-large-for-the-space television. Sliding glass doors could have allowed natural light into the space, but the chatter of the neighborhood children on his patio often prevented this. A-louder-than-necessary television volume was often Wesley's go-to when he desired to drown out the noise from outside or next door. It was a more-than-adequate bachelor's pad that was equipped with all the latest technological gadgets.

Having visited his Saturday friend earlier, he felt sated now. He savored in recollecting the afternoon. He enjoyed hearing his name repeated in moments of passion and the woman's willingness to please without inhibition. He had no problem leaving her a small financial stipend, which she eagerly accepted. Besides, he enjoyed that fact that she ensured her availability whenever he called.

I'm moving when my lease is up, he thought as he increased the volume of the television three more clicks. *I need a place where I can really relax when I'm home.*

The chime of a text message on his cell phone interrupted his thoughts.

"What time are you picking me up?" stated the message.

"Did we have plans to go someplace?"

"You said you were coming over," came the reply.

"I might stop by a little later."

"I don't want you to just stop by," the message stated. "You always stop by until the next time you stop by! I want to go out to dinner."

After a sigh, he replied to the message with, "Let me take a shower, and I'll be over."

Turning off the television, Wesley sullenly walked to the bedroom. He didn't want to ruin things with this female because he liked her. He liked all the females he talked to, texted with, took out, and slept with. But he wasn't interested in marrying any of them. Well, maybe that one who owned her own business. He hadn't given it much thought, but it seemed as if she had it going on.

"Oh yeah," he reminded himself. "She's a church girl too."

Besides, she really liked him. She got pointers for that. He chuckled to himself as he matched his outfit with the perfect shoes when again he reminded himself that they all really liked him.

None of the women knew about the other women. Each saw Wesley as their potential or exclusive partner. It was a game Wesley had mastered, although he didn't view it as such. Never take them to the same places, never frequent a place where they would come without him, always keep your phone on vibrate, lie whenever necessary, and, above all, deflect the blame when caught. Then when all else fails, remove yourself entirely from the situation. He saw himself as a man first and foremost.

As a man, he had to look out for himself. His upbringing had taught him that. A man makes his own way in every area of life. Financially, Wesley could hold his own. He had a marketable trade for a day job and an equally profitable side job as a flea-market vendor.

As for his personal life, he had tried the committed relationship thing more than once in the past. Those hadn't worked out in his favor. Not that he was a hundred percent committed or faithful either time. If asked, could he have done better? He readily admitted that he played a part in the demise of both relationships. Regardless, the answer to the question of what lesson he learned still evaded him. It happened, and he had moved on.

Clicking on the radio, a resolute sigh briefly swept over Wesley. For the first time in a long time, the thought of marriage crossed Wesley's mind.

Was this woman he was about to wine and dine really the right one for him? he pondered.

He had a good, successful life. He was single, but by choice. He imagined in moments of melancholia how his life may be different if only one of the relationships in his past had been successful. Not just successful but happy and successful.

Forcing these thoughts into the recesses of his mind, he pulled into the parking space of the apartment complex, took a deep breath, and began the short stroll to the door with flowers in hand.

An attractive woman, Denice, greeted him with a smile and a brief hug.

"You brought flowers," she said, eyeing the bouquet of daisies.

"I thought you might like these," he said with a smile.

"The flowers are nice. Thank you so much," she said sweetly, then absently placed them on the kitchen counter. "Let me just grab my purse, and we can go." She disappeared into the bedroom.

During dinner, Wesley listened to Denice's stories about work that week; how much money she wanted to make; the coworkers and neighbors in the apartment complex that were jealous of her car, her great body, and her beauty. Realizing that she had been doing all the talking with Wesley barely speaking a word, she paused.

"How did you do at the flea market today?" she asked after an uncomfortable silence.

"It was very good," he said proudly. "I left a little early." He left out the part about helping a friend take a shower.

"Really!" she exclaimed. "We can go shopping tomorrow since you made so much money!"

"Not tomorrow. I'm relaxing and watching the game," he said.

"The game won't be on until the afternoon. We can go shopping before it comes on," she snapped.

"Here's the check whenever you're ready," said the waitress, then turned to leave.

"Let me ask you a question," Wesley said seriously. "Where do you see yourself in five years?"

"Five years? Who knows? I'm living for today," Denice replied, staring at him in disbelief.

"That's your answer?" he asked, surprised.

"Yes! That's my answer! And by the way, I need some money to pay my cell phone bill."

"We've been on what, three dates, and after each date, you always need money for something."

"What do you expect? You think I'm free? You have to pay to be with me!" she said, drawing the attention of other patrons.

"Let's go," he said, settling the bill and tip.

"There's a new movie I wanted to see playing at the theater," she said once inside the car.

Without responding, Wesley drove without stopping until he reached the parking space in front of her apartment.

"Are you coming in?" she asked expectantly.

"No," he responded. "Have a good night."

With a huff, she exited the car, slamming the door as she stated, "Cheap asshole."

Quickly opening his door, Wesley confronted the woman as she reached the sidewalk. Without speaking, he stood toe to toe, staring into her eyes.

"Why aren't you coming in?" she questioned sadly.

"Should I?" he asked.

"You always come in. Why aren't you coming in now?" she continued.

"Why should I come in when you are acting like this?" he said with indifference.

"You know I didn't mean anything, Wess," she said, softly caressing his lapel,

"I'm upset right now," he lied.

"If you come in, I can make you forget," she purred.

"How are you going to do that?" he asked, knowing the answer.

"Let me show you," she said, leading him to the apartment.

Her comment hadn't bothered him at all. What he was feeling was relief. His earlier question of whether she was the one had been answered. It's not that he couldn't afford to give the money she constantly asked for. It was the fact that she never gave him the opportunity to give on his own. First, it was to get her nails done. Then it was her car note. Now she wanted him to pay her cell phone bill. Her hand was out with expectation as soon as she laid eyes on him, and her lack of appreciation for the small thoughtful things bothered him.

When he left her apartment, she was sleeping deeply, having tired herself out trying to make him feel better. He flung a few dollars on the dresser once dressed.

She earned it, he thought.

Later, settling back in his recliner, Wesley's mind returned to Ms. Nadine Swift. She was attractive, obviously educated, and financially stable. Her choice of automobile and her style demonstrated that she prefers the finer things. But what is she like on the inside and out of the public's scrutinizing eye? he wondered. He wondered if she could cook. It wasn't that he couldn't cook. But it would be nice to have a hot meal ready for him after a long day at work.

She probably orders takeout, he thought with a chuckle.

*****

Across town, Nadine dried her hands on a dish towel after loading the dishwasher. She glanced around her kitchen, making sure everything was in its proper place. She loved to cook and was very proud to have a large open kitchen to slice and dice in. The cooking channel had become a favorite pastime as she eagerly hoped to discover new dishes to try. Since she was cooking for one, it had become an unintentional habit to praise herself with the phrase, "Oh my goodness, Nadine! This is great!"

She headed toward the master bath for a quick shower before bed. She would love to have someone to share her love of cooking with but had long ago decided not to pine over what's not present. Rather, she chose to make the executive decision to praise herself for accomplishments. This approach allowed Nadine to truly enjoy her life with the absence of a significant other.

She snuggled into her down pillow and allowed the sound of the ocean on black screen to quickly lull her to sleep. It wasn't her alarm clock that woke her. It was her body's reaction to an extremely sexual dream with her ex, Antonio. She didn't hate having these dreams. She hated having them about Antonio.

After a sip from the bottled water on her nightstand, she lay there for a moment thinking of Andrew and the way he made her feel. She forced her mind and body not to linger on the thought. Fearing to do so would only complicate things. Soon she fell back to sleep.

Green Light

THE CLICK OF Nadine's stilettos on the marbled office floor drew the attention of every man and woman as she exited the elevator. She strode toward her office briefly, glancing left and right to give good-morning greetings. The corporate world had taught her to focus on the job and ignore the envy and the flirts. The initial gossip that she'd slept her way to a promotion had dissipated as soon as her attendance at the stockholders' meeting became office news.

It wasn't the coveted corner office that Nadine had been after when hired. It was ownership, business power, and the day when she could sell her stock or live the lifestyle she had created off a continuous flow of dividends. A wise male professor had long ago advised her to not only dress for the position she wanted but to take the necessary steps to make her desire a reality.

She began her career with the purchase of two shares of stock. After years of long office hours; personal sacrifice of her time, money, and social life; and coworker comments of her hating men and preferring women, she was finally offered the position of vice president of stockholder relations. She was the first female to compete with a male for a position in her company and get selected by virtue of the quality of her work. She was very proud because she knew that she had earned it. Now she strictly worked nine to five and not nine to whenever.

*****

Halfway across town, while Nadine continued to sleep, Wesley was beginning his day. As a senior project manager, he arrived at the jobsite an hour before his team. He prided himself on daily briefing himself on project's scope, schedule, and structure. His work ethic preceded him and was the primary reason his employer often assigned him as the overseer of their most lucrative projects. On several occasions, he had been assigned to reestablish controls including redefining baselines and overseeing and providing updated status reports.

With years of experience in construction, Wesley was very good at his job. He had a dedicated enthusiastic crew that had great respect for him. His leadership style wasn't to simply tell what he wanted. Wesley provided on-the-spot problem-solving and often demonstrated his expectations. It was his years of experience that had prevented him from reaching the pinnacle of director of project management with his company that he sought. Apparently, he was viewed as benefitting the company best being in the field rather than in an office.

"Hey, guys! You did a great job today as always," Wesley called out with a wave as he walked to his SUV.

"See you tomorrow, boss," the men replied.

Instead of taking the highway home, Wesley headed toward the suburbs. He wanted to review the jobsite of the next project he was scheduled to oversee within a few weeks. He was surprised that he was being assigned a residential project. He preferred commercial projects but was more than capable of managing this venture. Although he hadn't been provided the plans, he knew the location and the fact that this site was slated to be an upscale community clubhouse.

Turning into the community, he stopped a short distance away beside a five-acre partially grassy clearing. Scanning the area, he saw that the manicured lawns, tree-lined sidewalks, and an abundance of yellow tulips created an inviting entrance. Glancing at the community's name, Dolce Vita, he decided, a life of pleasure and luxury, probably accurately describing those that lived in the large two-story homes.

"Is there something I can do for you, sir?" asked an elderly gentleman driving a Mercedes. "Do you need directions?" he continued drawing Wesley's attention.

"No," Wesley responded with a smile. "I'm right where I need to be," he said, returning his gaze to the clearing.

The elderly man exited his car, looking perplexed and unsure of what to say next. The man waited for an explanation in silence.

Purposely ignoring the man, Wesley began walking back to his vehicle.

"I'm the man that will be overseeing the building of the community center," he said as he passed, having grown irritated by the man's continued presence.

"Oh! We have neighborhood watch in this community. That's the reason I asked," the man responded nervously.

"Nice," Wesley replied as he kept walking.

An approaching car prevented him from getting into his SUV and away from the nosy man. As he waited for the car to pass, he realized there was something familiar about the car. It was an Audi R8.

Can't be, he thought. He focused his vision on the driver.

It was.

Is this where little Ms. Nadine Swift lived? he wondered.

*****

It had been a great start to the work week for Nadine. No major business fires to put out. By corporate standards, it had been an easy day. Sign here. Return that call. Make a call. Check calendar. Review reports. Prepare reports. Approve this. Deny that. Yes, she had a secretary, but Nadine was not one to leave keeping up with her schedule completely to someone else. Saying that the secretary forgot to send a reminder was not an acceptable excuse by any standards.

With a sigh of contentment, Nadine turned into her subdivision.

Home, she thought.

There was an SUV and a Mercedes parked along the curb near the "coming soon" community center clearing. Slowing her approach, she noticed nosy Mr. Jameson. She felt sorry for the driver of the SUV. Old Mr. Jameson had declared himself as neighborhood watch. He walked and drove the community looking for someone he could question.

She had refused to endure his nosiness when she moved in. Informing him that she had purchased the house was all the information she chose to provide. When he continued questioning, not allowing time for an answer, she stopped his questioning and not politely.

"Look, sir, Mr. Jameson. I just bought this house. My name is Nadine Swift. You don't need to know anything else about me. I don't want to know anything about you. If you are a part of the neighborhood watch, fine. Now kindly watch from the street," she had said without taking a breath and turning to ignore his presence.

Focusing on the oddly familiar man waiting to enter the SUV, she slowed her car. Their eyes locked. A slow dimpled smile softened his features. He stepped directly in front of the car, forcing her to stop. His smile widened as he approached her window.

"Hello, lovely lady," he said after the window lowered. The scent of her perfume tantalized his senses.

It was impossible for her not to smile in return.

He wondered what it would be like to plant kisses upon her scented neck.

"Wesley Johnson," she responded, saying his name slowly with an equally wide smile. "What are you doing here?" she asked.

"I'll be working on the community center in a few weeks," he answered, allowing his eyes to glide over her face.

She was thoroughly made up for the corporate world, he noticed. Not a single stray hair. Just the right amount of makeup. Small diamond drop earrings hung from her ears. An unusual diamond infinite necklace encased her neck. The semisheer white blouse with white camisole underneath had been covered by the blazer that hung from the passenger seat. He visualized enveloping her in his arms.

"Really?" she said with raised brows, unsure of his thoughts at that moment.

"Yes," he replied with a chuckle. "Did you think I made my living as a flea-market vendor?"

"I…hadn't given it…," she stammered, realizing the statement would sound rude. "So what do you do for a living?" she finally asked, continuing to smile to hide her embarrassment.

"I work in construction. I'm a project manager," he replied, smiling at her obvious unease.

Most women he met were impressed when he disclosed his job title. Others were completely ignorant and asked him to explain. He knew Nadine was impressed but for a different reason. He was aware that her initial impression of him was extremely low. A no-money street hustler was what she had seen.

"Project manager," she repeated, nodding her head, assessing his attire.

Wesley smiled and remained silent, allowing her the freedom to inspect him. His company's logo was embroidered on his shirt. "Terner Construction," it read.

"Well, that's interesting," she added.

"If you say so, lovely lady," he said, holding her gaze.

"I should be going," she said softly.

"Are you visiting, or do you live in this community?" he asked, already knowing the answer.

"I live here," she confirmed, eyeing him curiously.

"Since that's the case, I'm sure I'll be seeing you, Ms. Nadine Swift," he commented, softening his voice when he said her name.

He saw her eyes dilate. She liked the way he said her name but tried to hide it. He could tell she was the caution type.

I'll have to take my time with her, he thought, gazing at her with sultry eyes.

"Yeah," was all she said before driving away.

He sat and watched her drive away. Their eyes met when she looked in her rear-view mirror.

His presence and the fact that she was attracted to someone she considered below her standard unnerved her.

Wesley liked challenges, and Nadine was going to be a challenge. She was going to be the challenge he enjoyed conquering.

"That's Ms. Nadine Swift," said Mr. Jameson.

The elderly gentleman had walked up to Wesley's SUV without him realizing.

"What?" he asked.

"That's my neighbor, Ms. Nadine Swift," the man repeated, leaning into the window.

"Yeah. Right," responded Wesley as he pressed the Start button.

"She moved in a few months ago. Businesswoman is what she is. Got no husband. No kids either," Jameson rattled on but was cut off before he could continue.

"Neighborhood watch, huh?" Wesley stated, staring at the old man. He began rolling up his window, forcing the old man to remove his arm before the old joker told Nadine's shoe size and bank account numbers. He wanted to discover her not be told who she was. That would ruin everything.

*****

Nadine glanced toward the entrance of the subdivision. She was relieved that Wesley hadn't followed her. She liked him but hated to feel as if she was being pressured. Gathering her purse, briefcase, and jacket, she was about to close the arched iron and glass door when she caught a glimpse of Mr. Jameson as he drove slowly past her driveway, peering at her house. With a roll of her eyes, she closed the door and typed in the security code to turn off the pending alarm.

Walking across the foyer, she placed her briefcase on the floor next to the fireplace in what would become her home office once furnished. She made her way to the bedroom, deciding to change her nightly routine by taking a shower before dinner rather than before bed. Then she'd relax in the hot tub with a glass of wine. The perfect way to end the day, she decided.

Reaching into the glass-encased shower stall, she started the water and checked the temperature. She began to remove the hairpins from the French bun and dropping them in a small container with a click. Stripping off her clothes and stepping into the shower, the warm spray began to relax her body. It also revived thoughts of the dual persona of Mr. Wesley Johnson. Professionally, he appeared unassuming. Personally, his flirty urban style was undeniable.

Interesting, she thought before squeezing shower gel onto a loofah. *Very. Interesting.*

She would never have imagined him being employed with Terner Construction. The company had over a billion dollars in revenue with over thirty office locations. She was impressed. She had participated in the final planning for the community center. Residents had been invited to provide feedback on the project and vote on one of three potential candidates. She had voted for Terner based on their reputation and recognition for creating complex, innovative projects.

"But why weekend flea-market vending?" she asked, pausing as she wrapped herself in a towel.

Later dressed in a bathing suit and sheer cover-up, Nadine spread fresh garlic butter onto a couple of slices of Italian bread as she listened to the interview of a politician on television. She critiqued the man's answers and decided he was an immoral liar. After placing the pan in the oven, she began to sauté thinly sliced chicken breast in crushed garlic for a salad. She was placing the last of the chicken atop the salad when the oven timer went off.

Perfect timing, she thought with a smile, turning off the kitchen television.

She ate her meal in the sunroom as she continued watching the newscast from a television mounted over a fireplace. It wasn't that she was a political fanatic, but she knew that political knowledge provided power. The power to possibly prepare and avert the negative personal impact of decisions made by political imbeciles. For Nadine, it was very important to be aware of what decisions those with decision-making power had made or were planning to make.

*****

Reviewing the community center jobsite had extended Wesley's commute home. A stop at Pat's Parlor for home-cooked takeout was a delay he wasn't going to grumble about. One slice of her sweet potato pie always sweetened his mood. According to him, she also made the best raspberry lemonade in the city. With two orders in hand, he finally headed home.

Wesley finished what he could of one takeout order. The leftovers would be his lunch the following day. The second order went in the refrigerator to be an already prepared dinner. Changing the television station directly to the sports channel, he took a sip of his beer and reclined in his La-Z-Boy. Taking a shower was the last thing on his agenda now. He'd do that right before bed. It would help him fall asleep. Not that he had any difficulty in that area. He had planned to catch up on the latest Dallas Cowboy's news. That endeavor would be left to social media since he was asleep within a few minutes.

A few hours later he woke to find a barrage of text messages on his cell. Heading toward his bedroom to shower, he decided to read the messages afterward.

Later, stretching his tense muscles before propping up on a pillow, he began to read the numerous messages. A meet-the-family picnic, a couple of offers to cook dinner, and several sleepover invitations were among the positive messages from females. The negatives included profanity-laced gossip about him being a user and womanizer.

"What does it mean when a man tells you that he has a lot of female friends?" he questioned aloud with a shake of his head. *Every red-blooded woman should realize that, that statement means whatever is being done with her is also being done with several other women*, he thought without remorse.

He responded to the positive messages. The negative ones he ignored, deleted, and blocked the messenger. The messages from his sister, mother, aunts, and potential customers were all viewed as priority. Quick callbacks that he was doing fine and had eaten was enough to ease family concerns. Customers received counterbids, pickup, or additional product information.

An hour later Wesley fell asleep thinking, *Tomorrow I'll call my Tuesday Suzy*.

After that, he could only be aroused by the sound of his 5:00 a.m. alarm.

*****

Taking a late lunch break the following day, Nadine walked the short distance to the luxury furnishings showroom. With no afternoon meetings, she could take a little extra time. Besides, her business phone made it possible for her secretary to reach her if necessary. The woman had quickly learned, when selected to assist Ms. Nadine Swift, to text her immediately and to call whenever the task wasn't typed, filed, or made an appointment.

"Welcome to High Fashion Furnishing!" a young female sale representative said as Nadine entered the showroom. "Is there something I can help you with today?" the woman asked with a smile after scanning Nadine from head to toe.

"Yes, there is," Nadine answered as her eyes searched the store for the appropriate sections.

"I'll be purchasing some items, and I'd like to have them delivered and assembled, if necessary," she said as she began to wander.

After walking the showroom twice with the saleswoman trailing behind taking notes, Nadine selected two eighty-eight-inch Larkin leather sofas for her oversized living room and a square Roscoe coffee table. Searching for a focal piece to go above the fireplace, her stroll was halted as the art piece she'd purchased from Wesley hung on display. Eyeing the price difference, she was unable to visibly identify any deviations to determine if his was original or a replica. Solution found. She'd hang the Glam Up art pieces she'd already purchased. Each piece was priced at a thousand dollars. He had charged only a few hundred dollars for the art.

The man has a possible eye for style, she thought with a smile.

With the living room started, she returned to the office furnishing section of the store. With her home office so close to the front door, the emptiness of the room was starting to annoy her. She selected a Curata metal leg desk and a Nobletex platinum bench with two arm bolsters. After checking the time, she chose a tall faux fig tree in a zinc planter.

Nadine sat with crossed legs, checking her messages while the woman calculated the sales total. There were no updates from Cassandra, her secretary, which meant an easy afternoon. There were three messages from Drew, her male acquaintance inquiring about her plans for the evening and requesting a callback. She knew what he wanted. For the last year or so, the two had a no-strings-or-expectation relationship.

"You've made some excellent selections today," the young woman commented with a smile as she mentally calculated her commission.

"Would you be interested in our in-store financing?" she asked.

Without responding or looking up from her phone, Nadine placed a gold American Express Card on the desk and proceeded to respond to a text message.

"My place. Eight thirty," she wrote, not bothering to check for a reply. She knew Drew would be there.

"When is a good delivery date for you, ma'am?" the woman asked happily as soon as the receipt began to slip from the machine, signaling approval and requiring Nadine's signature.

"The end of this week," was her reply, looking directly into the woman's eyes.

"I'll have to check with my manager to confirm that," she said nervously, knowing that two weeks was the usual turnaround time.

"I'm sure that won't be a problem," Nadine said confidently. "I've done business with William before. He'll make it happen."

William, the store manager, walked up seconds later. His appearance was always very austere.

"Ms. Swift, so nice to see you again," he said happily.

"You as well," she responded with a smile.

"I'd like my delivery no later than the end of the week, William." She turned to look directly at him. "Is that possible?" she asked, pausing before signing the credit card receipt.

"Your delivery will be there without fail, Ms. Swift," he stammered, noticing the yet blank signature line and the gold card on the desk.

"Perfect." She smiled, finalizing her purchase with her now coveted autograph, then retrieving her credit card.

"Now that's what I call a nice commission," the saleswoman whispered, watching Nadine exit.

"It always will be when she leaves the store. Take the rest of the day off, Kris. You've earned it," William said before turning to walk away.

Kris, which was a shortened version of Kristie, rushed off to grab her purse before he changed his mind. The commission that she'd make off the sale would make it possible for her to get her own apartment. No more sleeping on her sister's sofa. It wasn't that her sister treated her badly or gave the impression of being tired of her; she was just tired of the situation. Her sister was a single parent to two boys, and she was taking night classes. The two didn't go well together when she needed to study. In her mind, this was the start of the financial break that she needed.

*****

Wesley stood reviewing a spreadsheet with the job foreman, Miguel, when an approaching car distracted him. Recognizing the car, he knew it was Dan, his supervisor. After giving the foreman instructions on adjustments of specific angles, he walked toward Dan, the director of eastern operations.

"What brings you to the site?" he said, shaking the man's free hand.

The other was occupied with a manila folder and project binder.

"I believe I can find a hammer and tool belt for you," he joked.

"I'm here to have a talk with you, Wess," Dan replied.

"It must be pretty important for you to pay me a personal visit and not Skype me," Wesley said curiously.

"We had a meeting with Parker & Polanski and have decided to move the start date of the Dolce Vita community center project up," he said, waiting for Wesley's rebuttal. He knew that leaving a job two weeks before his scheduled departure wasn't Wesley Johnson's style. Finishing what he had started was the man's method of operation. This was a quality Terner liked and had come to rely on. This was also the reason Wesley was sent from one job to another and used to clean up what other managers messed up.

"A lot can be accomplished in two weeks," Wesley said after pondering the idea.

"That was our exact train of thought," Dan said with a smile. "That's why we decided to move the start date up in the first place."

"We can get a lot accomplished on this site as well in two weeks," Wesley said seriously.

"That's true," said Dan with his smile slowly fading.

"The fact is, after reviewing the updates that you've been providing weekly, we're confident that you can begin that project on Monday and provide support on this site for the next couple of weeks, especially since they are not that far apart," he reasoned. "Besides, this one is ahead of schedule."

"Twice the work but not twice the pay," Wesley said, looking Dan directly in the eye.

"I know that director's position is your goal, Wesley," said Dan with a sigh. "It's timing. Right now we have several projects slated to begin. And honestly, the company needs you out here where you are at your best. You simply must understand our position."

Wesley understood. He understood that he was being used to make the company richer while his salary remained the same. He also knew that if Dan was paying him a personal visit, it wasn't a say-no situation.

"Listen, we are prepared to adjust your contract. Effective immediately!" he said joyously, waiting for a reaction from Wesley, which didn't come.

How generous of you, Wesley thought.

"It's a 5 percent salary increase, a company car, and credit card for expenses," Dan said to break the silence.

"I'll need a business phone so I can stay in contact with both sites," he said finally.

"Done!" said Dan, pulling a pen from his jacket pocket. "I have the contract right here for you to sign. You'll see the increase in your salary this week. I also brought the plans for Dolce Vita since you'll be starting there next week."

He watched Wesley sign the revised employment offer.

"You'll be getting paid before starting the job," Dan said as if Wesley was profiting from the deal as much as the company.

"What about my crew?" Wesley asked.

"Whatever you need," Dan said with a smile.

"I want this crew. I'll start with a skeleton and work these guys in as this job nears to completion," he said.

"With that area...," Dan stammered. "I would think a more experienced crew would be best."

"These guys are experienced, dependable, and they get the job done" Wesley countered. "I want this crew."

"Well, we definitely want the job done," Dan said after a brief pause. "This crew it is."

After handing the project binder to Wesley and shaking his hand, Dan turned to leave.

"What's up now, boss?" asked Miguel, the foreman. "Good news or bad news?"

"Both," said Wesley as the two men stared at the departing car. "The good news is we'll all be moving to the Dolce Vita project. That also means you get to sleep in your own bed at night. The bad news is that it's starting two weeks early, and I'm managing both sites."

"What about this project?" asked Miguel.

"You'll be the lead person on-site here, and we phase the whole crew in as we go," answered Wesley.

"We get to work on the Dolce Vita project?" asked Miguel with a surprise. "I would have expected them to pick a completely different crew based on that area alone."

"They tried. I guess they think a minority crew in the land of heedless pleasure and luxury will distort the area some way. He relented in the end," said Wesley.

"Yeah. Beautify their area just don't think of becoming a member of their community," said Miguel with disgust.

"We're a corporate crew anyways. This will be a walk in the park for us," said Wesley, unsuccessfully attempting to lighten the man's mood.

He knew Miguel was right. Prejudices came with many faces and from every race and workplace. There was no avoiding or beating it. First, you understand your worth and simply endure and be strengthened but not manipulated.

With a sigh, Wesley returned to his temporary office. He was compelled to stand up for his crew. They weren't just good workers;

they were good men with families to support. They trusted him and had grown to rely on him to select them as his crew.

Dan was right about the current project being completed ahead of schedule. He and his crew had agreed to daily project completion goals. The reward was the possibility of a week off for them all before the start of the Dolce Vita development. Thanks to the decisions of those in offices, that was no longer an option. He was thankful that at least he'd have a dependable crew.

*****

Nadine spent the afternoon reviewing quarterly accounting records and working on a profits/loss presentation for a meeting the next week. It was vital that her reports be unquestionable since she was also a shareholder. It wasn't unusual for an executive to own shares in the company, but she intended to avoid any possible accusation of lacking fiscal responsibility, violating the company's constitution, or in any way not promoting the success of the company. To do so would be self-sabotaging considering the amount of stock in this company that she owned.

She had been very careful not to invest directly in a competitor as it could be viewed as a conflict of interest. Her investment portfolio was quite diversified. Her dividends were untouched and deposited into what she referred to as her retirement account. The addition of some commercial real estate was something she was contemplating for the near future. Glancing at her watch, she realized it was five thirty. The quiet of the office said everyone had gone home except the few that were trying to meet deadlines.

She had dismissively waved good night to her secretary half an hour earlier. Saving her work on both her laptop and a flash drive, she logged offline and headed to the parking garage. She drove home, deciding a dinner of eggplant parmesan with sweet Italian sausage would be perfect. Then she'd take a shower and wait for Drew's biweekly arrival.

*****

With resignation, Wesley reclined, took a swallow of his beer, and began reviewing the construction contract documents. This project's schedule was a lot longer than he imagined. The plans called for a building that housed a heated indoor pool, exercise room, small banquet room, an executive-style meeting room, and a kitchen. That was the first floor. The second floor called for three office spaces, a library with a balcony overlooking an outdoor putting area, playground, tennis court, and pool.

"This is a commercial style project in a residential area," Wesley said aloud, taking another swallow of his beer. He was thankful that he'd have his crew with him.

He remembered a site he was sent to get the project's timeline back on track. There, Dan had arranged the crew. Wesley had to deal with constant absences and insubordination. He resorted to firing and rehiring almost an entire crew.

He and the new crew had worked hours of overtime to get the project back on schedule and meet the deadline. It was then that he met the men he now referred to as his crew. That was three years ago. Setting the project plans aside, Wesley went into the kitchen to microwave his meal.

As he ate, he wondered how often he'd get to see Nadine while at the site. Maybe not daily but he hoped for a couple of times a week. His goal was to wear down her defenses slowly. She intrigued him. She was different from other women he'd dated.

*****

"Hi love," greeted Drew when Nadine opened the door.

"Hi," she responded, stepping back.

Handing her a small bouquet of flowers and a bottle wine, his hands were now free to properly greet her with a firm hug. He loved the scent of her perfume and the softness of her skin. More than that, he loved her soft passionate moans. There were a lot of things he loved about Nadine but refused to disclose. To do so would violate their agreement and possibly end their relationship as it was.

Although her hands were now the ones filled, she returned the greeting, displaying mutual acceptance of what would later take place. Their meetings, though sporadic, were more than hit and depart. They involved friendly banter and sometimes serious discussions over a bottle, sometimes two, of wine. It all depended on their moods. The one consistency was, if either of them sent a request, the other obliged. When he first attempted to make the meetings weekly, upon his arrival, Nadine forced a review of the original agreement. He was however able to increase them by requesting a "need to see you." For now, he was satisfied with that.

Interference

AS NADINE DROVE past the site for the community center on her way to work, her exit from the subdivision was hampered by a large truck setting up a portable building. She assumed it would be used as a temporary office space for the construction crew. They were starting early. Two weeks early to be exact. She was fascinated to watch the progress of the project. A couple of the men stopped what they were doing to stare at her car as she drove by. Ignoring the stares, she continued her commute.

*****

After checking with Miguel, who assured him that everything would run smoothly for a couple of hours without him, Wesley decided to visit the other jobsite. With only two and a half days to prepare for next week's start up, he wanted to make sure everything would be a go. Presenting a costly change order was something he tried hard to avoid. If one was submitted on one of Wesley's sites, most likely, it was the client making that request.

The portable office was in place, and the final steps to connecting the electricity was taking place when Wesley arrived on-site. A stay-at-home mom stood on her patio ensuring that the property line was not breached as the plastic construction barrier was erected. Backhoes, mini excavators, and forklifts were staged at the back perimeter of the site. A huge construction waste receptacle was being improperly placed at the front of the site.

With a loud whistle, Wesley got the driver's attention before he could complete his task and drive off.

"I'm going to need you to move that to the other side of the portable building," he directed a young driver whose music blared from his cell phone.

"Move it?" the young man asked in disbelief, taking a Black & Mild cigar from his mouth.

"Yes. Move it," Wesley repeated.

"I only take orders from the foreman or project manager," the man said with a look of condescension, taking a pull of his cigar.

"Then I guess you'll be moving it since you're talking to the project manager," Wesley said with a smile.

Realizing who he was speaking to, the young man hurriedly turned off the music.

"Sorry, sir," he said, fumbling with his cigar, unsure if he should hold on to it or dispose of it out the window. "As you can see, I have two more receptacles to deliver. I was just trying to make sure each site had what they needed," he stated nervously.

"Is that so?" asked Wesley. "Well, if you check your paperwork, you'll see that this site is slated for two."

Grabbing his clipboard, the man nervously apologized for the blunder.

"Put them both on the other side of the utility pole beside the portable building," said Wesley, turning to walk away.

After checking to make sure the electricity inside the office worked, Wesley went outside just as the temporary fencing was being installed for safety reasons. With the chain securely locked, he headed back to town for lunch and to see if any issues had arisen during his absence. He was confident in Miguel's ability to lead, but he knew that he would be blamed for any mishaps.

Before pressing the Start button for the ignition, the vibration of his phone stopped him. Taking a glance at his phone, a smile crept upon his face. It was hump day; and this female, Wanda, had no problem putting a hump in her back for him anytime, anyplace, anywhere, and any way he said.

"I'll be over right after work. I'll be needing some fuel," he wrote with a smile before driving off. *The next week and a half is going to be hell*, he thought as he drove away.

*****

Downtown, Nadine sat engulfed in the task of reviewing a presentation she had created when she was interrupted by her secretary.

"Ms. Swift, you have a call from a Mr. Antonio Williams," said her secretary, peeking into her office.

"Thank you, Cassandra. I'll take it," Nadine said without looking up.

"Hello. Nadine Swift."

"Nadine! How have you been?" said a friendly male voice.

"I'm good, Antonio. Thank you for asking. How have you been?"

"Are you busy?" he asked.

Why wouldn't I be busy? I'm at work, she thought sarcastically. "Yes, I am. But I can talk for a minute. What's going on with you?" she asked.

"We hadn't talked in a while, and I just wanted to check on you," he said.

"It has been a while, but like I said, I'm doing good."

"That's good. I'm glad to hear that," he said kindly.

"Okay, Antonio, spill the beans. I'm sure you didn't just call to ask how I'm doing. What's going on?" she said, growing irritated by the pace of the conversation.

"Well, I moved back to town and was hoping we could go out for dinner," he said, knowing she wasn't one for small no-nonsense talk in the middle of the day.

"Dinner? Me and you?" she asked skeptically.

"Let me be honest," he began. "Things didn't end well for us. I was an idiot, and I'd like the opportunity for the two of us at the very least to be friends. We had fun together. We made each other laugh. We could talk. We understand each other on many levels."

Nadine listened and silently agreed with him. She especially agreed with the part about things not ending well for them. She had been hurt—badly. At one time she was very angry. The mention of his name created internal turmoil. That was two years ago. She realized, listening to his voice, that she wasn't affected at all. He was just another recognizable voice on the phone.

"Sure. We can do dinner," she said finally.

"Great!" he said joyously. "Is Da Marcos, okay?"

"Yes. That would be lovely," she replied.

"I'll pick you up at, let's say, six thirty?"

"Six thirty is fine, but I don't live in the condo anymore," she said.

"Really! You sold the condo?" he asked.

"I'll meet you there," she said, ignoring the question.

"Okay," he said after a short pause. "Looking forward to it."

"See you there," she said before hanging up.

Returning immediately to her work, Nadine didn't give the call or caller a second thought. She was confident there was nothing Antonio could do at this point to impress her. She could be a friend, a friend that kept her distance.

*****

Antonio sat motionless at his desk. He was both happy and nervous about seeing Nadine again. Two years earlier, he had been working hard to establish his security company. Nadine had been both motivating and encouraging from the start. They had dated for a couple of years prior to the incident and, by all accounts, were a happy couple—until his company started to grow.

Antonio had started to feel and look successful. While out of town, setting up a third location, he began seeing a woman, Shawn, from his past. It had been fun at first, bragging about his success. Six months later, she decided the two of them should move in together.

"Take the first step in making things official," she had said.

He had tried to break off the affair before Nadine became aware. Two years ago, fate wasn't kind to him. A few weeks after her cohabitation declaration, Shawn showed unannounced at his apartment. He and Nadine were enjoying a pizza, wine, and movie night. Once the door opened, the jealous woman began screaming affirmations of love to him and confirming their six-month long affair to Nadine, who watched the encounter in shock. That had been the deal breaker to their relationship.

The true hurt came with the announcement of being pregnant with his child. He would never forget the devastated look on Nadine's face. She stood for a moment, never uttering a word. She just stared at him with tears that never fell. Then she turned and walked out of the apartment and his life.

The pregnancy had been a lie. Antonio had never gotten the opportunity to tell Nadine. She blocked his calls to her cell phone that night and refused all calls at work. She also denied him access to her building. After trying every day for a couple of months, he finally gave up. He hadn't taken her seriously when she said that once she was done with a person, she would cut them off from every access to her. He was both amazed and happy that she had accepted his call today.

*****

That evening, Antonio sat nervously awaiting Nadine's arrival. He was a handsome sight, dressed in all black. He didn't know what to expect. He wondered if she was still angry. He knew she had every right to be. Anxiety caused him to repeatedly glance at his watch.

He had arranged for the restaurant to deliver a bouquet of flowers to their table. He glanced at his watch again. He remembered how she used to love flowers. He wondered if she was going to be late, but then he remembered he had been ten minutes early. He took deep breaths to calm his nerves. At exactly six thirty, he glanced up to see the maître d' escorting her to the table.

He rose from his seat as she approached. She was just as stunning to him as she was two years ago. She looked directly at him as she approached. Wearing a black one-shoulder-strap Alieva bandage dress with crystal embellishments, the eyes of other patrons tracked her approach.

Nadine allowed Antonio to greet her with a kiss upon her cheek before being seated. The waiter immediately came with freshly baked bread, poured wine, and left menus.

"You look lovely," he said honestly.

"Thank you. You look rather dashing yourself," she said jokingly.

"I was beginning to wonder if you were going to show up," he confessed.

"I'm a woman of my word. You should know that," she said, looking up from the menu.

"Yes. You are," he agreed, never taking his eyes from her face.

"Everything looks and sounds good," she stated as she read the menu.

"I agree," he said. "Everything looks very good."

Glancing up, Nadine realized he was not referring to the food at all.

Placing the menu on the table, she said, "Remember, this is a friendly dinner."

"Friends?" he asked with a hopeful smile.

"Friends, it is," she answered, smiling in return with a slight nod of the head.

A vase of yellow roses was placed in the center of the table just before the meal was served.

"A gift from the gentleman, madame," announced the waiter, smiling.

Nadine stared speechless at the flowers before looking at Antonio.

"I know you love flowers," he said, smiling.

"Friends," she repeated, unsmiling, continuing to look at the flowers.

"Yellow for friendship," he said, reaching across the table to grasp her hand.

She smiled a "thank you" but slowly withdrew her hand.

The rejection stung, but Antonio knew he deserved much worse.

Throughout dinner, the two shared their latest achievements. Neither of them mentioned their personal lives. Business and home were the silent conversation agreement. Keep it simple.

Antonio shared that he was branching into cybersecurity and returned home to establish a headquarters location. He considered his as a small but successful business. Nadine congratulated him. She shared her promotion news and home purchase in the Dolce Vita Community. Although the tension was present, they were both genuinely happy for the progress of the other.

The evening ended the way it began—with a kiss on the cheek. They agreed to keep in touch, with Nadine making sure he knew that it would be as friends. He readily agreed knowing that she had stepped outside of her comfort zone having dinner with him. There was something different about her now. He wasn't sure what it was, but she was not the same Nadine he knew two years ago.

*****

The following day Wesley and his crew worked ferociously attempting to complete two days' worth of work in a single day. If they could maintain the pace, the men would be rewarded with a four-day weekend. Completing this project became a paramount endeavor for them. They not only wanted but deserved a few extra days off. Wesley, however, would not have the opportunity to enjoy such a luxury. It was a price he had to pay for the salary increase.

His company credit card, phone, and automobile (an F-150) were delivered by a Terner Construction courier. The men were impressed, but both Wesley and Miguel understood that these perks meant increased infringement on his personal time.

For the next two days, he would travel to the other jobsite after work to make sure it remained secure. The neighborhood had children of various ages. Wherever there were children, especially teenagers, Wesley knew there would be curiosity and mischief. He decided to put in a request for temporary security cameras just to be safe.

It was the time of day that his mother referred to as being the cool of the evening when he arrived at the site. Unlocking the gate, he walked the grounds, making sure nothing had been disturbed or vandalized. Upon his return, he was greeted by none other than Mr. Neighborhood Watch Jameson.

"Good evening," Jameson called out happily.

"Good evening," Wesley replied with a tired-sounding voice.

"Making sure everything is safe and secure are you?"

"Always," Wesley answered as he relocked the gate.

"I saw you when you locked up yesterday. I've been keeping an eye on things ever since," he said proudly.

Turning to look at the old man, Wesley could see the pride on his face.

"You enjoy being the neighborhood watch, don't you?" he asked the elderly gentleman.

"I certainly do," the elderly man said, attempting to puff out his chest.

"Keep up the good work, Mr. Jameson," Wesley said with a smile, then walking to his SUV, ignoring the ringing of his phone.

Before driving away, he briefly watched Mr. Jameson, with his hands clasped behind his back, slowly stroll toward his home. He figured the man to be a lonely widower who walked the neighborhood looking for someone to interact with. Being the neighborhood watch gave purpose to the man's life. Quickly glancing at his phone, he read, then answered a text message.

"Round two?" the message read.

"Be ready when I say," he wrote in response.

Glancing toward Mr. Jameson, Wesley made a mental note to be patient with the old man. Then he headed home for a shower before visiting Cora, the day-care owner. She was slightly older and carried a little more weight than he preferred, but she had her own money and was deep into the church. Besides, she gave him money and gifts although he didn't need it. He liked that about her.

*****

Nadine's Friday was one meeting after the other. First, she was a presenter at a workshop for new hires. Then she attended a remote planning meeting to share updates for the shareholders meeting the following week. That was followed by a one-on-one meeting with the president of the department to share the same information.

She noticed that all participants, including the president, could best be described as walking bundles of nerves. It was understandable for the new recruits to display nervous tension. They were new graduates starting their careers and wanted to make a good impression. Out of the group, she had identified a few cutthroats based on their reaction to the comments of others.

In the planning meeting, everyone either had major or minor discrepancies in their presentations and/or reports. She watched as seasoned executives scampered around, calling for their secretaries to adjust their presentations and correct their reports. Many of the assistants appeared weary and confused, the obvious result of being assigned a task beyond their ability level.

Cassandra, her secretary, glanced at Nadine with sorrowful eyes right before it was their turn to share with the group.

"Is something wrong?" Nadine asked. "If you forgot something, don't worry. I have my copies."

The woman looked as if she would burst into tears at any moment. The feeling of incompetence was growing inside of her.

"I have everything printed and bound for you, ma'am," the woman began sadly. "But I didn't review for discrepancies," she whispered.

"Is that what's bothering you?" Nadine asked in a surprised tone. "I reviewed everything," she said reassuringly. "More than once. We're fine."

At that moment, Cassandra understood why many of the executives requested all secretaries attend this meeting. Unlike the others, this was her first time in attendance. She knew her discomfort was visible to Ms. Swift. It pained her to watch her coworkers scramble to obey the wishes of the executives. "Yes, sir," "Right away, sir," "Nearly finished, sir."—these were the phrases that rang out repeatedly throughout the meeting. Turning her head back and forth, trying to keep up with the commands was giving her a headache.

Nadine had prepared a short visual presentation and mini reports for this meeting, which only highlighted vital information. The longer, detailed presentation would be presented at the stock-holders meeting. Cassandra watched as Nadine stood and spoke with confidence during the introduction phase. When directed with a nod to ensure that each executive received a report, she stood with confidence and passed out the reports. A smile from Ms. Swift eased her jitters and boosted her confidence. She was beginning to understand how Ms. Swift operated in meetings.

*****

It was a relief for Nadine to be at her desk the final hour of the workday. She felt as if she had been in constant motion from the moment she arrived. Sitting at her desk, she took a final review of her to-do list. She thanked the Almighty there was nothing left. Picking up the phone, she dialed High Fashion Furniture and asked for Kristie, the saleswoman.

William picked up, stating that Kristie was off and wouldn't return until Monday. He eagerly offered his assistance. Nadine thanked him for his kindness and asked him to have Kristie give her call at her earliest convenience. She was surprised when moments later Cassandra informed her that a Kristie Elliott was calling.

"Nadine Swift," she said, answering the call.

"Ms. Swift, this is Kristie Elliott from High Fashion Furniture returning your call."

"Did William call you on your day off?" Nadine inquired.

"It's perfectly all right, Ms. Swift," she said. "Did something go wrong with your purchase?" she asked nervously.

"Absolutely not. The delivery isn't scheduled until tomorrow," Nadine reminded her.

"That's good," she said with a sigh of relief.

"I called because I want to purchase some additional items," Nadine said.

"Really!" exclaimed Kristie. "I'd love to assist you."

"Very good," said Nadine.

"The only problem is that Mr. Simmons will have to approve immediate delivery," she said cautiously.

"Immediate delivery isn't necessary. As soon as possible is satisfactory."

"Great!" said Kristie.

"I just wanted to make sure that you get the commission," said Nadine.

"Really? Thank you so much," said Kristie sincerely. "I've only worked there a month, and I can really use the commission."

"I'm going to transfer you to my secretary. Give her your cell number, and I'll text you the items I'm interested in."

"Thank you, Ms. Swift. Thank you so much," Kristie said happily.

Nadine snapped a picture of the list of items she'd seen online and texted them to Kristie, informing her that she'd stop by on Monday to finalize the purchase. She had seen the youth and inexperience in the girl. It had reminded her of her younger self. The years she struggled financially, attending school, then trying to forge her career in what can only be described as a hostile environment. Back then, she wished someone would have given her a break. She hadn't been that lucky.

*****

Kristie reviewed the list sent by Ms. Swift. She carefully wrote everything down, then rushed to her computer to check the prices. She smiled, realizing that with the commission from both sales she could move to her own apartment next month.

Who cares about furniture, she thought. *I'll have my own place.*

Wrapping her arms around herself, she closed her eyes and said a silent prayer of thanks. She knew commissions like this were rare. She was willing to take on a part-time job on the weekends to make sure she kept her place. She knew that choice would leave little time for studying. If it had to be done, it had to be done. Deciding that there was no time like the present, she glanced at the clock, deciding she'd study until eleven thirty. If she could make this a routine, it wouldn't be hard once she moved.

*****

While the song "Living for the Weekend" played on Sirius radio, Nadine bobbed her head as she sang along. She was tired yet rejuvenated by the thought that her living room and office furniture would arrive the following day. Once Kristie filled her second purchase, her downstairs echo hopefully would be a thing of the past.

Cassandra had recommended a restaurant that served great home-cooked meals called Pat's Parlor. Following the directions of her navigation, she scanned the area as she turned into the parking lot. It wasn't what she considered the bad side of town. It just wasn't her side of town. Parking next to an F-150, she pressed the alarm on the fob and entered the restaurant.

Once inside, she noticed, a couple of males sitting to her left. Ignoring their presence, she immediately began to scan the large displayed menu. After placing her order and receiving a number, she turned to take a seat. She intended to play on her phone while she waited to avoid interaction with the men. She was tired and didn't feel like being rude.

"What brings you to my side of town?" a familiar voice asked.

Looking up, she discovered that not only was the voice familiar but also the face. It was the face of Wesley Johnson smiling at her.

"The recommendation of great home cooking," she said, returning the smile as she took a seat across from him.

"Is this going to be our first date?" he joked.

"Hardly," she replied, smiling.

"How was your week?" he asked.

"The week was good. Today was tiring," she confessed. "How was yours?"

"The week was productive. Today, I'm tired," he too confessed.

"I'm glad you were productive. I'm sorry you're tired."

"Got any plans for the weekend?"

"My furniture is being delivered tomorrow," she said with visible excitement.

"Are you redecorating or what?"

"I'm just starting to furnish my downstairs area," she said, noticing his surprised look.

"Honestly, I'm a bit surprised."

"I know. Three months is a long time to start furnishing downstairs, but I wanted to take my time."

"I take it you don't have many visitors."

"I'm very selective about who I allow in my home," she said seriously.

"That's very smart since you are not married and have no children," he stated with a smile.

"And what makes you think I'm not married?" she asked.

"Mr. Jameson spilled the beans," he said with a broad smile.

"That man," she said with a shake of her head.

"He means well."

"If you say so."

"Which rooms will be furnished tomorrow?" he asked.

"My office and living room. They won't be finished until after my second delivery next week or so."

"So how often do you eat take food?" he asked.

"Hardly ever," she confessed. "I love to cook."

"Is that so?" he asked, eyeing her. "What do you like to cook?"

"I like trying new dishes," she said. "I love watching the cooking channel too," she added playfully.

"I would have imagined you ordering from some fancy Italian restaurant," he said.

"Dinner at an occasional fancy restaurant is fine, but honestly, I like cooking for myself."

"Really?" said Wesley surprised.

"If you go all of the time, it loses its appeal," she said indifferently.

"You're an interesting lady, Nadine," he said, eyeing her.

"How often do you eat out, Wesley Johnson?"

"Whenever I'm tired," he confessed with a laugh.

"I imagine that means you've eaten out every day this week?" she joked with a broad smile.

"I have," he said, thinking how much he loved seeing her smile.

"Are you serious?" she asked, staring at him.

"Right now, I'm in the field twelve hours. I can cook simple meals. But when I'm tired, that's the last thing I want to do," he confessed.

"Completely understandable," she said.

"Number 41!" called cashier, then handing an order to one of the two men sitting to their left.

Nadine noticed Wesley's eyes were tracking the man who returned to his seat rather than exiting the restaurant. Turning to look in the same direction, she noticed the men smiling and speaking in undertones.

"Is everything okay?" she asked Wesley.

"Everything is fine," he said with a smile, returning his gaze back to her. "You, lovely lady, tends to draw attention. That's all."

"Whatever," she said with a dismissive roll of her eyes.

"Number 42!" called out the cashier, then handing the second of the two men his order.

Together the two turned as if about to exit the restaurant. Nadine was relieved they were leaving. The latter of the two turned unexpectedly and walked over to Nadine.

"I just wanted to say that you are a beautiful woman," the man said.

Nadine stared at the man with an incredulous look.

"Thank you," she said, returning her attention back to Wesley. "What were we talking about?" she asked Wesley, silently dismissing the man.

After a moment, he walked away, joining his friend as they exited together. Once outside, they stopped briefly to admire her car. Wesley kept an eye on them from the window.

"I didn't see your vehicle outside," she said, glancing out the window.

"You parked next to me," he said.

"You bought a new truck?"

"Company truck," he said coolly.

"Why so indifferent?"

"A perk that's supposed to make a twelve-hour day easier," he explained.

"Promotional perks work that way. They should be called employment bribes," she said.

"Number 43!" the cashier's voice once again called out.

Wesley walked to the counter for his order.

"You must be number 44," he said, retaking his seat.

"I am," she said, checking her ticket. "Hopefully mine won't be much longer."

"I'll wait with you," he said with a smile.

"How kind of you, sir," she commented with a smile.

A few moments later Nadine and Wesley strolled to their cars.

"Well, Ms. Swift, I hope you enjoy your meal," he said.

"I'm sure I will, and I hope you do as well," she said with a friendly smile.

"I guess I'll be seeing you," he said seriously.

"Yeah," she said, smiling pressing the button to start the ignition.

As Wesley's truck turned left into traffic, he gave his horn a tap of goodbye to Nadine. She turned right and responded with a tap of her horn. The noise drew the attention of a gentleman that was installing a security camera across the street. Antonio glanced up to see an F-150 and an Audi. Concentrating on the car's driver, he realized it was Nadine.

Quickly glancing back toward the truck, he became agitated at the thought that she was seeing someone else. Why was she meeting him at a lowly diner? He wondered if this was the best place that man could afford to take her. Had her standards dropped to this level? He stood, thoroughly perplexed, staring down the street. He couldn't let her get trapped by this ordinary guy.

She deserves better, he thought. *She deserves me.*

*****

Sitting at the table in the breakfast nook, Nadine enjoyed Pat's home cooking. She reveled at the fact that, again, Cassandra had been right. The food was very good. With her feet resting in one of the chairs, she ate while watching the television over the fireplace. Because she lived alone, she had a television in every room. They were her substitute for companionship. Her concentration on the newscast was interrupted by the ringing of her cell phone.

"Hello," she said, covering her mouth to chew and swallow quickly.

"Hey there, lovely. What are you up to?"

"Antonio?" she asked after a short pause.

"Yes. It's Antonio. You sound surprised."

"I am."

"Why? Can't friends call to check on each other? Besides, you didn't change your number, so I took a chance."

"I suppose friends can give each other a call," she said, wondering what he was up to.

"Sounds like you are eating," he commented with a chuckle.

"I'm sorry. I'm finished," she said embarrassed.

"No! Please continue. It's not like I haven't been around you while you ate before." He chuckled.

"This food is really good," she confessed.

"I can tell," he snickered.

"So what prompted this call?"

"Just thought I'd give you a call to see what's the latest in your life," he said, hoping she'd share who the guy in the truck was.

"Well," she began, "my furniture is being delivered tomorrow. I'm so excited!" A small squeal escaped her lips.

Antonio laughed at her excitement. "So which rooms will be furnished?" he asked, hoping for a description of the master bedroom.

"Only the living room and office. And they will only be partially furnished."

"I know you've lived there a few months. What the holdup on furniture?"

"I'm the holdup," she confessed. "I want to take my time and enjoy the process."

"Can you tell me why you bought such a large house?" he asked.

"It's an investment for one thing. Also, I wanted space and privacy."

"You're in the suburbs, so you'll get plenty of privacy. Is the community gated?"

"It will be in the very near future," she said.

"So when do I get an invitation to see your new haven?" he asked, hopeful.

"That's a good question. We'll see," she dismissively. "Got any plans for the weekend?" she asked, changing subjects.

"My nephew has a football game this weekend. I'm going to show my support."

"That's nice."

"Can I convince you to accompany me?"

"Maybe another time. I'm not sure how long the delivery will take and… I'm sorry," she apologized sincerely.

"How 'bout a rain check?" he asked.

"A rain check I can do," she replied.

He was disappointed because he wanted to spend some time with her. At the same time, he didn't want to appear pushy.

"Did you cook that great meal you were eating? I know you love to cook," he asked, attempting a new strategy.

"This time I didn't," she answered. "I picked it up at a restaurant in town."

"Oh really. You eat there often? Would you recommend it?"

"I definitely recommend it. The food is fabulous."

"So you do eat there often," he restated, fishing for additional information that wasn't unnoticed.

"The place was recommended to me," she said with a laugh. "Listen. I should be going," she said before he could continue questioning her.

*****

He needed to get some air. Disappointed that he didn't get more information before the call ended, Antonio sullenly walked to his patio. The breeze felt good on his face. He stood for a moment, taking a drag of his cigarette, thankful she talks to him. He allowed his mind to reminisce for a moment back to the days when the two of them were in love. He and Nadine were inseparable. They walked holding hands and whispered secrets to each other while others looked on. He remembered when being in each other's presence was comfort enough. Words were not required. He remembered when the sight of him transformed her flawless business appearance into soft, radiating love. Now the sight of him had no effect. She remained friendly but impassive.

She was different, he just wasn't sure how. She had loved him deeply two years ago, and he had trampled on her heart. Taking a longer pull on his cigarette, he tried to stamp out how badly his past actions bothered him. He assumed that if he was still bothered, Nadine had to feel the effects as well. It was odd because if she did, she hid the hurt well. That too bothered him.

He didn't necessarily want her to hurt; it just seemed as if he had no effect on her at all anymore. That hurt him. Flicking the cigarette away in agitation, Antonio returned to his condo. He had to come up with a way to get close to her. He needed a place where he could explain and apologize for the past. Hopefully, he would be able to patch things up and start on a path toward the future, a future the two of them often spoke of and dreamed about in the past. He had to find a way to fix this.

*****

A signal from the motion detector alerted Nadine to visitors. Rushing to the door, she swung it open just as the delivery driver was extending his finger to press the doorbell.

"You're here!" she exclaimed.

A muscular young man gave her a quick scan from head to toe, then plastering a toothy grin upon his face.

"Yes, we're here," he said. "Want to show me where you'd like everything?"

Leaving the door ajar, she led him across the foyer to her office.

"The desk, lounger, and plant will go in this room. I'd like the desk placed so that it's facing the window. The lounge should be placed directly under the window with the plant beside the fireplace," she said.

"And the sofa and table?" he inquired.

"Follow me, please," she said, leading him again across the foyer.

"I'd like the coffee table placed in front of the fireplace with the two sofas placed at angles," she said.

"At an angle?" he questioned.

"Here and here," she said, using her body and arms moving from one position to another to demonstrate the exact placement.

"Kind of like a *V* in front of the fireplace," he confirmed.

"Exactly," she said with a smile.

"I hope you don't mind me saying, but this is a very nice home you have," he said.

"Thank you," she said with a smile.

"We'll get to it then," he said with a smile.

After the furniture was set in place and the delivery guys all gone, Nadine set out hanging the artwork she'd purchased from Wesley over the fireplace in the living room. Climbing down from the small step ladder, then stepping back, she admired the room.

"Perfect," she said proud of herself.

From there, she walked into her home office. There wasn't much she could do in there except put her briefcase in one of the drawers of the built-in and place the iPad she'd purchased on the desk. It wasn't much, but still, she was proud. She stood for a moment, imaging what the room would look like once the other items arrived. She was proud because she was making progress.

She wanted this place to have an inviting atmosphere. After a while, she realized the condo downtown was modern and sleek, but there was a coldness about it. She liked order, everything in its proper place. Just not to the point where a person felt the need to sit with a stiff straight back and hands clasped in their lap.

Having been in the house all day, she decided on a workout at the fitness center. Before changing, she called up her best friend, Everett.

"You know I should curse you right now," Everett said in his usual female tone after answering the phone.

"Don't," she said. "I've been so busy lately."

"Too busy to call your best friend?"

"You are my best friend, my very best friend," she said with exaggerated sorrow.

"You better be glad I love you," Everett replied. "You're forgiven."

"Good," she said happily.

"So what's going on, chick?"

"I need to get out of this house for a while."

"Honey, you called the right person. So what do you feel like doing? Food, exercise, get a mani-pedi, walk through the mall and check out all the latest male eye candy?"

"Male eye candy?" asked Nadine, barely holding back her laughter.

"Girl, that's what I call them. They are sweet to look at, but you better not take them home because the tummy ache they give will head straight for your heart."

Nadine's laughter could no longer be stifled. "Shut up!" she exclaimed.

"Girl, you know I'm right. So what's it going to be?"

"All of them," she said. "Only let's put food at the end of the list."

"Let's do this," replied Everett.

"Great! Just let me get changed," Nadine said hurriedly.

"Don't rush. You're picking me up since you live in the suburbs now with the hoity-toity people," said Everett.

"Be there in forty-five minutes," she said before rushing off to get dressed.

*****

Nadine and Everett were hired at the same time but worked in different departments. They had similar taste when it came to fashion. On the job, Everett was always professional and debonair. Off the job, however, he was feminine and unpretentious. The two had become inseparable from the start. They'd gotten to know each other initially by sharing lunch breaks as new hires. Over the years, their friendship grew to the point where many assumed they were related.

"Why are you talking to that slug Antonio after what he did to you?" Everett asked as the two walked on treadmills.

"For a lot of reasons," answered Nadine.

"Promise me I won't throw up," he said, rolling his eyes.

"I'm not mad. I'm no longer hurt. He has absolutely no effect on me. And most importantly, I'm not attracted to him in that way," she explained.

"Good for you, girl," said Everett with exaggerated enthusiasm.

"And what's that supposed to mean?" asked Nadine.

"Listen. He's not mad either. That's because you didn't do anything. The only thing that hurt him was getting caught. The truth of the matter is that you still affect him. And most importantly, he is still attracted to you and wants you back. Please tell me you knew this," he ended, rolling his eyes once again.

"Antonio always has an ulterior motive," said Nadine.

"So why are you playing into his little game?"

"He's playing the game alone. I have no interest in rekindling anything with him. I can talk and be civil and that's it. I want him to know that I've moved on from him and the hurt. And I'm not bitter."

"Well, let me just say this right now. When shit hits the fan, and I know it will," he began. "I'm here for you, girl. I'll kick his ass."

"Really?" questioned Nadine with a stare.

"Well, me and a few other guys maybe. Is he still buff as hell?"

"Yes, he is still buff." Nadine laughed.

"I can't stand his ass, but he is some great male eye candy," he said, fanning his face.

After leaving the fitness center, the two headed across the pavilion to get mani-pedis. Everett shared his newest male endeavor. Nadine was shocked to discover the relationship was getting serious. Christopher was his name, and he had heard all about Nadine. With starry eyes, Everett spoke of gentleness, passion, and for the first-time commitment.

"Are you in love?" she questioned cautiously.

"Of course not, I just like him a lot."

Nadine didn't believe that for even a moment. She continued to stare at her friend.

"What?" asked Everett.

"Do...you...love...him?" she repeated slowly.

"Well, maybe a little," Everett said, avoiding eye contact.

A broad smile spread across Nadine's face.

"What the hell are you smiling at?" Everett asked with visible embarrassment.

"My place. Next Saturday. Dress casual," said Nadine.

"Do you have furniture yet? Last time, the only place to sit was in your bedroom."

"I'll have furniture," said Nadine.

"You don't have furniture yet!"

"I have furniture! I have some furniture anyways. I'll have more by then, I promise. Just be there by seven."

"Oh, honey, we'll be there. Who's going to be your date?" asked Everett, wiggling his eyebrows.

"Don't worry," she began. "I'll invite a friend."

"If it's Antonio, I won't be responsible for my actions," he joked.

Caution

WESLEY SET ABOUT arranging his display of merchandise. He enjoyed being a flea-market vendor. It provided him the opportunity to interact with people while at the same time providing a service at an affordable price. It also gave him unlimited access to woman. He was aware, however, that this would probably be his last opportunity for a while because of the Dolce Vita's project scope.

"Where is this vendor with the great electronic deals?" Antonio asked his nephew.

An electronic device of choice for good grades had been a promise Antonio had made to the youngest of his sister's children.

"He's this way, Uncle Tony," the boy answered with excitement, rushing through the growing crowd.

"I think you said that five minutes ago," Antonio responded, though desiring to stop at several setups they breezed past. He'd come back another time on his own, not wanting to ruin his nephew's excitement.

"There he is!" the child shouted before attempting to run off.

"Never show how anxious you are," said Antonio, grabbing the boy's arm. "You should always act cool. As if you're not really interested. Remember, they want to sell to you just as bad as you want to buy."

"Hi there, little man," greeted Wesley with a smile. "Looking to make a purchase?"

"I'm just looking," the child responded after glancing at his uncle.

"Let me know if you see something you like," said Wesley, realizing the man was teaching the child how to barter.

"Uncle Tony," the child said pointing to a PS5.

"Is this a new or refurbished gaming system?" asked Antonio.

"It's brand new. Never opened," replied Wesley.

"I didn't realize they sold brand-new electronics at flea markets," said Antonio, examining the box.

"I buy my inventory wholesale so I can pass on the savings to my customers," stated Wesley.

"We are interested. What happens if it doesn't work?" Antonio asked. "Is there a money-back guarantee?"

"This is a flea market, sir, not a department store," Wesley clarified. "The only guarantee I can give you is a guarantee that the system is new.

"How much are you asking?" Antonio inquired.

Wesley stated the price. Then pulling out his phone, he displayed the retail price for the man and child to see.

"That's a 20 percent saving," stated Wesley, tucking his phone back into his pocket.

"You want this one?" Antonio asked the child. "We can go to the mall and get a brand-new system if you want."

"But, Uncle Tony, he said it is new. And you said if we had money left over, I could get a new outfit too!" the child stated, wearing a confused expression.

Wesley looked on with a smirk, unable to hide the amusement he felt. Nor did he miss the embarrassment on the uncle's face.

"We'll take it," was all the man said before reaching for his wallet. "Cash or card?" he asked.

"Your choice. I prefer cash but will accept a card."

Pulling out the necessary bills, Antonio handed them to the vendor. He liked the man's business style. It was his natural confidence and choice of attire that he didn't care for. The gold chain with large pendant and earrings in both ears were overstatements in his opinion.

Wesley began placing the gaming system into a large bag. Right before handing the bag over to Antonio, he held out three video games giving the child a choice. The boy made his selection, wearing a huge smile.

"Thank the man," instructed Antonio dryly.

"Thank you, sir," the boy said, smiling while hugging the video game.

"Thank you for your business, little man," Wesley responded to the child with a smile.

After walking off, Antonio queried the child on his knowledge of the vendor.

"How did you know about this vendor?" asked Antonio.

"Mom bought her computer, the TV in her bedroom, and an iPad from him. I heard her tell Angie he gave her a good deal."

"Angie?"

"Angie used to be Mom's best friend. But they don't talk anymore," the child said.

"Oh," said responded Antonio, wondering what had ended the friendship.

"I heard Mom on the phone," the child added. "She told somebody Angie was saying bad things about her."

"What kind of bad things?" asked Antonio.

"I don't know. I was sitting looking at TV and heard her say something about Angie said she didn't need a second iPad. I wouldn't get mad if my friend had two iPads. Would you, Uncle Tony?"

"Not over two iPads, buddy," he answered, knowing it wasn't the iPads that had caused the rift but the man selling iPads. Either one of the women was dating the man, and the other made a move or they were both after him. Then again, he thought, maybe the man was leading them both on. He looked every bit of a ladies' man. He supposed there were women that found the vendor's type as attractive. He was sure he didn't know any.

*****

"Ma! Look what Uncle Tony bought for me!" the child yelled with excitement.

"Expensive!" his mother responded, eyeing her brother. "Why don't you go try it out?"

"Here, he got a new outfit out of me also," joked Antonio, handing a bag to his sister.

"Tony, I appreciate the gifts," Tracie said. "I don't want him getting used to things like that. I have two others I must provide for also."

"Stop worrying. We got a good deal from some flea-market vendor," Antonio said, gauging her reaction.

"Flea market? Did you buy from Wesley?" she asked.

"He didn't introduce himself," said Antonio.

"What did he look like," she asked.

"A man," said Antonio dryly.

"If it was Wesley, you'd know." She chuckled.

"What makes this Wesley so memorable?" he asked.

"Well, he smells good." She smiled, not impressing her brother with her statement.

"Okay, you're a man and wouldn't notice those things," she said with a roll of her eyes.

She was wrong because Antonio had noticed.

"He dresses very urban. He wears gold chains. He has dimples," she said again, smiling.

"Yeah, that's him," he said, cutting her off.

"You got a good deal then. He sells quality merchandise."

"I take it you've bought from him before."

"I have. Several items to be exact. He beats the retail price for sure."

"Was it the deals that kept you going back or the man?" he asked, turning to look at her.

"Both," she answered honestly. "Why?"

"Just asking," he said, careful not to disclose what his nephew had overheard.

"Mom, can I invite Trent over to see my PS5?" the child asked, interrupting their conversation.

"Go ahead," she said.

"Make sure you let him know your uncle Tony bought that for you and not me," she added before he could run away with cell phone in hand.

"What difference does it make?" asked Antonio.

"Trent's mom and I used to be close," she began. "That was before she recommended Wesley as a place to shop for great deals. Then she got it in her head that I was trying to take him away from her."

"Were they dating?" he asked.

"Not officially," his sister explained. "More like bootie calls. But apparently, she was hoping for more."

"So what happened?" asked Antonio, confused.

"I think she misunderstood his nice demeanor. She took it as flirting, and it very well could have been. In the end, she was just a female customer, and he's that way with everyone. When she heard that I had made repeat purchases, she assumed I was after him like she was."

"Were you?" Antonio asked, gauging her for a lie.

"Honestly, I don't know much about the man. Truthfully, I wouldn't mind finding out. But he was no more interested in a relationship with me than he was in her. I was a customer just like her. And no, I wasn't after him."

"He didn't flirt with you?" asked Antonio, wearing a doubtful expression.

With hands on her hips, she said, "On my second visit, I had to wait while he finished with another customer. He smiled and flirted with her to the point I'm sure she bought a couple of items she didn't need. Once it was my turn, he did the same thing. That's how he makes his sales to women. I'm sure he has a different approach for every gender. He's a salesman after all."

"I guess you're right, sis," he said with a satisfied chuckle.

"I don't want any drama with Angie. I'm planning to move when my lease is up. So I'm trying to keep all the theatrics to a minimum."

"Good for you, sis. Buying or renting?"

"Finally, I am buying," she said proudly.

"Let me know if I can help," he said.

"What are you about to do?" she asked.

"Go home. Watch the game," he said.

She noticed his sad expression. She also knew the source.

"Why watch alone? Stay here and watch with me. I have chicken wings, nachos, and pizza," she said, smiling.

"No beer?" he asked.

"What's a football game without beer? Of course, I have beer."

"You don't have to ask me twice," he said heading into the living room.

A few of Tracie's neighbors joined them to watch the game. Antonio had met some of them in the past. Kristina and Kristie were sister and new to him. Kristina had two boys. They all cheered for their respective teams and talked sports trash. It was fun. And for a short time, Antonio forgot about his sadness.

Tracie hadn't dared touch the subject of Nadine for fear of irritating her brother. Halftime and a big announcement did that for her.

"Attention, everyone! Attention! I have a big announcement," said Kristina, smiling at her younger sister.

"Please don't," begged Kristie, looking embarrassed.

"My baby sister, after only a month on the job, is the top person in sales commission this month!" announced Kristina.

Cheers, claps, and whistles rang out.

"Not only that. Her commission has earned her the honor of moving into her own apartment next month!" she added.

Again, cheers and congratulations rang out. Kristie smiled and thanked everyone.

"That must have been some commission," said Tracie. "How'd you pull that one off?"

"What does he look like?" another female asked jokingly.

"Actually, it was a female," Kristie began. "She came in, knew what she wanted, and basically paid for everything on the spot."

"I thought you said she paid with a credit card," questioned Kristina.

"She did. But with an American Express gold card," said Kristie. "With that card, you don't pay overtime," she clarified.

"You should've given her your business card," said one of the guys with a chuckle.

"I didn't have to. She called back asking for me. Gave me another huge order, saying she only wanted me to get the commission! Can you believe that?" said Kristie, smiling.

"You must have made a nice impression on her," Antonio said, finally joining in.

"I don't know what caused it. When she called, all I could say was, 'Thank you Ms. Swift. Thank you so much.'"

"Ms. Swift!" said Antonio and Tracie in shocked unison.

"Yes. Ms. Nadine Swift," Kristie replied, noticing their shocked expressions.

They looked at each other.

"Do you know her?" asked Kristina, also noticing their expressions.

"Yes," said Tracie, finally forcing a smile. "I know Nadine quite well."

"She seems like a very nice lady," said Kristie defensively as Kristina placed a reassuring hand on her shoulder.

"No. Nadine is very nice," said Tracie apologetically. "She and I were very close for some years, then we just lost touch. I was just surprised when you said her name is all. Honestly, she was almost like a part of the family."

"Has it been that long, sis?" he asked, drawing his sister into his game to glean information from the girl.

"At least a couple of years," she said, following his lead.

"Now that was a lady with class," he commented, looking directly at Kristie to add to his comment.

"I totally agree," added Kristie, taking the bait. "She furnished her entire living room and home office in two purchases!"

"Not piece by piece like I would." Kristina laughed.

"At first, I thought she was all stuck-up and snooty," said Kristie joyously. "But she's not."

"You just have to get to know her," added Tracie with a laugh. "She is stuck-up and snooty too. But only with people she doesn't know. Once you get to know her. She's sweet and caring."

"She wouldn't even let the manager help her. I'm glad she didn't because I wouldn't have gotten the commission," said Kristie.

"You impressed her. Once she likes you, she likes you," said Tracie, glancing at Antonio. "Right, bro?"

"Right," agreed Antonio slowly with a nod. "And she obviously likes you."

"She's coming in to finalize her purchase tomorrow," said Kristie, smiling.

"Is that right?" said Antonio, taking a sip of his beer with a far-away gaze upon his face.

He had hoped for more details from the girl. Did Nadine come in with a guy? If so, was it the guy in the truck? He wanted something more than what he had already been told.

Who the hell was that guy? he wondered.

"Nadine sold her condo?" asked Tracie after the gathering as she and Antonio cleaned up.

"I guess so. I know she bought a house in the suburbs," he said as he tied a bag of trash.

"How'd you find that out?" she asked.

"We've talked a couple of times since I've been back," he answered, noticing her smirk and stare.

"It's not like that. She's cordial but distant," he clarified.

"Don't take this the wrong way," she began. "But cordial is good. All things considered."

"Yeah, I know. I'm thankful for cordial," he said sadly.

"Give it time," she said encouragingly. "If it's meant to be, it'll be."

*****

Wesley watched the game alone. Tomorrow he'd be supervising two sites and decided against entertaining. He sat, having no problem screaming at the television. While checking his messages during halftime, an inquiry about a PS5 reminded him of the sale he'd made earlier that morning. The preppy dude and his nephew. The little guy reminded him of a previous customer. What was her name? Tracie. The child looked just like Tracie's son.

He considered Tracie as a cutie-pie. She flirted like all his female customers. She tried to be subtle, but he knew. He flirted back because that's what he does. His goal wasn't the woman though; it was the sale. Besides, she had three boys and the two oldest were quite mischievous. That had been a deal breaker for him right away. He'd sell her merchandise, but that was it.

Wesley didn't dislike children. He just didn't have any yet. He wanted to mold the lives of his own offspring. He had no interest in trying to reverse years of lackadaisical parenting. Tracie's boys needed the guidance of a man. He just wasn't that man.

He used to have moments of loneliness. He learned to fill those moments with calls to one female or another. Lately, he avoided calls and opted for texting instead. He decided the who and when. He fell asleep in his recliner, waking in the middle of the night in search of his bed.

*****

A few miles away, Antonio lay staring at the ceiling unable to sleep. He knew he was being impatient. He'd just feel better if he could confess to Nadine. She wasn't being unfriendly; she just gave him the impression of being unfazed. He couldn't understand it. She used to love him so deeply. He expected a completely different reaction after dinner. Sighing deeply, he closed his eyes, willing sleep to come upon him. Eventually, it did.

*****

That same night Nadine also watched the big game. Like Wesley, she screamed and cheered for her team but not alone. Eating pizza and drinking wine in her sitting room was Drew. She and Drew laughed and talked sports trash to each other. They had a meeting scheduled for the coming weekend but agreed to add another day.

The halftime show and third quarter would have to be viewed during replays because the two were engaged in their own passionate scrimmage. By the end of the game, she was glad her bed was so close. Crawling into bed with Drew, feeling tipsy, tense free, and elated because her team had won, she fell asleep without delay, snuggled next to him.

*****

"Secure Systems," said Antonio, answering the office phone.

"Good morning. This is Andrea Cummins calling from Terner Construction. I'd like to speak to someone about installing some cameras at a construction site," said a woman's voice.

"I'm the owner, Antonio Williams, so I can answer your questions," he responded.

"Great. Tell me about your services?" she asked.

"We offer a variety of camera styles. We install and provide twenty-four-hour monitoring and tech support," he said.

"Just what we need. The specific camera type will be selected by our project manager, Mr. Wesley Johnson," she began. "The two of you can decide on the camera's locations and any other needed adjustments I haven't mentioned. Once that's completed, Mr. Johnson will send the invoice to me, and I'll take care of it," she finished in a friendly tone.

"How soon do you need them?" he asked.

"As soon as possible," she stated. "Mr. Johnson will be on site today. Are you able to have a technician meet with him?"

"I'll make that visit myself," he said.

"I'm sending him a message right now informing him to expect you," she said in a friendly tone.

"What's the location of the jobsite?" he asked.

"It's the Dolce Vita residential community. Can I send the email on your website to send the address?" she asked.

"Yes, please," he answered.

A notification on his computer screen informed him that Ms. Cummins was prompt. He hoped she was just as prompt with payment.

"I have the address and should arrive within the hour," he stated, then ended the call.

Antonio performed a silent cheer, then danced in his seat. A call from Terner Construction was evidence that his business was growing. Puffed with pride, he didn't stifle his smile. Not only did he have a lucrative contract he'd also see exactly where Nadine lived. Somewhere in the suburbs was all that she'd disclosed.

Things are getting better, he thought.

*****

The sound of heavy machinery drew Nadine's attention as she exited the community that morning. Glancing toward the portable, she spotted Wesley's truck but refrained from searching for him. His urban style prevented her from imagining him as a project manager for Terner. He looked completely different when he wasn't standing behind a vendor's display.

Ignore his urban style of dress and he has great social skills. She chuckled. *Everett is going to have a hissy fit*, she thought as she drove. That is, if Wesley accepts the invitation.

Having just received a message from Andrea, Wesley looked up just in time to catch a glimpse of Nadine as she headed out to work. Standing on the opposite side of the site, he smiled as she looked in the direction of his truck. Quickly looking away before anyone noticed, she drove past.

She's looking for me, he thought with a smirk as he headed to look at the site's plans again. He wanted to select some specific camera locations before the technician arrived.

He was just finishing a call to Miguel when a car pulled onto the site bearing a magnetic logo that read Secure Systems. After a brief pause, the driver correctly parked next to his truck. As he headed in that direction, he noticed the driver staring at his vehicle.

It can't be, he thought. The nerd he'd sold the PS5 to that past weekend. Wesley couldn't help but smile.

"Good morning. Can I do something for you, sir?" he asked as the man continued staring at the truck.

"Yes," said the man before introducing himself, then pausing. "You're the guy from the flea market," Antonio said before realizing his statement was rude.

"Yes, that's me," said Wesley continuing to smile. "Can I help you?"

"I'm Antonio Williams from Secure Systems. Can you point me in the direction of the project manager? I have a meeting with him," Antonio stated, scanning the site.

"You're speaking to the project manager," Wesley said, smiling, then extending his hand. "Wesley Johnson."

At a loss for words, Antonio slowly shook the proffered hand.

"Shall we get started?" asked Wesley, amused by the man's reaction.

"Yes," Antonio responded, trying to conceal his surprise.

Walking the site, Antonio took note of the man's leadership. He answered questions, gave instructions, explained, corrected, and gave brief demonstrations constantly. He did this while pointing out key locations for cameras.

"Ms. Cummins indicated an as soon as possible installation date," said Antonio. "Are there concerns regarding material or equipment?"

"Not at all, Mr. Williams," said Wesley, halting any further movement. "My crew consists of loyal, hardworking family men. They would never jeopardize their family's livelihood."

"My apologies. I didn't mean to imply anything," he said, angry at himself for allowing jealousy to cloud his judgment.

"There are children in this community, Mr. Williams," Wesley began to explain. "Children are curious regardless of how wealthy their family is. My job is to complete this project on time while at the same time protecting this community and my crew. Yes, the property, material, and equipment of Terner Construction is important. But if someone is playing with the equipment after hours, one of my crew could be injured. In this field, every element affect something else."

"I understand," said Antonio, nodding his head with respect. "I agree with you 100 percent."

"Do you have any suggestions regarding camera placement?" asked Wesley.

"Not for camera placement," said Antonio. "I would however suggest our recording and storage feature. Once the cameras are turned on you will have access to not only a live feed, but also continuous recording with cloud-based storage that can be accessed at any time remotely by you, Terner, or both."

"I like that. How soon can get me an invoice and begin installation?" asked Wesley.

"Does before the close of business today on the invoice work for you?" said Antonio.

"Can you have technicians here first thing tomorrow morning?" asked Wesley.

"I can, but shouldn't we wait for corporate approval?" asked Antonio skeptically.

"It was approved before you got the call," said Wesley, looking the man in the eye.

"I'll get that invoice to you," said Antonio, shaking the man's hand.

A smug butt-wipe was the description Antonio allotted to Mr. Wesley Johnson as he walked to his car. Closing his car door, he seethed with resentment. It was difficult to determine the man's birthplace because he spoke with a combined North/South accent. He was the opposite of his friendly flea-market persona. Today, he was arrogant and aloof.

"It was approved before you got the call," Antonio mimicked in a feigned voice. He doubted the approval would be as swift as Wesley would lead him to believe. He learned the hard way that installation begins after the invoice is approved and signed. This invoice was priority once he reached his office.

*****

Right after lunch a fax slid out of the machine and onto Wesley's desk as he reviewed the materials list to begin the structural outline of the building. He was about to put in a call to the supplier for some additional lumber and hardware. Pausing to pick up the sheet, he smiled.

The nerd sent the invoice, thought Wesley with a chuckle.

The man had rubbed Wesley the wrong way, insinuating that his crew stole from the jobsite. It angered him when all minorities were judged by the few. Honest men and crooks resided in every race. He found himself defending his crew constantly for one slur or another. He considered for a moment what would happen to his crew if he got the director's position he had been chasing. The thought unnerved him. Erasing the thought with a shake of his head, he picked up the phone and informed Andrea that he received the invoice for the cameras and was faxing it over.

*****

"Secure Systems, Antonio speaking."

"Mr. Williams, this is Andrea Cummins from Terner Construction. We spoke this morning about installation of security cameras for the Dolce Vita jobsite."

"Yes, Ms. Cummins, what can I do for you?"

"I just wanted to inform you that I'm emailing you the approval to begin work with an acceptance of your quote."

"Thank you, ma'am, for getting this approval taken care of so swiftly," he said, smiling.

"No need to thank me." She chuckled. "The company had already given Mr. Johnson prior approval for anything he needed."

"I see," said Antonio.

"Honestly, it was approved before you received a call." She chuckled. "I'm just finalizing things."

"Is that so?" stated Antonio.

"Lastly, Mr. Williams, Mr. Johnson would like for installation to begin first things in the morning. Please have your technician at the jobsite promptly at eight," she said with a serious tone.

He realized that one phone call from Wesley Johnson, and he'd lose this contract. That was something he didn't want to happen. His resentment he realized was misplaced. He had no proof this was the same man that blew at Nadine. There had to be hundreds of F150s of that color in the city. He may be upset for no reason. Tomorrow morning he'd apologize again for his offensive statement.

*****

The eyes of all the sales personnel turned at sound of the door's chime. In walked Ms. Nadine Swift wearing a crisp white Tom Ford pant suit with a silk bronze camisole underneath. She wore her hair loose but away from her face. Chanel's Extrait De Camelia hoop earrings hung from her ears while the matching necklace accentuated the entire ensemble. She stood briefly as if looking for a specific person.

"You look exquisite today, madame. Is there something I can assist you with?" asked Gary, known as the commission thief. He had knowingly stolen the commissions of several of his coworkers in the past regardless of the wishes of the customer.

Having looked up moments too late, Kristie saw Greg, the thief, approaching Ms. Swift. Dropping what she was doing, she rushed over.

"No," said Nadine, walking past him having spotted Kristie rushing toward her.

"Ms. Swift," she said, knowing the woman saw her sudden fear.

"Stop worrying, this commission and others will be yours. Deal?" said Nadine, extending a hand of agreement.

"Deal!" Kristie smiled, shaking the woman's hand.

"What's the status on the second purchase?" asked Nadine, taking a seat at the sales desk.

"Great news! All items are in stock and can be delivered as early as Thursday afternoon, if that's a good time for you," said Kristie.

"That's perfect if you make sure it's the last delivery of the day. That will give me time to get home from the office," she said.

While Kristie typed the delivery instructions into the computer, Nadine sat with crossed legs, skimming through her messages.

"I see Kristie was able to assist you again," said William, standing beside the desk with the appearance of an aged sitcom butler.

"William, please make sure the delivery instructions that Kristie is placing in the computer are adhered to," she said ignoring his annoying gaze.

"Without fail, Ms. Swift," he said, moving behind the desk to look at the delivery instructions and the purchase total. "Without fail, Ms. Swift," he repeated, unable to conceal his joy.

Kristie had already prepared the paperwork based on Nadine's previous purchase. She slid the paper across the desk, which Nadine immediately endorsed.

"Thank you, Kristie," said Nadine, then rising to leave, then paused.

"You're very welcome, Ms. Swift. Thank you for your business," replied Kristie with a combination of happiness from the sale and nervousness from the proximity of the manager.

"William," Nadine said, facing him directly.

"Yes, Ms. Swift," he said with hands clasped behind his back.

"Make sure that Kristie receives the commission for this and all of my purchases," she said with meaning.

"Without fail, Ms. Swift," he said with a smile and nod.

They watched Nadine exit the store in silence.

"Take the rest of the day off, Kristie," said William, then returning to his office.

She didn't argue, although she didn't agree either. She knew he was cutting her hours based on the amount of her commission. She was supposed to be a full-time employee and a part-time student. Her commission was more than her normal paycheck. It wasn't guaranteed money though. Once Ms. Swift had made all her purchases, Kristie was afraid she'd be left with part-time hours to support full-time responsibilities. She was starting to worry as she slowly walked to her car.

I'll have to be careful and start to save more, she thought with a sigh before starting the ignition.

*****

"Hello," answered Wesley.

"Hey, boss, it's Miguel."

"How did everything go today?"

"The day was smooth. We're still on schedule. Met our daily goal. No problems at all," said Miguel.

"That's a relief," said Wesley.

"How are things at that site?" asked Miguel.

"We set the forms set for the foundation to be poured. Security camera getting installed tomorrow," answered Wesley.

"That's progress," said Miguel.

"Slow but steady," Wesley said.

"Listen, boss. You can go straight home this evening if you want. Everything is fine over here. I'll make sure the site's secure," said Miguel.

"That great, Miguel. What I'll do is drop by there first before heading over here in the morning," said Wesley.

"I'll come in a little early tomorrow, and you can let me know what you think. Okay, boss?"

"Sounds great. I'll see you in the morning," said Wesley.

He was grateful to have Miguel as his foreman. He was especially thankful now with having to manage two sites. After checking his emails, placing an order for additional materials, and reviewing the schedule, Wesley left his office to walk the site, check inventory for the following day, and then lock up the site and head home.

As he headed to his truck, he glanced up to see Nadine turn in to the subdivision. She slowed and stopped her car next to the curb.

After exiting the car, she began walking in his direction but stopped just in front of the office. Dressed in a white pant suit and bronze-colored top, she was a refreshing yet out-of-place sight.

"Hi, there," she said, smiling.

"Hi, there to you," he said, returning the smile.

"Checking up on me?" he joked.

"You wish," she responded with a laugh.

"So what's going on, Ms. Nadine Swift?" he asked, smiling.

"Please call me Nadine," she said with a friendly wave of her hand.

"Okay, Nadine, what's up?" he asked, still smiling.

"I'm having a small friendly gathering," she began. "A very small gathering this Saturday and was wondering if you would be interested in attending?"

"I'd love to come," he said, completely surprised by the invitation.

"Great," she said. "It's at seven. Extremely casual and, like I said, a small gathering."

His silent stare began to make her feel uncomfortable.

"Well," she began. "I guess I'll see you then."

"Nadine," he said softly.

"Yes?" she replied, curiously.

"Are you going to give me the address?"

They both burst into laughter.

"Yes," she said, laughing. "Is it okay if I text it to you?"

"You still have the number?" he asked.

"I do," she said. "I have the business card."

"I'll be on the lookout for that text," he said, watching her walk away.

"You know Mr. Jameson will bring you straight to my door," she jokingly called out.

Giving him a friendly wave, she was in her car and soon out of sight.

After locking the gate, Wesley looked up to see Mr. Jameson strolling in his direction. He waved to the man, who returned the wave. Wesley was too elated by Nadine's invitation to cook his noodle specialty, so he headed to Pat's for a real meal.

Parking his truck in what he referred to as his usual spot, Wesley walked into the restaurant and placed his order for two meals. He pulled out his phone after taking a seat and found that Nadine had texted her address as promised.

"Eat here often?" a man's voice asked interrupting Wesley's thoughts.

Looking up from his phone, standing before him was the nerd aka camera guy, Antonio Williams.

"Actually, no," said Wesley, annoyed by the man's presence.

"Oh, so this is your first time?" Antonio asked.

"Is this an interrogation?" Wesley asked, glaring at the man before him. Placing his phone on the table, he began to wonder what was issue that this dude had against him.

"I saw you sitting here, and I wanted to apologize for my rude comment earlier today. I was also hoping you could make a recommendation," said Antonio.

What he really wanted was to know if Wesley was the guy in the truck blowing at Nadine.

The cashier motioned to Wesley that his order was ready.

"I accept your apology, Mr. Williams," said Wesley, standing. "I don't eat here. I always order take out. Have a good evening."

Wesley walked away, leaving the annoying man standing beside the table.

Antonio sat watching Wesley as he drove away. That was the type of truck he had seen. He was sure of that. If he could somehow confirm that Wesley was the man, then he would be able to develop a strategy.

"Sir, your order is ready," a young, impressionable female called to him, smiling.

Opportunity, he thought. Hanging her a ten-dollar tip, he smiled.

"Do you know the guy that left a few minutes ago?" he asked.

"You mean Wesley?"

"Yes, Wesley," Antonio said, smiling. "He just told me that he orders here a lot. Is that true?"

"It's true," confirmed the girl. "At least once a week."

"A friend of mine says she met him here a couple of weeks ago," he lied.

"You mean the real pretty bougie lady with the fancy car?" she asked.

"That would be her," he said, nodding.

"I saw them sitting together and talking," she confirmed. "They left at the same time too."

A call from the kitchen ended his questioning. His curiosity had been satisfied anyways. Antonio couldn't believe that this flea-market-vending project manager thought he was good enough for his

Nadine. The man could barely speak properly for goodness' sake. Not only was he arrogant, he was also rude and much too urban to consider himself within the same class as Nadine.

Antonio headed home with new confidence thinking that Wesley was no competition. He had been worrying all for nothing.

Roadblock

"LOOKS LIKE THIS project will be completed earlier than expected," said Wesley as he and Miguel walked the site.

"The guys have been working hard to meet their daily goals," said Miguel proudly.

"I'll schedule all of the inspections," Wesley said. "I'll check back before I head home this evening."

"We're aiming to finish this evening," said Miguel.

"At the rate you guys are going, that looks like a real possibility," said Wesley.

"If that happens, boss, do we start over there tomorrow morning?" asked Miguel.

"No, you and the guys take the rest of the week and show up over there on Monday. I'll get all the inspectors out here to do their thing. I will need you guys to be prepared to come in and fix anything they identify though."

"Not a problem, boss," Miguel said with a smile.

"I don't anticipate anything, just think of it as being off but not really off if you're needed," warned Wesley.

"You can count on us, boss," Miguel said, smiling. "I'll be sure and let the guys know."

From his truck, Wesley waved to several of his crew that were arriving to work.

"Boss!" yelled a carpool of men.

Wesley responded with a thumbs-up out the window.

On the second jobsite, he was the first to arrive. After unlocking, he opened the gates wide so the crew and trucks would have easy access. Entering his office, he opened the blinds, stored his lunch in the mini fridge, and made a pot of coffee. The earth work had been completed, and today the ever-important foundation work would begin.

It wasn't his preference to use this temporary crew for the masonry work. Having to do so meant constant supervision since their work ethic and quality of work was unknown to him. It would have been easier to go ahead and start to phase in his crew immediately. He reluctantly decided against that option. The men had come in thirty minutes earlier and left thirty minutes later to finish that site ahead of schedule. They deserved a day off.

The repeated sound of the time clock informed him that the crew had started to arrive. He staged an area in his office for the camera monitors once installed. After placing extra gloves on a table and filling a cooler with ice, he walked over to the crew to give instructions on the goal of the day. The expressions of a few made it obvious that this was something they were not used to hearing. But this was Wesley's style of leadership.

"Excuse me, Mr. Johnson, I have a question," said one crew member after hearing the daily goal.

"You have a question. I have an answer," said Wesley.

"That is a pretty big goal for one day, sir," said the man.

"It is. So what's your question?" asked Wesley.

"How are we going to complete all of that today? Are we not taking lunch and breaks?" the man asked, looking at the rest of the crew for verbal support.

"You are allotted a thirty-minute lunch and two fifteen-minute breaks, sir. I expect the daily goal to be completed by you and everyone else here through teamwork. I expect an honest day's work for an honest day's pay," Wesley responded.

"It just seems like a lot," the man said, softly realizing he wasn't getting any coworker support.

"Sounds like working at this site is going to be a problem for you," said Wesley.

"Not at all," the man replied for fear of being told to leave. "Not at all."

"Then let's get to it," said Wesley, dismissing the meeting as two concrete trucks pulled into the site followed by a Secure Systems minivan.

The temporary site foreman directed the concrete trucks while Wesley went to meet with the camera technicians. Williams was one of the two technicians. It was a lucrative contract, so he understood why Antonio was there. He greeted and shook both men hands.

"I had the men install poles at the locations we discussed," said Wesley to Antonio.

"Great," Antonio said, glancing in the directions indicated.

"I'll let you gentlemen get to work," he said. "If you need anything, just let me know."

After unloading their equipment, Antonio checked the stability of the first pole, then he and his assistant began the process of installing the wireless cameras. They checked and adjusted the camera's perspective using an iPad before moving on to the next. After a few hours, with only a third of the site completed, he and his assistant were wiping sweat from their brows.

The project was larger than he anticipated. He sent his assistant for additional cameras right after lunch. His instructions were, "Do not delay. The project must be complete by close of business." After his assistant pulled away in the truck, Antonio couldn't help but notice the steady work pace of the men. Wesley was right in the midst assisting, directing, and, in some cases, instructing. Completing the cameras became urgent for Antonio.

Antonio was finishing his last installation when the assistant returned thinking he'd take a break seeing the amount of sweat on his brow. Without delay, the two moved on to the next camera after a quick check of his watch. With a meager four hours remaining, Antonio instructed his assistant to begin working independently. After a couple of hours, they approached Wesley with an update.

"If you have time, I'm ready to set up the viewing station in your office," he said, wiping sweat.

"We have two coolers filled with water and Gatorade," Wesley said to the profusely sweating assistant. "Help yourself." He led the way. "Let me show you the area I prepared in the office," he said.

Then pausing to point the coolers, he said to Antonio, "Please feel free."

After quenching his thirst, Antonio followed Wesley into the air-conditioned office. It was a nondescript portable building on the outside. Inside the appearance was of an executive office. Placing his cell phone on the desk, Wesley walked to the refrigerator to get a bottle of water. A text message flashed across his phone just as he turned his back. Glancing at the screen, Antonio was able to quickly read a part of the message.

He pretended to admire the office when Wesley turned to face him.

"Very nice office," he said.

"Thanks. It serves its purpose," Wesley commented, walking to the area he'd designated for the computer monitors.

"Is this space adequate?" asked Wesley.

"Definitely," answered Antonio, visually judging the space.

"I'll let you get to work then," said Wesley, then walking to his desk. Picking up his phone after taking a seat, a smirk crept upon his face, which wasn't missed by Antonio. He quickly responded to the message and placed the phone back on his desk. Antonio quickly installed and connected the monitors. He provided Wesley with a demonstration and allowed him the opportunity to practice.

"Here's what I call our cheat sheet in case you forget something. On the back is the number for our twenty-four-hour tech support," he said, handing over the pamphlet, then extending his hand.

"Everything looks great. Thank you," said Wesley, giving his hand a firm grip.

"Don't hesitate to call if you have any questions," said Antonio, before walking away, wiping sweat from his brow.

A few minutes later an alarm sounded, alerting the crew that the day had ended. Standing near the time clock, Wesley congratulated the men on a great day's work.

The tapping horn of a passing car drew everyone's attention. It was Nadine on her way home. She stopped when she spotted the waving of Wesley's hand. As he walked to the car, the hushed voices of his men admiring her car and the fact that he knew the driver could be heard.

"Hi there, lovely lady," he said with his usual dimpled smile.

"Hi yourself," she responded, smiling back.

"Getting home a little late, aren't you?" he inquired.

"I stopped by the market. I needed a few things for this dish I'm trying for the first time."

"Want a test subject?" he asked, gauging her reaction.

"It's nothing fancy. A simple dish actually," she responded.

"I do simple. Unless I make you nervous," he said.

"No, of course not. If you don't mind a taco bake, I'll see you at the house when you finish up here," she said.

"See you in about thirty minutes then," he said with a tap on the car door.

Walking back to where the men stood in a huddle, Wesley noticed the smirks and looks of astonishment on their faces.

"A friend of yours, boss?" asked one man, smiling widely.

"Yes," he answered, picking up the coolers to place in the office.

"Your friend drives a nice car," commented another man when he came back for the second cooler.

Wesley glanced around, realizing none of the men had left.

"You've all seen a beautiful woman driving a nice car before," said Wesley, secretly enjoying the attention. "Get out of here and go home."

The men dispersed, heading toward their vehicles. Wesley glanced after then. He overheard a few commenting that the woman was probably his personal lady friend. He chuckled to himself knowing that it wasn't true at the present but was confident that it would be in the very near future. He took his time finishing up to give Nadine time to change out of her work clothes.

*****

Wesley climbed the steps of a Mediterranean-style house and pressed the doorbell. He was standing, admiring the cul-de-sac when the door swung open. Turning, he saw Nadine standing before him dressed casually in a loose-fitting gray ribbed square-neck jumpsuit. Her hair was pulled up into a high ponytail.

"Hi, there," she said, smiling.

"Hi," he said.

"Come on in," she said, stepping back to allow him to enter.

Stepping into the two-story foyer, Wesley glanced up, admiring the coffered ceiling. He noticed the diagonal pattern was repeated on the stone tilework of the floor below.

"It's still a work in progress," said Nadine, apologizing for the emptiness of the space.

"Mind showing me what you've done so far?" he asked, continuing to admire the space.

"The office is here," she said, walking toward glass French doors.

Wesley admired the way Nadine used light colors, abstract artwork, and modern furniture to brighten the dark mahogany of the room. A fireplace created a comforting space to not only work but to also create. Because the room was large enough for two desks, Nadine solved the problem by incorporating two Eliot swivel client chairs.

"Very nice," he said, admiring the space as he walked.

"Thank you," she said. "This will allow me to work from home some days."

"Requires discipline to work remotely," said Wesley.

"It does," she agreed.

"Think you can handle that?" he asked, glancing in her direction.

"Looking forward to it," she said. "Let me show you the living room."

He admired the sway of her hips as she walked away.

"Is that?" he asked, pointing to the painting over the fireplace.

"It is," she said, smiling.

"I rarely get to see some of my merchandise once it's sold," he lied, smiling.

"I think it ties everything together, don't you?" she asked.

"You did a great job," he said, taking in the room. "It's elegant but comfortable."

"That was my goal," she said, appreciating his assessment. "Come on." She headed toward the kitchen.

Taking a seat at the breakfast bar, Wesley picked up a remote and pressed the Power button. To his surprise a television began to broadcast a news show. Two glasses and a bottle of wine was placed on the counter in front of him along with a corkscrew.

"You mind doing the honors?" she asked, gesturing toward the wine.

"Not at all," he said.

After washing her hands, Nadine busied herself seasoning then cooking ground lamb, then dicing vegetable toppings as Wesley watched. The two chatted about her plans for decorating additional rooms and comments from his crew about her car. He shared that he was an only son in a family of three girls. He left out the part about how protective they were. She shared that she had been adopted and had a half-brother, Daniel, that was also adopted. She left out a lot of details, maintaining an impassive expression as she spoke.

Handing Wesley two plates for the table, she gathered napkins and silverware and directed him to the sunroom.

"Another television, Nadine?" he asked.

"Hey, I live alone," she commented with a smile.

"Mind if we turn this to sports?" he asked.

"Not at all. Go ahead," she said. "I'll get the food."

When she returned, he was listening intently to the latest updates about the Dallas Cowboys. She plated the food, not wanting to disturb him.

"I love the Cowboys," he said, turning to face her.

"I would've never guessed," she said with a smile.

"Shall I say grace?" he asked.

"Please," Nadine said, impressed by his action.

"This is really good," he said after taking a bite.

"You really like it?" she asked.

"Yes, I do," he said, taking another bite.

"I'm glad," she said, taking a sip of her wine.

"Do you always have wine with dinner?" he asked.

"Not always," she said with a smile. "But I do like wine."

"Good to know. What else do you like?"

"Well, you already know I like to cook," she said.

"From the look of every room, I've seen so far you like flowers too," he added.

"I do," she said softly with a smile. "I plan to have a little flower garden."

"So you grow flowers too?"

"I plan to do my best," she added with a dreamy look in her eyes.

"Where do you see yourself in five years, Nadine?" he asked.

"Retired, managing my own business from home, hopefully in a serious committed relationship," she said without hesitation.

"What about you?" she asked.

"In five years, I would like to be the regional director, move my business online somehow, maybe purchase a home somewhere," he said after some thought.

"How long have you wanted the director position?" she asked.

"Been chasing it for a few years," he said with a sigh.

"What has been the hold up?" she inquired.

"Me and the company," he answered.

"I'm not sure I follow you."

"The company believes they benefit more from me being in the field than in an office."

"Aren't you managing two sites right now?" she asked.

"I was. We completed the other site," he said sadly.

"Then show them you can do the same thing from behind a desk," she suggested.

He glanced at his phone when he received an alert from the cameras.

"I'm sorry. I had cameras installed at the site today so I can always see what going on," he said. "It was just a cat."

"Problem solved," she said with a huge smile.

"What do you mean?" he asked.

"Install cameras at all of the sites and manage from a desk," she said with a victorious smile. "Request to manage another site, have cameras installed, manage both sites. One in person one remotely. Show them you're capable of more."

He stared at her, pondering her suggestion. A slow smile crept upon is face.

Could it work? he asked himself.

"Just think about it," she said.

"I will. That's a great idea," he said, looking at her.

"To the first steps toward your promotion," she said with a smile, raising her glass in a toast.

*****

As Wesley drove home, he thought of his evening with Nadine. Not only was it relaxing, but enlightening. Not only was she beautiful, but she was also smart. She was interested in his dreams and helping him achieve them.

Nadine was different from the other women he dealt with. His goal to get her in bed hasn't changed. She was just different. The main interest his other conquests was what was in his wallet first. His prowess in bed was their second focus. His main interest was getting them in bed and as often as he could. The few dollars he threw their way was viewed as pennies by him.

He had encounters with successful women like Nadine but tended to avoid them. As soon as statements like "Move in," or "I can take care of you" came up, he would remove himself from the situation. He refused to be dominated by a woman financially or any other way. He noticed that earlier Nadine stated, "Committed relationship" and not marriage. *Very interesting*, he thought. He wondered if she was opposed to marriage. More to be discovered, he decided.

*****

The text message seen by Antonio had been from a female asking if Wesley was coming over. He wondered if Nadine was aware that the guy was already involved in a relationship.

The ringing of his cell phone interrupted his thoughts.

"Hello," said Antonio.

"Hey man, this is Charles. I heard you were back in town."

"What's going on man?" Antonio asked happily.

"Nothing. Just sitting here looking at a little TV and sipping on a beer. What about you?"

"Man, I'm beat," said Antonio. "I had a big install today at a construction site in the suburbs."

"Oh yeah?"

"Yeah, man," said Antonio. "That project manager is a real piece of work."

"Is he?" Charles laughed.

"Yeah, man," said Antonio. "Dude by the name of Wesley Johnson. An arrogant-to-the-bone type of dude."

"Wess, the ladies' best." Charles laughed.

"You know him?" asked Antonio.

"Yeah, I know Wesley," said Charles. "He's arrogant, but he's a good dude."

"Saw a text from some woman asking if he was coming by," said Antonio.

"What, are you checking out the dude's phone?" Charles asked, laughing.

"Naw, man. It was lying on the desk. I was standing right beside it when the text flashed across the screen. It just caught my attention," Antonio explained.

"What can I say, the dude's a real chick magnet," said Charles with a chuckle.

"Is that so?" Antonio chuckled, hoping for more information.

"I know it sounds like I'm ragging on the man, but there's no other way to say it except he's a straight man whore," said Charles.

"Really?" asked Antonio.

"Yeah, man. Wesley got a lot of women. Supposedly, none of the women know about the other women. They each think Wesley is their man exclusively. It's all a game with Wess," said Charles.

"A womanizer," said Antonio.

"Well, we're all guilty of our past little indiscretions," added Charles.

"Yeah, but it sounds like you're saying he has multiple women," said Antonio.

"I'm pretty sure he does." Charles laughed. "I've known him for a few years. Seen him out on a few occasions with different women. Looks like he never takes them to the same places. But that's his thing you know. I'm settled down now with a wife and a baby on the way."

"Congratulations, man. I'm happy for you," said Antonio.

"Thanks, man. I'm happy. I really am," confessed Charles.

"I plan on joining you," joked Antonio.

"Seriously man, when are you going to settle down?" asked Charles. "A few years back I thought you were going to beat me to the altar. You and that one girl you were seeing. What was her name?"

"You're talking about Nadine," Antonio said.

"Yeah. You guys were like the lovebirds of the century," remembered Charles.

"We were," agreed Antonio with a smile.

"Whatever happened to her?" Charles asked.

"We kind of stopped seeing each other," said Antonio, then going silent.

"Was it you or her?"

"It was me," confessed Antonio.

"Can it be fixed?" asked Charles.

"I'm trying, but I think Wesley has his eye on her too," added Antonio.

"Oh wow," said Charles slowly. "She seemed like a smart lady. Once she figures out, she's not the only woman, that won't last. Just hang in there if she's what you want."

"I intend to. It was good talking to you," said Antonio, feeling melancholy.

"Listen, come over Sunday. You can meet my wife, and we'll watch the game together," said Charles.

"Okay, thanks for the invite," said Antonio, hanging up, not feeling very sociable.

*****

In the suburbs, Nadine smiled as she responded to a text from Drew asking her to confirm their appointment. She did, but also asked if he would be interested in attending her gathering that was scheduled for earlier in the evening. The reply of yes came immediately. Before she could place her phone on the charger, Everette texted, asking if it was okay to bring another friend, a female. Nadine agreed, thinking it would even the male-to-female ratio for the evening.

Nadine was excited because it was going to be the first gathering she'd had since moving in. She'd have to remember to have Outdoor Elegance deliver the Rustic Deep patio furniture and a couple of chaises she'd located online. It was perfect for after dinner conversation.

*****

The following day, after giving the team their daily goal, Wesley busied himself scanning upcoming projects. Pairing the right project with this current one was vital to successfully implement Nadine's suggestion. Wireless headsets would be needed for immediate communication with his foreman. He put in a requisition to Amanda for sets. For now, he decided to utilize a walkie with the security cameras while he worked in his office.

*****

Across town, Antonio unloaded equipment to begin an installation. Coming out of the bank a few doors away was none other than Nadine's closest friend, Everette.

"Fate should not be so cruel," came a female-toned male voice.

Glancing up, Antonio saw Everett standing in front of his van, looking especially feminine although dressed as a professional male.

"Everette?" Antonio said, surprised.

"None other," Everett responded, looking Antonio over with a contemptuous expression.

"What's going on, man?" Antonio responded with a chuckle, not bothered by the man's antics.

"Life is good, for me anyways. I can see you're not doing too bad either. No one has broken your legs yet," he answered, smiling after his last comment.

"You're right I'm not doing too bad," responded Antonio with a chuckle and shake of his head.

"So what the hell are you doing here?" Everette inquired.

"I'm about to do an install," he said.

"I see," said Everett, glancing at the storefront. "I guess Nan's idea about you going commercial is paying off."

"It is. I'm indebted to her for helping grow my business," Antonio responded sincerely.

"You must have forgotten," Everett said with feigned surprise. "You paid her back with a broken heart. I'm sorry you forgot about that."

"I haven't forgotten, Everett, and I plan to explain and make it up to her."

"Oh, pa-leez," Everett said with genuine disbelief.

"Look, I know you're Nadine's best friend. So I'm going to say this to you. It was all a misunderstanding," said Antonio.

"Let me get this right," said Everett. "You misunderstood that you were sleeping with another woman and got her pregnant while at the same time, making Nadine think the two of you were an exclusive couple on the way to marriage."

"I guess you've never made a mistake," accused Antonio.

"You mean mistakenly break someone's heart that truly loves me by having an affair that resulted in a pregnancy?" asked Everett. "Can't say that I have. You got me on that one."

"Yes, I had an affair. Yes, I broke Nadine's heart. Yes, I regret it every minute of every day. But there was no pregnancy. It was all a lie," admitted Antonio.

Everett stared at him while he spoke. Suddenly and frantically, he began reaching into his pocket in search of something. Pulling out a coin, he handed it to Antonio with contrived sadness.

"Here, call 1-800-NEED-SYMPATHY because I have none for you. Besides, Nan is having her first gathering this weekend, and I must find an outfit. Bye, loser," he said, almost skipping away.

I hate that guy, Antonio thought as he walked toward the building. He was counting on Everett spilling his guts to Nadine the moment he got to his office. That pleased him. What disturbed him was knowing that she was having a gathering and hadn't thought to invite him. He preferred an evening alone with her. A setting where the two of them could talk.

He did two more installations that afternoon before deciding to give Nadine a call to see if she would mention the get-together. The call didn't go as he had hoped. Nadine mentioned the gathering indicating that it was very small because the house was still mostly unfurnished. She did however raise his hopes by stating that as soon as a few more downstairs rooms were furnished, she'd have him, Tracie, and the boys over to see the house.

"Hey, Tony. What's going on?" asked Nadine.

"Just thought I'd give my friend a call," he responded.

"That was sweet of you," she said, rolling her eyes.

"So how's the decorating coming?"

"It's coming along. I should have the living room and office finished off this week," she said.

"What's next after that?" he asked.

"I want to do the media room next, so I'll have a relaxed area to entertain in. Right now, I'm trying to keep gatherings small because I only have the living room, kitchen, and sunroom that are presentable," she explained.

"Sounds like you're planning a small gathering," he inquired further.

"I am. Vee has someone special that I need to check out his qualifications," she joked.

"Everett's feisty. You need back up?" he asked, laughing hopefully.

"Oh no, I've got this," she responded confidently. "When I get the media room set up, I am going to invite you guys over for a tour of the place."

"That sounds like a plan," he reluctantly accepted.

*****

As Everett returned to his office, he wondered how much of Antonio's rantings were true. Normally, he'd be on the phone immediately spilling the gossip to Nadine. With only one day until the gathering, he decided to wait and see who the mystery guy was. Besides if he was a sleaze like Antonio, then he'd surely make a move on Denice.

Everett had invited Denice as a distraction. He wanted to know if the guy was really into Nadine or could he be distracted by a pretty face and body. He was counting on Denice being herself. Her goal was always how much money she could get out of a guy and by any means necessary. The night was going to be interesting. While Nadine would be busy sizing up his guy, he would be doing the same to hers.

*****

Denice dressed in a form-fitting jumpsuit with jeweled sandals. Everett, whom she didn't know very well, had invited her to a gathering in the suburbs. He came into the salon to get his hair done regularly. The fact that he was gay and had money was no secret. Men with money were the kind of men she liked, and she planned to nab one.

When Everett had invited her, she was more than a little surprised. The man remarked about how pretty she was and asked if she worked out. She answered no and laughed at the thought of her sweating in a fitness center. She exercised and sweated too, just not in the way that he imagined.

*****

Nadine set glasses in the freezer to chill before her guests arrived. She glanced around the sunroom to make sure everything was up to her standard. This would be her first-time meeting Everett's special friend and the unknown guest. She wanted to make a good impression.

Nadine made her way to the door when the motion detector informed her that the evening was about to begin.

"Hey, love," said Nadine at the sight of Drew.

"Evening, beautiful," said Drew, stepping into the threshold embracing her. "Where is everyone?" he asked, handing her a bouquet of roses and a bottle of her favorite wine.

"You're the first to arrive, dear," she said. "Let me put these into a vase."

He followed behind, admiring the way she dressed. It was apparent to him that she wore thongs as always under the pretty little pink off-the-shoulder floral dress. The taupe block heels with ankle straps accentuated the shape of her legs.

"How early am I?" he asked, taking a seat at the breakfast bar.

"Only a few minutes," she said, arranging the flowers in a vase, then setting them on the kitchen table where she had staged bottles of wine.

The doorbell sounded again just as she set a chilled bowl of fresh strawberries on the table.

"The evening begins," she said with a smile, going to greet more guests.

"Shall I pour some wine?" called Drew from the kitchen.

"Yes, please," she replied.

"We're here!" announced Everett as soon as the door opened.

"Hey!" exclaimed Nadine, then embracing her friend tightly. "Come on in." She smiled brightly. "Welcome. Welcome."

"Nan, this is Chris, my boo," said Everett, stroking the man's arm as he spoke.

"It's so nice to meet you," Nadine said, shaking the man's hand.

"Don't be fooled, love. She plans to grill you with questions before the evening is over," said Everett with a roll of his eyes.

"He is exactly right," confessed Nadine, laughing.

"Nan, this is Denice. Denice, this is my best friend, Nadine," introduced Everett before heading to the kitchen.

"Hello," said Denice, looking around the foyer in amazement.

"Hello to you," said Nadine, smiling, surprised by the woman's reaction. "Please come in."

"And just who the hell are you?" asked Everett, seeing Drew seated at the counter.

"I'm Andrew," he responded with a chuckle, extending his hand. "And you are?"

"I'm Everett, Nan's best friend." He shook the man's hand. "You'll never convince me that she hasn't mentioned me," said Everett incredulously.

"She's mentioned you." Andrew laughed. "She talks about you all of the time."

"She hasn't mentioned your ass at all," said Everett with hands on hips. "Why is that?"

"Nadine and I are private when it comes to our personal life," explained Andrew with a smile.

"Bitch, I know everything there is to know about Nan," said Everett, accepting a glass of wine.

Nadine and the others entered the room and introduced themselves. Everett glared at Nadine questioningly, which she ignored with a smirk. Drew handed a glass of wine to Nadine and then the newest guest. This little act did not get pass Everett without being noticed.

As Everett glanced round the room, he just realized the dynamics were off.

The doorbell sounded, and Nadine scurried off to meet what Everett assumed was the final guest of the evening.

"So, Andrew, what do you do?" asked Everett as soon as Nadine was out of sight.

"I work in corporate acquisitions," he answered without hesitation.

"What about you?" Drew asked, reversing the question.

"I work in finance. Nan and I work for the same firm."

"I imagine you guys have been friends for a while," said Drew.

"Years to be exact," clarified Everett. "And you?"

"Babe, come on," interrupted Chris with a smile.

"A couple of years," answered Drew.

"So what are your intentions?" asked Everett.

Before he could answer, Nadine entered the room with a handsome dimpled-faced gentleman. Everett was surprised by the man's urban casual style. He completed the look with what Everett would later describe as a monstrous gold chain and medallion. He wore earrings in both ears to finish off his look.

As Nadine made introductions, Everett didn't miss the looks that passed between Denice and the new guy, Wesley. They knew each other, he was sure of it. Something else that didn't go unnoticed was the huge bouquet of flowers Nadine held when she entered the room. Drew was visibly not pleased but tried to hide his displeasure.

"Put some music on please, Drew," said Nadine with a slight touch on his shoulder. Her touch seemed to ease his discomfort.

As he moved across the room to comply, Denice followed close on his heels.

"You said you work in acquisitions," Denice began. "Would that be in real estate or stocks?"

Turning, Drew was forced to steady the woman because she was standing so close. She gazed at him with a sultry look. The smell of her cheap perfume annoyed his nose.

"That would be corporate," he said, careful not to brush against her as he moved away.

As he and Nadine made eye contact, a smirk of humor crept upon her face. Whenever the woman came near Drew, he would subtly withdraw closer to Nadine. He whispered something to Nadine, and she responded with a huge smile.

"Denice, tell us about yourself. What do you do?" asked Nadine.

Three faces waited for a response. Everett sipped his wine, already knowing the answer. Wesley looked at the floor, then glanced up.

"I'm a stylist," she responded to the three faces waiting for an answer. "A hair stylist."

"And she's very good," added Everett. "She must be. She does my hair every two weeks."

"So you own the salon where babe goes?" asked Chris, giving Everett a loving hug.

"No," she stammered. "Right now, I just work there. I plan to open my own shop though."

She's been saying that for years, thought Wesley, looking up, having heard that lie numerous times when put on the spot.

"We all begin somewhere," said Nadine, seeing the embarrassment on the woman's face.

"Yeah," said Wesley and Drew in unison, then glancing at each other, both sharing a knowing smirk.

Nadine nudged Drew, who reacted with a one-armed hug. She sent Wesley a motherly stare that said, "Behave."

He smiled and gave her a slight nod of compliance.

"I know Nadine has wine for the evening, but would any of you guys like a beer?" asked Drew.

"Here, here," said Wesley and Chris as all three moved to the patio for manly conversation.

"Vee talks about Nadine daily," said Chris, taking a swallow of his beer.

"They're inseparable." Drew chuckled.

"How long have you and Nadine been together?" asked Chris.

"Year and a half," said Drew.

"Is it serious, or you guys just waiting to see where it goes?" inquired Wesley.

"It's serious," said Drew. "I know where it's going."

"That wouldn't be the altar, would it?" asked Chris, grinning.

"All the way," replied Drew.

"You're serious about her if you're talking like that," said Wesley.

"Nadine's mine. She always will be," said Drew, confidently looking directly at Wesley.

Back inside the house Nadine, Everett, and Denice sat at the breakfast bar sipping wine and talking.

"Since it's just us girls, give us a tour of the furnished rooms," said Everett.

"You have a beautiful home," said Denice.

"Thank you," said Nadine.

"Since it's just us girls, I'll show you the master bedroom," said Nadine, leading them upstairs.

"I've already seen it," said Everett, sounding bored.

"See it again," snapped Nadine. "This way, Denice." She smiled.

"This place is unbelievable," said Denice as the three women returned to the kitchen to find the guys all nibbling strawberries.

"Lovely lady, strawberries, wine, and beer is nice. But some meat would be better," Wesley joked as he approached Nadine.

"Drew, grab the salad from the fridge," Nadine said, smiling after Wesley, who whispered something as he walked past her.

"There are steaks and potatoes in the warmer. Can you get those for me, Vee?" asked Nadine.

"I'm on it," Everett said, moving across the kitchen to obey.

"Everything goes on the table in the sunroom," she said as she warmed up the rolls.

"Wesley, can you please grab the butter and salad dressings from the fridge?" she asked. "Denice, honey, go ahead and have a seat outside."

Denice glanced back at Wesley before exiting the room. Nadine saw the look and smiled at Wesley.

"Don't start," he joked.

"I think she likes you," she whispered.

"I was about to say the same thing about your friend, Andrew,' he whispered back.

They both snickered, then put on nice faces before leaving the kitchen with butter and warm rolls.

"I hope no one is allergic to seafood," said Nadine.

"I love shrimp salad," commented Denice with a smile.

Drew and Wesley again exchanged glances but neither commented knowing it was a seafood salad.

"The food is delicious," said Chris, reaching for another roll.

"Thank you. I'm glad you like it," she said, smiling.

"I told you my girl can cook," said Everett.

"You cooked all of this?" asked Denice, surprised.

"Yes," said Nadine. "I love to cook."

"The food is delicious, love," said Drew.

"Thank you for the compliment," she said, giving him a look.

"We know this isn't your first time," said Everett, fishing for information.

"You're right. It isn't," Drew said, smiling continuing to eat.

"How about you, Wesley? Have you tasted her cooking before?" Everett continued questioning.

"Okay, Vee!" said Nadine, smiling. "Let him enjoy his meal without you interrogating him."

"Is it okay if I interrogate him?" asked Denice to everyone's surprise.

"By all means" said Nadine, motioning with her hands with a surprised expression.

"Have you tasted her cooking before, Wesley?" she asked.

"I certainly have," he confessed with a broad smile. "And it was just as delicious. My compliments to the chef," he said, raising his glass and everyone joined in.

Denice raised her glass with a faked smile. Her head, however, was spinning with questions. She and Wesley had been weekly bed partners for over a year. They had even gone on a few dates. Deciding to be more observant, she noticed his frequent and lingering glances at the hostess.

Wesley and Nadine's friendly playfulness was visible as soon as he arrived and obviously irritated Drew, who remained silent. Before dinner, Denice had noticed that Andrew began to frequently adjust his proximity or touched Nadine's shoulder or hand in some slight way. Politely, she responded with a quick glance and a smile of reassurance. Wesley appeared too comfortable in the space. It was evident that he'd been there before but kept his distance because of the other man.

She wanted to stir the emotional pot a little more but didn't want to appear low class. She'd get her information from Everett, who clearly had more knowledge and freedom to pry. With the ladies clearing the table, the guys, not including Everett, took the gathering to the patio where they lounged on the plush but firm cushions.

"Nadine, forgive me asking," began Denice, "are you and Andrew engaged?"

Everett burst into laughter and looked at Nadine for an answer.

"Yes, please tell us. Are you two engaged?" he asked, smiling broadly.

"We're not engaged," Nadine answered, glaring at Everett. "We're just friends," she explained softly, redirecting her glance to Denice. "Why do ask?"

"I was going to comment that you could be, if you were interested," Denice said, smiling sneakily.

"He does seem into her, doesn't he?" added Everett, wiggling his eyebrows.

"Oh, please," said Nadine dismissively. "Drew is a nice man, but we're just close friends."

"He better not be classified as the best friend," snapped Everett, with hands on both hips.

"Relax, honey," said Nadine, smiling. "You're the only one who gets the honor of that title."

"Damn right," responded Everett. "I'd hate to go out there and have Chris beat his ass."

"Have Chris do it?" asked Nadine.

"Please, don't pretend you can't see the biceps and pectorals on that guy," remarked Everett. "Hell, I can't touch that."

The two other women burst into laughter.

"What about Wesley?" Denice asked, fishing for more information.

"Someone's got lots of questions," said Everett, spotting the ruse.

"Like Drew, Wesley is also just a friend," said Nadine, trying to end the interrogation.

"Not exactly like Drew, I hope," mumbled Everett with a shiver. "Do you know Wesley?" he asked, directing his question to Denice.

"Um, well, yes," she stammered, unprepared for the role reversal.

"Do you?" asked Nadine, surprised.

"Now this is interesting," commented Everett. "How do you know him?"

"He's a flea-market vendor. I bought some merchandise from him a while back," the woman explained, fidgeting. She wouldn't dare disclose the fact that he only came and went at night. One night a week to be exact.

Nadine and Everett exchanged glances but didn't comment.

"A flea-market vendor?" said Everett, looking at Nadine with astonishment. "Seriously?" he said to Nadine's amusement.

"Let's join the guys," said Nadine, laughing.

The men were in a serious conversation about football when the women joined them. Chris immediately gave Everett's hand a quick kiss after he settled beside him.

"Wesley, forgive me for asking, but what do you do for a living?" asked Everett.

"Babe," reprimanded Chris.

"It's fine," Wesley said with a chuckle, reclining on a chaise. "I'm a project manager for Terner Construction."

"Project manager?" asked Denice, stunned by his answer. "I thought you were a flea-market vendor!"

"You know him?" asked Chris and Drew in unison, glancing between the two.

"This shit is as thick as unstirred glue," mumbled Everett.

"I sell merchandise on the weekends at various flea markets," answered Wesley without hesitation. "She probably saw me there or bought something from me." He gave Denice a look that dared her to answer differently.

"What a relief," said Everett with exaggerated female gestures before taking a sip of wine.

"Project manager today, director tomorrow, right, Wess?" said Nadine, noting how Denice's outburst bothered him.

"That's right," he said, smiling as she reached across and patted his hand.

Denice stared across the patio at Nadine. She realized the woman wasn't chasing Wesley. They really were just friends to her. Still, she couldn't stomp down the jealousy. She could tell by the way he looked into the woman's eyes that Wesley wanted Nadine.

He never looked at her that way. The looks he gave her were purely sexual. The only time she could remember him looking at her seriously was when he asked about her five-year goal.

Dumb-ass question, she thought.

"I hate to do it, Chris, but it's time for your interview." Nadine smiled.

"Bring it on," snapped Everett. "You're about to hire my babe. Besides, we had a prep session before we got here."

"Tell me about yourself?" she asked seriously.

"Well, I work as a real estate broker. I have no kids, and I've never been married," he said.

"How long have you known Vee?"

"A little over a year now. A year and a half to be exact."

"Where do you see yourself in five years?"

"Married to Vee, maybe adopt a couple of kids, a homeowner like yourself, taking on life and whatever it brings as a team," he answered, looking directly at Nadine.

"Let me say this," Nadine said, moving to the edge of her seat with Drew's hand resting on one of her knees. "Vee is my best friend. He's been there for me through every up and down I've encountered. If you do anything—"

"I can see you are serious," he said.

"I am."

"I promise you. My heart and my intentions are all in the right place," he said sincerely.

"Good," she said, relaxing in her seat with a broad smile. "I'd hate to have Wess and Drew kick your ass."

They all laughed.

"You're cool and all man," began Drew. "But if she says do it—"

"Then we have to do it," finished Wesley.

The two men bumped fists in agreement.

"You're hired!" yelled Nadine, raising her glass in a toast.

*****

The evening was a success. Wesley left first after saying his goodbyes to the other guests. Nadine walked him to the door. He gave her a tight hug, which she reciprocated.

"I'll call you tomorrow," he said after a kiss on the cheek.

Moments later, Nadine walked Drew and the others to the door together.

"I have a long drive. Quick restroom break," he said before rushing off.

"Um, you know the way," she said, following his lead.

"We'll chat," said Everett before the three of them descended the stairs.

Drew and Nadine chatted as the two tackled the task of righting the kitchen.

"I think your friend Wesley is interested in you," he said.

"I think Denice was interested in you," she countered with a smile.

"Definitely," he said sneeringly. "Like Capital One, what's in my wallet."

"Did you see her reaction when she discovered he wasn't a flea-market vendor?" Nadine laughed.

"I almost spit my beer." Drew chuckled.

"You think they sleep together?" whispered Nadine.

"Of course! And why are you whispering?" he asked.

"I don't know." She laughed.

"Did you see that look he gave her?" he asked.

"I did," responded Nadine. "It looked as if she wanted to say more."

"She did," said Drew, folding a dish towel. "I almost wanted her to."

"I'm pretty sure he may have said something embarrassing if she had," Nadine stated.

"It wouldn't have bother me." Drew laughed. "She was border-line annoying."

"She was pretty though," said Nadine.

"She is pretty but not the marrying kind," he said, noticing Nadine's stare. "What those kinds of women don't get is that, yes, as men we want to see, but not all at once. When you put it all out there like that, you're sending the message that it's open and available to the highest bidder. We fuck those kinds of women. We don't select them for serious relationships, and we don't marry them. No man wants every other man looking at his goods."

"Well, that was enlightening," said Nadine, grinning

"Let's go to bed," said Drew, leading her upstairs by the hand.

"So what'd you think about Vee?" Nadine asked as she adjusted her body next to his.

"I think he's quite entertaining for one thing." Drew chuckled.

"He'll grill me on why I haven't mentioned you and a thousand other questions," she said, smiling.

"Why haven't you mentioned me?" he asked, sounding serious.

Readjusting to face him, Nadine could see the hurt in his expression.

"Come on. How do you explain what we've been doing without it sounding cheap and meaningless?"

"Is that how you see us?" he asked.

"Of course not. But that's how it began. That's how I began it. I cringe thinking about how you must have viewed me when I came to you," she said, shaking her head.

When he looked at her, he saw self-degradation. Balancing on his forearm, he tilted her face so he could look into her eyes.

"When you presented me with your proposal that night, I'm not going to lie, I was surprised. But as you waited for my response, I could tell you were in unchartered territory and was taking a chance. You were not only nervous, you were scared, and had no clue about what to do once you'd finished your little presentation," he said.

"You knew?" she asked surprised.

"Yeah, I knew. That's why I took the lead. It was never cheap and meaningless, Nadine," he said. "Did it begin as an agreement? Definitely. But it stopped being that that first night, the moment I entered you and we looked at each other. It was mutual commitment, not to the agreement but to each other. I'm still committed."

"We can't complicate things, Drew," she whispered with a shaky voice.

"Too late. We're in too deep," he finished, then kissed her deeply.

Roadblocks

ANTONIO SAT AT his desk reviewing tech support calls from the night before. He had a company that handled that, but he liked to follow up with his customers. The chime of the door alerted him to a customer.

"Hi, Tony," said the woman standing just inside the threshold.

"What are you doing here?" he snarled.

"I heard you were back in town and thought I'd drop by to see how you were," the woman said softly.

"I'm back. I'm fine. You've seen me. Now you can go," he said, turning back to the monitor.

The woman didn't move.

"What do you want, Shawn?" he snapped.

"I wanted to apologize."

"Apologize for what? Apologize for refusing to accept that our fling was over? Apologize for breaking up a relationship that meant the world to me? Or maybe you wanted to apologize for lying about being pregnant?" he ranted.

"Wait a minute," she retaliated angrily. "I do apologize for lying about being pregnant. And I also apologize for not accepting the end of us. I refused to accept it because at that time I loved you. But I won't apologize for breaking up your relationship with that other woman. You did that when you started seeing me knowing you were involved with her."

"Okay, I accept your apology. Now can you just get out of here and forget you ever knew me," he said with exasperation.

"I can see you are still bitter. After what? Two years," she said, shaking her head.

"The sight of you makes me bitter," he snapped.

"You act like you were the only one hurt," she said.

"I tried to end it nicely," he said. "You just couldn't stroll off into the sunset. You had to complicate things."

"Your lies complicated things," she snapped.

"Okay. I'm bitter, Shawn. Are you happy now? Does that just make your day?"

"No, Tony. Your bitterness does not make me happy. What does make me happy is the fact that I'm married now to a good man that loves me and I am pregnant this time with his child," she said proudly.

"Congratulations and I hope he gets a DNA test before he signs the birth certificate. Goodbye," he said, turning his back.

Turning toward the door at the sound of the chime, he was relieved to find her gone. He clinched his fists at the thought of her being happily married and moving on with her life while he woke every morning drowning in the guilt of his past. *It's not fair*, he thought. He was a good man that made a horrible mistake. Worst of all, he couldn't move past it.

He hadn't lived a celibate life after he and Nadine broke up. He'd dated and slept with women. He just couldn't connect with them the way that he wanted and needed. He missed everything about her—her smell, her smile, her presence. With a determined mind, he picked up the phone and pressed a saved number.

"Nadine Swift."

"Nadine, it's Antonio."

"I know." She chuckled. "What's going on?"

"I need to talk to you," he said seriously.

"Is everything okay?" she asked, concerned.

"No. It's not. I really need to talk to you," he pleaded.

"Lunch or dinner?" she asked, truly concerned.

"Dinner, I guess," he said. "Nothing fancy. A place where we can talk."

"There's a sports bar on the first floor of my building. How about we meet there right after work?" she suggested.

"I'll be there," he said, hanging up immediately.

*****

"What's the meaning of that look?" asked Everett, entering her office.

"I just got the strangest call from Antonio," she said.

"Don't tell me he's knocked up someone else?" said Everett, rolling his eyes.

"Shut up!" Nadine laughed. "What are you doing down here?"

"Personally, dropping off financial statements to my bestie because I know how she likes to get a jump on things," he said, handing her a binder.

"You know me so well," Nadine said, taking the binder and placing it on her desk.

"I didn't mention it, but I saw Antonio on the street a few weeks ago," confessed Everett, taking a seat.

"That's not a big deal. At least you got the opportunity to see that he's still Mr. Muscle Mania." She laughed.

"He said something strange," said Everett.

"Oh yeah, what was that?" asked Nadine as she saved something on her computer.

"He claimed the pregnancy situation was all a lie," said Everett, causing Nadine to pause.

"A lie?" she asked.

"That's what he said."

"Did you believe him?"

"I don't know. I was being an asshole as usual, and he ignored it," said Everett thoughtfully. "He seemed sincere."

"He wants to talk. Do you think that's what he wants to talk about?"

"If I had to guess, my answer would be yes."

"I don't want to relive that," whined Nadine.

"You've already agreed to listen, I'm sure. So listen. Just listen with open eyes and not a bleeding heart," advised Everett, rising to leave. "You know I'm going to be calling you," he said before closing her door.

*****

Nadine sat nibbling on nachos and salsa and sipping a whisky sour. She attempted to dissipate her apprehension. Glancing across the room, she inhaled deeply at the sight of Antonio strolling in her direction.

Here we go, she thought.

"Thanks for coming," he said, giving her a kiss on the cheek.

"Of course, I'd come," she replied. "You sounded so serious over the phone."

"It is, Nan," he said.

His use of the pet-name told her just how serious.

"I'm listening. What is it?"

"Promise me you'll listen first," he pleaded. "And please don't walk out."

"I promise," she said after a short pause, then took a sip of her drink.

"Two years ago, I made the biggest mistake of my life. My business was growing. I was feeling successful and on top of the world. I felt like I had everything right at my fingertips. I was just waiting for it to come into fruition. I ran into Shawn, a girl I dated in high school when I was setting up the first satellite location. He had a few drinks, exchanged numbers, and reminisced. That night we both drank too much and ended up in bed."

Nadine leaned back in her seat and continued to listen.

"I regretted it the next day. I did. Then every time I came to town, she'd call, and the whole thing just kept replaying. I know it sounds bad, but I didn't love her. It was just sex to me. I felt like a stupid teenager doing something I know I shouldn't be doing, but I was getting away with it. Then she calls one day when I get to town talking about the two of us moving in with each other, and I panicked. That wasn't what I wanted. She wasn't what I wanted. I was just having fun. I had told her I was involved with someone, but she acted like she hadn't heard a thing. So I blocked her from calling, thinking it was over, I was done, and you and I could go one with our lives like we planned.

"That's when she followed me home. She told me this after you left that night. Before kicking her out, I told her to meet me at the clinic the next day for a test. I arrived. She never showed. She texted to tell me it was a lie and that she just wanted to hurt me like I'd hurt her," he said, finally going silent.

"Wow," said Nadine softly, then finished off her drink. She sat for a few minutes, then motioned for the waitress to bring two.

"I live with the guilt of what I did with every breath," he said. "I understand it's an unbelievable story. And what I did is unforgiveable. I know how much you loved me. And I loved you the same. I still do. I don't deserve your forgiveness, but I'm begging for it."

Immediately taking a swallow of her drink, Nadine looked across the table, not speaking. She saw the truth of his words in his eyes and heard the guilt in his voice. The evidence of it was on his face. Finally revealing the truth to her seemed to age him.

"I believe you, Tony," she said finally. "I can also see how it all happened."

The breath he'd been holding finally escaped him.

"What I can't understand," she added, "is why you continued for so long? You cheated with her for six months. Did you expect her not to develop feelings?"

"I don't know what I was thinking. There's no other explanation other than the truth. I wasn't thinking, at all. I was feeling myself. Thinking I was top dog, having my cake and eating it too. I had a woman at home that I loved and that loved me, and I had this trick on the side stroking my ego making me feel like I was invincible."

"I agreed that we could be friends, Tony. Why are you telling me this?" she asked.

"Because you deserve to know the truth. And I can't continue living with this guilt," he confessed. "It's killing me inside."

"Then stop," she said softly. "Stop feeling guilty. It happened. Now let's move on."

"I love you, Nadine. I've always loved you. I still love you," he confessed, grasping her hand across the table.

"I loved you too, Tony," she said not withdrawing her hand. "With everything within me, I loved you. You know I did. For a long time afterward, I continued to love you. You hurt me so badly I thought I'd never recover. But I did. And I forgive you. I forgive you for the past. It happened. We can't change that. It's out in the open crystal clear. Now you must forgive yourself."

"You forgive me?" he confirmed.

"I do," she said.

"I still love you," he said.

"I know you do," she said, leaning in. "I care for you, Tony. But I don't love you. I'm afraid to love you. I'm afraid you'll hurt me again."

"Are you afraid of me, Nadine?" he asked directly.

"What do you mean?"

"Are you afraid of being around me?"

"I was afraid of this conversation and how it would make me feel," she answered honestly. "But I'm not afraid of you."

"And now?" he asked.

"I'm glad we had it, and I'm glad it's over," she confessed.

"So where do we go from here? Now that you know how I feel."

"We're friends, Tony. We're still friends," she answered with a modest smile that didn't reach the sadness in her eyes.

"Tracie asked about you," he said, trying to lighten the mood.

"Did she?" asked Nadine, thankful for the subject change.

"I told her you'd bought a house."

"I'm going to invite her and the boys over to watch the game one Sunday," she said thoughtfully.

"Is it okay if she calls? She keeps asking, and I told her I wasn't sure how you felt about all of that."

"Yes, please. Tell her it's okay. It'll be good catching up," she said, smiling.

"She'll be glad to hear it."

"I'm going to head out. I think after this conversation, a bubble bath and a glass of wine is calling my name," she said, standing.

"I give great massages," he whispered as he hugged her goodbye.

"I remember," she said with a smirk, then walked away.

*****

Antonio bypassed his condo and headed straight for Tracie's apartment. He felt as if a weight had been lifted from his shoulders. With overexcitement, he recalled the encounter to his sister, who smiled, nodded, and listened to his story.

"Be careful, Tony," she said.

"Careful of what?"

"I don't mean to sound doubtful, but Nadine was devastated. That gay friend of hers called here asking for you mad as hell. He was ranting about her being close to a breakdown!"

"Everett. He's dramatic," said Antonio dismissively.

"I don't think he was being dramatic. He sounded seriously concerned," she said. "He made me concerned for her."

"It was bad," he admitted. "I could see it in her eyes when she looked at me."

"She may say you guys are friends," she warned. "But trust me, bro, she has a titanium wall up around that heart of hers when it comes to you."

"You know that Wesley guy?" he asked.

"Wesley Johnson, the vendor?"

"He's after her. And he's not a vendor. He's a project manager for a construction company."

"You're kidding!" she exclaimed.

"I installed security cameras at his site a few weeks ago."

"How does he know Nadine?"

"He's overseeing the construction of the community building in her subdivision."

"Get the hell out of here! Seriously?"

"Seriously."

"Project manager? What do they do anyways?" she asked.

"He's the boss of the whole set up. He leads an entire crew of men in constructing a project from start to finish. And he has pull with the company," said Antonio.

"He must be good," she said.

"From what I could see, he is."

"Think he makes good money?" she asked, smiling deviously.

"No doubt."

"Well, if she doesn't want him, I'll take him," said Tracie. "No pun intended."

"Really, Trace?" said Antonio.

"I'm just saying." She smirked. "So she said it's okay if I call?"

"She did."

"Good because I want to see that house," she said, walking toward the kitchen. "Are you staying for dinner?" she called out.

"I'm heading out. Let me know how the call goes," he yelled back before leaving.

*****

When Nadine turned into her community, Wesley was just locking the gates. Turning, he walked into the street, preventing her from moving forward.

"What's wrong, lovely lady?" he asked the moment he looked at her.

"Just a rough day," she lied.

"Looks like more than a rough day at work," he said, eyeing her suspiciously. "Want to talk about it?"

"I'm okay," she said, forcing a smile.

"Listen. No judgment, just ears, and it stays between us," he said.

"Okay," she said softly, then driving away.

*****

Nadine was just depositing her briefcase in the office when the doorbell sounded.

"Come on it," she said, moving aside so he could enter.

"I'll wait in the kitchen," he said. "I'll let you get changed."

"Thanks," she said, disappearing up the staircase to an area he had not been privileged to explore yet.

After turning on the television, he checked the fridge to see if any leftover beers remained. To his surprise there were several. Grabbing a bottle, he searched the drawers for an opener.

Nadine entered to find him sipping on beer and eating Chex Mix as he listened to a news broadcast.

"Sorry it took so long," she said.

"I hope it's okay," he said, raising the beer and gesturing to the snacks.

"Feel free," she said. "I hate beer." Then she explained, "I cook when I'm aggravated."

"Please," he said. "Just make sure it's enough for two."

Grabbing a pack of sweet Italian sausage, some boneless chicken that was thawing in the fridge, pasta, and a bottled whiskey sauce. Nadine set about preparing a meal.

Wesley turned off the television to avoid interruptions. He watched her cook and listened as she began to recap the events of her conversation with her unnamed ex. Midway through her story, he poured her a glass of wine because he could tell she needed it.

"Okay. Comments? Something," she said.

"Listen to me, lovely lady," he began. "In relationships, none of us are perfect. We make mistakes. Some of them we can correct. Others we can't. You forgave him. You even agreed to be his friend. That says a lot about your growth as a person. It's time to move on. Time to open your heart and love again."

"You make it sound so easy," she said, plating their food.

"I know the hurt of being cheated on when you love and trust a person," he admitted. "It's happened to me twice."

"Did you find love again?" she asked sadly.

"I'm looking. And I hope to find it real soon," he smiled, forcing her to reciprocate.

"Are you still in love with Tony?" he asked, then took a bite of food.

"No, I don't love him. I just care about him," she admitted.

"You know, Nadine, I'm into you on so many levels," he admitted. "You're an intriguing woman."

His directness momentarily stunned her.

"What you do say to me and you, hanging out, spending more time together, getting to know each other?" he asked seriously.

"Me and you?" she asked with food on her fork but not placing it within her mouth.

"What? Am I not your type?" he asked with a smile.

"It's not that. It's just that I never thought about us like that," she said.

"We're already friends. Let's just hang out and see where things go," he suggested.

"Us?" she asked.

"Yes, us. You and me. Nadine and Wesley," he said, smiling. "I'm a fun guy. Now put that food in your mouth."

They both laughed.

As she chewed, she looked at him. "Friends?" she repeated.

"Imperfect friends trying to enjoy life," he said. "Who knows?"

"Okay," she agreed slowly.

*****

The next day a bouquet of roses was delivered to Nadine's office. They were from Tony. Not wanting to talk to him, she elected to send a "Thank you" text message instead.

"You're everything to me," was his reply.

She read it but was not moved.

"I was waiting for your call last night," said Everett, entering her office. "Chris forced me to give you some time to digest it on your own."

"Thank you, Chris," said Nadine.

"Okay, bitch, by now you should've digested it and expelled the waste. What happened?"

"You were right. He made a full confession," said Nadine.

"So the tramp lied about being pregnant?"

"Followed him home and then lied," said Nadine.

"Are you kidding me?"

"Apparently, she confessed to him via text the next day," said Nadine.

"Girl, wait! This man must have a golden dick," said Everett, wearing shocked expression.

"We're not going there," said Nadine with a shake of her head. "Supposedly, her goal was to hurt him the way he had hurt her."

"Well, shit. Kudos to her," said Everett. "I hate you got hurt in the process. But his ass totally deserved every bit of that."

"He did," agreed Nadine.

"So why come clean now?" asked Everett.

"Evidently, the guilt was getting to him."

"There is a God," said Everett, looking up, then mouthing, "Thank you."

"He asked for forgiveness."

"And you did," said Everett with a roll of his eyes.

"I did," said Nadine. "I'm over it. It happened. It hurt. Now I want to move on."

"With Andrew?" asked Everett with a grin.

"Maybe, but not exactly," she said sheepishly.

"Wesley!" he exclaimed louder than intended. "Wesley?" he repeated in a whisper.

"I'm thinking about it."

"No! Not him," pleaded Everett.

"What's wrong with Wesley?" Nadine asked.

"Girl, he's a cheat waiting to happen," said Everett.

"He's nice though," said Nadine.

"A pony's nice. But he'll kick the shit out of you too," reasoned Everett.

"Don't make me laugh," said Nadine, struggling not to howl with laughter.

"What's wrong with Andrew?" asked Everett. "He is definitely into you."

"He is. But we have an understanding," said Nadine.

"What you mean is, the two of you have a fucking understanding," clarified Everett.

"Can you be any more vulgar? Besides, he was just a bridge," she explained.

"Not the way he was acting the other night," commented Everett.

"He's always like that," responded Nadine.

"A bridge, you say? Does he understand this?" asked Everett.

"Of course," said Nadine. "We had a big discussion more than a year ago."

"And he hasn't pushed the issue? Is he married? Does he live with someone?" asked Everett, confused.

"No, he isn't married. No, he doesn't live with anyone. And yes, he pushes the issue all the time, especially lately," she said.

"Wake up. The man's in love with you," exclaimed Everett.

"Oh please, Vee." Nadine sighed.

"Do you want a serious relationship, Nan?" asked Everett.

"I do," she answered. "I'm scared, Vee."

"Of what?"

"Tony hurt me so badly, I can't go through that again. I just can't," she said sadly.

"Listen to me," he said, leaning closer. "You must let that hurt go. Stop letting it control you because that's what it's doing. It's okay to take a chance. It's okay to love again."

"Maybe you're right," said Nadine, wanting to end the discussion.

"Listen, spend some time with godforsaken Wesley if you must," said Everett. "But also spend some quality time with Drew. Just see where your heart leads you. Your heart will respond to true love. Your heart will lead you in the right direction. Okay?"

"Okay," said Nadine.

"And let them both know I'll kick their asses if they step out of line," he said, then left.

*****

While shopping for plants for her patio and balcony, Nadine smiled as she received a message from Drew.

"What are you up to, beautiful?" he asked.

"Plant shopping. What's going on?"

"I was gifted tickets to the football game this Sunday," he replied.

"Gifted? Nice work," she wrote.

"They're box seats. Care to join me?" he wrote.

"It's a date," she responded.

"I'll pick you up at six."

A thumbs-up emoji was her reply.

"Just take it slow," she reminded herself.

She had avoided romantic dates with Drew. Instead, she accepted casual food sites and picnics. She had been in guarded mode most of their relationship. He knew she had been hurt bad and was extremely patient. She had shared enough of the painful experience for him to know that the hurt had been crushing. He was aware that she cared for him but refused to allow herself to love him. He didn't give up because he had grown to love her.

*****

"Hey, Nan. It's Tracie."

"Hey! How are you?"

"I'm good. How are you?"

"I'm great. How are the boys?"

"Growing like weeds. Did I catch you at a bad time?"

"No. I'm just watering my plants."

"You grow plants now?"

"I'm trying to grow plants. I just bought them," Nadine said with chuckle.

"I hear you bought a new house."

"I did. I'd love it if you and the boys could come out and watch the game one Sunday."

"That would be great! We're free this Sunday," Tracie replied, hopeful.

"I won't be home this Sunday. How about the following Sunday?"

"We'd love too! I can't wait to see the new place!"

"I can't wait to show it to you."

"I've missed you, Nan."

"I've missed you too, Trace," said Nadine.
"We'll make up for it. Agreed?"
"Definitely," agreed Nadine.

*****

Drew was prompt on Sunday. The two held hands when they walked, his arm casually draped across her shoulder when they conversed with his coworkers. He laughed with astonishment when she jumped and cheered for her team. They were a perfect couple. She complimented his life in an exquisite way.

"Is this the one?" a coworker, Jason, asked Drew.

"She is. She just doesn't realize it yet," he answered, looking at Nadine from across the room with pride.

When their eyes met and held, the connection was obvious.

"She knows," Jason said, taking a sip from his glass to conceal his words, then moved away.

*****

In the weeks that followed, Nadine and Drew went to the movies, an amusement park, and their first romantic dinner. She went speechless when he invited her to church. She accepted all the invitations to his delight. Church was the most uncomfortable because he failed to reveal that his entire family attended the location.

Apparently, Sunday dinner at his parent's home was a regular event. The entire affair was very relaxed. They were all curious about her and genuinely happy Drew had finally decided to bring her to meet the family. She enjoyed the friendly sibling banter and parental rebuke. For the first time, she realized that Drew loved children. His nieces and nephews were all over him. He patiently listened to, coddled, and played with them all. Nadine was impressed.

"I take it you two haven't talked about kids yet," whispered his mom as Nadine watched the interaction between Drew and the children.

"No, we haven't," said Nadine with a smile.

112

"He's been talking about you for months," the elderly woman said. "Never would bring you over though."

"The timing. I guess the timing had to be right," she said, thinking quickly.

"Strange," replied his mother, eyeing her. "That's what he said."

"I guess the two of you finally got it right, huh?" said the woman, continuing to eye her quizzically.

"We did," responded Nadine, smiling. "We did."

"That's good," said the woman, patting Nadine softly on her shoulder and moving away.

From across the room Drew gave her a look to see if she was okay. With a smile and a nod, she reassured him to continue enjoying the children.

"My boy really likes you," said Drew's father after taking a seat next to Nadine. "Hope my cigar doesn't bother you." He glanced in her direction.

"No, I actually enjoy the smell," she said, smiling.

"My Lucille said the same thing thirty years ago," he said, then taking a puff.

Nadine smiled at the old man, noting the father-son resemblance.

"He told me all about the two of you," the man revealed. "Don't go getting all embarrassed," he said without looking at her directly. "Just two men talking about the women they love. Nobody else involved."

The man handed her a can soda. She proceeded to immediately take a large swallow to hide her mortification.

"You do know that he loves you, right?" the man said, never looking directly at her.

"I do," she whispered.

"How 'bout you? You love him back?" he asked, looking directly at Nadine.

"Well...I...," she stammered.

"Of course, you do," he said, redirecting his gaze. "Couldn't be doing what the two of you been doing for this long and not feel something. Not to mention, neither of you bothering to date anyone else. Don't know why you waited so long to give love a try. And no, he didn't tell me. Just know that we've heard so much about you for so long that you're already considered a part of this family whether you accept it or not." He gently patted her knee, ending the conversation as a grandchild crawled into his lap.

Drew saw the horrified look upon Nadine's face.

Dad, please don't scare her away, he silently pleaded.

"Hey, beautiful. Let's get some air," Drew said, taking her hand and leading her outside.

*****

"Are you okay?" he whispered, taking her face in his hands. "You can tell me," he urged. "What is it?"

"It's nothing, love. Really," she said, smiling.

"I love you, Nadine," he confessed for the first time.

"I know," she admitted sadly. "I've always known."

"Don't run," he said.

"I won't," she said softly.

"Don't give up. Give it some time. Okay?"

"Okay," she responded.

With that Drew took her into his arms and kissed her. It was their first kiss outside of the bedroom. To Nadine's surprise, the passion was still there. Only this time, she tasted his love, and it stunned her.

*****

It was a few weeks before Nadine was able to schedule a Sunday with Tracie and the boys. She had texted her address and prepared lots for football food to nibble on. With the media room all set up and comfortable, she went to answer the door.

With a squeal, she and Tracie embraced each other. The two hadn't seen each other in more than two years.

"Oh my goodness!" she exclaimed, hugging the boys, each scrambling to get a hug.

"I've missed you guys so much," she said with teary eyes. "Come on in."

It was at that moment she realized Tony had invited himself. Her grin faded to a smirk.

"Hope you don't mind," he said.

"Um, no. I wasn't expecting you. Please come in," she said politely.

He and Tracie exchanged glances but remained silent.

"We brought sodas," said Tracie while Nadine closed the door.

"Let's get them in the fridge, and I'll take you guys on a tour of the furnished part of the house," she said, rubbing her hands on her thighs nervously.

"This is a super big house, Auntie Nan," remarked the oldest.

"It is," she agreed, grinning at the child as his head turned back and forth trying to look at everything.

"I'm scared I'll mess up something," said the youngest.

"I have a great place set up for us to watch the game, so you won't have to worry about that," she said, giving him a reassuring hug.

"This place is amazing, Nan," commented Tracie. "What in the world are you going to do with all of this space?"

"I have a few ideas floating around in my head," she said with a smile, leading the group to the media room.

"This place is absolutely amazing, Nan," commented Antonio.

"Thank you," she said.

The doorbell rang just as she picked up the remote.

"Are you expecting someone else?" asked Tracie surprised.

"Actually, I am," Nadine said, walking away.

"I see they're here," commented Drew, hearing the voices of children when he entered.

"Yes, and she brought an uninvited guest with her," said Nadine with annoyance.

"Can't blame a man for trying," said Drew. "That's why I insisted on being here. I knew this was going to happen."

"Please don't be mad," she said.

"Hey, it was going to happen sooner or later," he said, giving her tight hug followed by a kiss of reassurance.

They made their way to the media room holding hands.

"My final guest has arrived," announced Nadine as she entered the room.

"Everyone, this is Drew. Drew, this is Tracie; her brother, Antonio; and Tracie's boys, Travis, Ray, and Corey."

"Hello, everyone," said Drew, then moving across the room to shake Antonio and Tracie's hand.

"Hi, little men," he said to the boys, smiling.

"Little men, I like that," said the oldest.

"Babe, put the game on, please," said Nadine. "Tracie, can you give me a hand?"

The two women left the room to get the platters of food and drink. Tracie glanced back at Antonio nervously as she left.

Alone in the kitchen, Tracie was compelled to pry a little.

"So who's this Drew?" she asked.

After taking a moment to find the correct words, she answered, "Drew is someone very special to me."

"Special in intimately special?" she asked directly.

"Yes, he is," said Nadine, smiling.

"Are you happy?" Tracie asked. "Does he make you happy, Nan?"

"I am happy, Trace," she confessed. "And yes, he makes me very happy."

"I'm glad for you, Nan. Really, I am."

*****

Things were not as amicable in the media room.

"Drew, is it?" asked Antonio.

"Andrew actually. Nadine shortens it."

"And you're Antonio," said Drew as he located the correct channel, receiving a cheer from the boys once the game displayed.

"I'm not sure she's mentioned me," said Antonio.

"She's mentioned you," said Drew with cordial indifference.

"Did she mention that we've known each other for quite some time?" he asked, implying something that was no longer true.

"Actually, she's told me all about you, you and her, everything," said Drew.

"You're just a bridge," said Antonio smugly.

"You really think so." Drew grinned.

"Food!" the ladies sang out, placing the food on the coffee table.

"Coin-toss time!" the boys yelled.

"Eat up, everyone," said Nadine. "Don't be shy."

"I'll be right back," Drew whispered to Nadine, leaving the room.

She glanced after him, hoping Antonio's behavior hadn't disturbed him.

The boys piled food upon plates and settled on the area rug in front of the television. Tracie did the same. As she sat back, she could feel Antonio's tenseness and glanced in his direction.

Not good, she thought.

"Eat up, Tony," urged Nadine. "I honestly don't want to eat football food for a week."

He smiled at her, then began to fill a plate.

Drew entered carrying a couple of beers in each hand.

"Here you go, man," Drew said, handing two beers to Antonio, who looked up surprised, then accepted the bottles.

He settled in the seat next to Nadine, taking a few bites off her plate as the game began.

Overall, the evening was a success. Everyone collectively cheered, berated the referees for bad calls, ate, drank, and conversed without discord. Antonio threw sharp stares in Drew's direction whenever he spotted anything he construed as affection. Nadine and Tracie however chatted nonstop during halftime, catching up on everything from promotions, shopping, and Everett's new love.

Pulling out his cigarettes, Antonio stood, needing a smoke break. Drew offered to show him to the patio where he could smoke. The two men disappeared without the women noticing.

"She seems happy," Antonio commented without looking at his nemesis.

"She's getting there," replied Drew as the two stared past the pond.

"Did you do it?" asked Antonio.

"I wish I could take the credit, but I can't," he answered honestly. "She did it. I was just around during the process."

"You seem pretty confident," remarked Antonio.

"I'm confident in the woman that she is and the love she knows I have for her," he said.

"I'm not giving up," Antonio said.

"Didn't expect you to," Drew said, smiling. "I wouldn't."

"Sounds like an impasse," said Antonio.

"No. You lost two years ago, man. You just haven't realized it yet," said Drew, then walked away.

*****

By the time her guests left, Nadine was ready for a shower and bed. Drew helped her put the house back in order. He knew she wouldn't rest if something was in disarray.

"Overall, things went well. Would you agree?" Nadine asked.

"Tracie and the boys are great," Drew said.

"We were only in the kitchen for a minute. Did he say something horrible?" Nadine inquired.

"Oh yeah, informed me that I was merely a bridge," said Drew.

"Are you kidding me? How rude!"

"I'm competition in his mind, love," said Drew with indifference.

"I'm sorry," she apologized.

"Don't be," he urged. "We both knew this was going to happen."

"I just can't believe he was so blatantly rude."

"Do you still love him?" Drew asked, searching her face.

"Absolutely not," she answered without hesitation, meeting his gaze.

"Do you love me?" he asked.

"I do," she answered softly.

"Then there's nothing to worry about," he finished.

They showered together, igniting a passion that was quenched between the sheets, then fell asleep in each other's arms.

*****

With business and casual clothes in Nadine's closet, heading to work from her house was no longer an issue for Drew.

Wesley was shocked to see a vehicle parked in Nadine's driveway. She never had overnight guests or none that he'd seen the few times he drove by early in the morning. Taking note of the car, he drove back to the construction site. A few hours later, as he stood talking to Miguel, the car drove by. A man was driving. It was Andrew from the gathering.

The thought of some other man in bed with Nadine irritated him. He scolded himself for a moment knowing that he slept with numerous women, and one of those women was a guest in Nadine's house just weeks earlier. Moments later, Nadine drove by, only she didn't look in his direction as she normally did.

Interesting, he thought, walking back to his office.

*****

Deciding to have a real home-cooked meal for breakfast, Antonio walked into a popular diner and took a seat. The waitress immediately came over with coffee and a menu. He placed his order and began pouring cream and sugar into his coffee. Then in walked a very pregnant Shawn and a man he assumed was her husband. Her face had the glow that only pregnancy gives, and she smiled with happiness.

She deserved to be happy, he thought. But so did he. He smiled remembering conversations he and Nadine had years earlier about baby names. His thoughts were tainted when the face of Andrew came to mind. He had to admit that the way the guy acted the night before he loved Nadine. He behaved attentively and was caring. Their interactions reminded him of the relationship that he and Nadine had once shared. He decided that it was all a show because the man knew Antonio was watching. Noticing the time, he concentrated on finishing his meal. He had an appointment to install security camera at a recently completed location.

After parking next to Miguel's truck, Wesley looked around at the completed site with pride. It had passed all inspections, and cameras were being installed tomorrow. He was glad to finally be able to cross this off his list. He had located two other sites that he wanted to simultaneously oversee. He had a Skype meeting with Dan scheduled for later in the afternoon.

"Morning, boss," said Miguel.

"How's it going?" responded Wesley.

"What time is the camera guy supposed to show up?" asked Miguel.

Before Wesley could answer a Secure Systems minivan pulled into the parking lot.

"Now," said Wesley, looking in the direction of the approaching vehicle.

Antonio exited, surprised to see Wesley. His appointment was with the foreman. He assumed that was the Hispanic man since he knew Wesley was a project manager.

Does this guy oversee every construction site in town? he silently questioned.

"Good morning," he said, approaching the two men.

"Morning," they responded in unison.

"Mr. Johnson," he said, offering his hand, which Wesley readily accepted in a firm grip.

"This is Miguel Rivera, the foreman," introduced Wesley. "Miguel, this is Antonio Williams. He'll be responsible for installing the cameras."

"Boss says you do good work," said Miguel with a smile.

"We have a system to fit your every need," said Antonio, smiling.

"Let's do this," said Wesley, leading the way.

Antonio took notes and measurements on locations and type of camera. He knew the start and completion dates would be yesterday when dealing with Wesley. When Wesley stepped away to make a phone call after receiving numerous text message, Antonio discussed the installation with Miguel. He vaguely attended to what the man was saying because he was straining to hear what he could of Wesley's phone conversation.

"Stop texting me, I'm at work," Wesley had snapped into the phone. "Look, I don't owe you anything."

"I don't care what you do."

"You know what? You're dismissed," he said, ending the call and pressing a few extra buttons obviously blocking the caller.

Wesley went back to the men with an irritated expression. "Are we all set here, Williams?" Wesley asked.

"I'll fax over the invoice and start installation this afternoon," said Antonio, smirking.

"Great. Miguel, head back to the site and keep things going. I need to take care of something," Wesley instructed.

"Sure thing, boss," replied Miguel.

Turning out of the parking lot, Wesley headed downtown, needing a few moments alone after the aggravation caused by the call with Denice. He wasn't the type to argue with a bootie-call chick when he had so many to choose from. And he certainly didn't owe any of them explanations on why he hasn't called, came over, or responded to a message. The way he viewed things were, if he does, then he does; if he didn't, then he didn't, end of story.

Driving along, he noticed two familiar individuals coming out of an office building walking in his direction. It was Nadine and her friend Everett. The two laughed, leaning into each other like schoolgirls. Pulling into the nearest parking space, he stood in front of his truck, waiting. They were a few feet in front of him before they realized they knew the man blocking their forward progress.

"I could use a good laugh," he said, smiling at the two.

"I was about to wax on, wax off your ass," said Everett with his usual feminine gestures.

"Please don't hurt me," commented Wesley with hands raised and a smile.

"You know, Wesley," began Everett, looking the man up and down, "if I didn't love Chris, I'd wax you on and off really good."

"Thank God for Chris," Wesley replied, smiling, taking a small step backward.

"Oh, honey, please. I don't want your ass. Nadine can have you. I like my man smooth all over. You got bulges everywhere," Everett replied, waving his hand, then grinning.

"Hey, Wess. What are you doing down here?" asked Nadine.

"I needed to mail some reports to home office," he said.

"Why didn't you do it electronically?" asked Everett.

"I did, but sometimes the data get unaligned on the spreadsheets," he clarified.

"We know all about that," the two responded in unison.

"We're taking an early lunch. We have meetings all this afternoon. Want to join us?" asked Nadine.

"I think I can handle that," said Wesley.

Khakis and a company shirt weren't the proper attire considering his dates were dressed in designer business suits. He didn't care because Wesley knew it wasn't the clothes that made the person. They each ordered the seafood salad, not wanting to be overstuffed in the middle of the day. He and Nadine opted or the raspberry tea while Everett selected a soda.

"So what's the latest?" he asked, starting the conversation.

With an extended hand, Everett showed off a diamond band.

"We're engaged!" he announced, grinning.

"Now that's an announcement," said Wesley, smiling. "Congratulations!"

"Thank you," the man responded. "You already know who the matron of honor is."

"Let me guess," he said with a frown. "Nadine?"

"None other," said Everett, then took a sip of his soda.

"Plan on diving for the bouquet?" joked Wesley to Nadine.

"Don't count on it," replied Nadine, smiling, then a roll of her eyes.

"Marriage not your cup of tea?" he inquired.

"Just not something I lose sleep thinking about," said Nadine flatly.

Warm rolls and softened butter were placed on the table by a waitress.

"Wesley?" said a woman, drawing everyone's attention.

Looking up, Wesley found himself face-to-face with Saturday Sabrina.

"Hi, Sabrina," he said, staring uncomfortably at the woman.

"I'm sorry," the waitress said to Nadine and Everett before continuing. "We know each other."

"Apparently," said Everett, smiling while staring between the two.

"Yeah, we know each other," explained Wesley. "I'll give you a call this evening."

"You must have lost my number," she said, quickly scribbling on a napkin, then handing it to Wesley. She stood briefly as if wanting to say more, then decided it wasn't the appropriate time.

"Yeah, thanks," he said, closing his fist around the napkin. "I'll give you a call," he said dismissively as Nadine and Everett grinned at each other.

"You know," began Everett pretending to rearrange his silverware, "it's so annoying when you can't just fuck 'em and leave 'em."

"Oh my god," said Nadine, smiling with embarrassment.

"Well, it is," continued Everett. "They just get addicted to the dick."

Wesley could only stare at the man and grinned. "You are something else," he said.

"What's so funny?" Everett asked Nadine. "Nan, you know."

"Don't put me in this," Nadine warned with raised hands, barely containing a laugh.

"I can say this now because you're over it," he continued. "Go and ask that freak Antonio was screwing with. She got addicted to the dick."

"Please," begged Nadine, struggling not to laugh aloud.

"Wesley knows too," said Everett. "How many you got chasing your dick?"

With that comment, Nadine covered her mouth with a napkin to smother her laugh.

Wesley shook his head while staring at Everett, grinning.

"Is he always like this?" Wesley asked Nadine.

Unable to reply, she nodded a yes while wiping tears of laughter from her eyes.

The trio enjoyed their lunch break, then parted ways. Nadine and Everett began to walk the short distance back to their office building when they were spotted by Antonio.

"Must have been a great lunch break the way the two of you are smiling," he said.

"It was until this moment," said Everett sarcastically.

"And hello to you too," Antonio said to Everett.

"It was a great lunch," said Nadine. "We're headed back now."

"I won't hold you up," he started.

"Good," said Everett.

"I was wondering if you knew that Tracie is having a birthday party for one of the boys?" he asked Nadine.

"Yes. She called me," said Nadine.

"Think you'll be able to make it?" he asked her.

"I'll be there. I'll be a little late, but I'll be there," she said.

"Bye," said Everett, starting to walk away.

Antonio stared after the annoying man, then said, "I'll give you a call this evening, Nan."

"Okay." She chuckled, then disappeared into the building.

I can't stand that dude, thought Antonio as he walked back to the minivan. Everett was a loyal friend to Nadine, and Antonio appreciated that fact. It was Everett's sarcastic condescending comments that annoyed him. If he wasn't Nadine's friend, Antonio would love to show him how real men react to disrespect.

*****

Wesley was sitting waiting for Dan to log on to the Skype meeting. Just as he was checking the time for the third time, Dan's face popped online.

"Sorry I'm late, Wess," said Dan, looking flustered. "I read your proposal."

"So what do you think?" asked Wesley.

"Well," he sighed. "It's going to be a challenge."

"If you'll notice, I've covered pretty much all the angles. They are in roughly the same areas. The cameras will allow me and you to see in real time what's going on. I'll be able to communicate with the foremen immediately. It will be a much easier setup to manage dual sites at once. It will also allow us to take on more projects," Wesley explained.

"Honestly, Wesley, it sounds great. I like the idea. Let me run all of this by Jim, and I'll get back to you by the end of the week," said Dan, then logged off.

Yes, thought Wesley. If they agreed to this plan for dual management, he would be in a prime position to go directly to Jim about the director's position after he completed a triple site management. Leaning back in his chair, he felt victorious. Antonio? Wesley remembered that Everett had referred to an Antonio during lunch. He wondered if it was the nerdy security camera guy.

Wesley wouldn't place him in the category of a ladies' man, but any man could fit into the category of a cheater. It didn't matter to him one way or another. All he really wanted was a few hours in Nadine's bed. He wasn't interested in marriage to her or any of the women he slept with. It was just sex, pure and simple for him.

What else can they offer me? he thought smugly.

*****

"Hey, beautiful," said Drew.

"Hey, love," responded Nadine.

"I just wanted to give you a heads up that I was planning to come over this evening," he said.

"Drew," said Nadine softly, "I don't need a heads-up. If you're coming, just come."

"I'm glad we've finally come to this point," he replied.

"Me too," she said.

He was quiet for a moment, then said, "I like coming home to you."

"I'm starting to look forward to it myself," she confessed.

"Really?" he asked.

"Really."

"You ever think about us doing that on a consistent basis?"

"I've thought about it," she said with a sigh.

"But?"

"No buts. We'll know when the time is right," she said. "I don't plan on going anywhere. I know that."

"Neither do I," he said.

"Ms. Swift, your meeting starts in ten minutes," said Cassandra from the doorway.

"I have to go love," she said.

"I'll see you at home," he said, then ended the call. He replayed those words in his head. "See you at home." That was what he wanted with Nadine.

*****

That weekend Drew had a meeting with a client and Everett was planning his honeymoon, so neither was able to accompany Nadine to the birthday party. Dreading having to deal with Antonio alone, she asked Wesley. To limit the time at the party, she urged him not to forego his flea-market hours.

As they drove up, the size of the party surprised both Wesley and Nadine.

"I guess, she goes all out," said Wesley.

"Not that I remember," said Nadine, looking at all the parents and children running around.

"Nan!" exclaimed Tracie, giving her a hug. "You're just in time for blowing out the candles.

"This is my friend Wesley," introduced Nadine.

"You sold me some merchandise at the flea market," she said with a smile.

"That I did," he said, smiling and shook her hand.

"Travis! Travis!" Tracie screamed. "Auntie Nan is here."

Wesley and Nadine looked at each other, bewildered by the loud announcement.

"Auntie Nan!" the child yelled, running into her arms.

"Birthday boy!" she responded, laughing.

"When are we coming back to your house?" he asked.

"Real soon, love. Real soon," she said. "Here put your present on the table with the others."

"This is a pretty flat present," the boy said.

"Well, here's a bigger one," said Wesley, handing over a present to which the child cheered and ran away.

Glancing around, Nadine spotted a familiar face. It was Kristie. The two headed in each other's direction with Kristie grabbing a similarly looking but slightly other woman.

"Ms. Swift," she said.

"Please, Nadine when we're not working," she said, smiling.

"I want you to meet my sister, Kristina," the girl introduced.

"My sister talks about you all of the time," Kristina said, shaking Nadine's hand.

"Good things, I hope," said Nadine with a smile.

"All good things," said Kristina.

"This is my friend Wesley," introduced Nadine.

"Hello. You look familiar," he commented.

"I get that all of the time," Kristina said with shake of her head. "I have a twin sister, Sabrina. You may have seen her."

"Does she work downtown?" asked Nadine, smiling.

"Yes. She's a waitress at that new restaurant that opened," explained Katrina.

"Right. I've seen her there," said Nadine, grinning at Wesley.

"It was nice meeting the two of you," he said, ushering Nadine off.

"Don't you dare go Everett on me," he whispered, smiling. "Look around and see if you see her."

"I will not," said Nadine, laughing.

"Nadine, is that you and Wesley?" a female voice asked.

"Denice, right?" asked Nadine, smiling, turning toward the voice.

"Yes, it's Denice," the woman said, looking at Wesley. "Imagine the two of you being here," she said. "Together."

Confused by the woman's reaction, Nadine was momentarily taken aback.

"Travis is my godson, and Wesley is my guest," said Nadine, looking confused.

"Well, I'd like to talk to Wesley alone," the woman said, waving her hand dismissively in Nadine's direction.

"Then do it on your own time," snapped Nadine. "Wesley is with me."

Tucking her arm in Wesley's, the two strolled away.

"Ruffled your feathers," whispered Wesley with a smile.

"That hairdresser better recognize who she's talking to," said Nadine angrily.

Walking to the refreshments table once again, the two were accosted by another female.

"I haven't seen you in a while," said a female unknown to Nadine.

"Hello, Angie," said Wesley dryly, returning to pouring drinks for he and Nadine.

"Aren't you going to introduce me to your lady friend," asked Angie, looking Nadine over.

"Nadine, this is Angie," said Wesley, only this time he tucked his arm in hers and walked away.

"Are we going to have to fight our way out of here?" joked Nadine, staring at him.

"You made it," came Antonio's voice from behind the couple.

"Your turn," joked Wesley to Nadine as they turned around.

"Hey, Tony," said Nadine with a friendly smile.

"This is my friend—" she said, before having her sentence finished for her.

"Mr. Wesley Johnson," said Antonio dryly.

"You two know each other?" asked Nadine surprised.

"The company hired him to install security cameras at the site," explained Wesley.

"And I bought a PS5 from him at the flea market," added Antonio.

"Well, isn't this a small world," said Nadine, grinning.

"So how do you two know each other?" Antonio asked Nadine.

"He's my friend," said Nadine, smiling.

"I thought Andrew was your friend. So is it Wesley here, or is it Andrew?" he snapped at her jealously.

"It's none of your business," she snapped back and walked away.

"I wonder what Andrew is going to say about this?" he mumbled, watching her leave.

"I think she cleared that with him before she asked me, man," said Wesley, smiling before walking after Nadine.

"The infamous ex?" asked Wesley.

"One and the same," answered Nadine.

"Here," he said handing her a wine cooler. "Your nostrils are flared. Calm your nerves."

They both burst into laughter, drawing the attention of other party attendees.

Wesley noted Antonio keeping an eye on Nadine. He chuckled at the man's jealousy. He had cheated on her and now acted as if he owned her. It relieved him that she had someone else. It would limit the amount of time he'd have to put in. Besides, one night with her was all Wesley really wanted.

Once the birthday song had been sung, the candles were blown out on the cake, and the gifts were being opened, Nadine and Wesley were preparing to say their goodbyes. His plan was to entice her back to his place and seduce her. Unfortunately, things were detoured by an unexpected guest. Andrew showed up.

Nadine had texted him the address without Wesley being aware. The guy showed up with a gift for the child and a kiss for her.

The knight in fucking armor, thought Wesley with agitation.

It was at that moment that a commotion drew everyone's attention. Three women were engaged in a heated argument about a man each of them had been seeing at the same time. Wesley didn't wait around for details.

"Okay, buddy. It's time to open the rest of your gifts," Antonio said to his nephew.

"I guess I'll open this little one from Auntie Nan," the boy responded sadly.

In the past she had always arrived with a huge box. Now that he was older, he expected some dumb gift cards.

"What is it?" asked his younger brother.

"It's three tickets to the playoff game!" the child screamed. He immediately burst into tears and ran into Nadine's arms.

She whispered something into the child's ear. He nodded, and the two wiped his tears.

"Oh my god, Nan," said Tracie, wiping tears, then giving Nadine a tight hug.

"Stop it," coaxed Nadine, struggling not to cry herself. "Go. Help him with the other gifts."

Drew held her close and gave her a kiss on her temple. "You're an amazing woman," he whispered.

"Thank you, Nan. That was extremely generous," said Antonio sincerely.

"You'll have to take them," she said.

"I will."

"It's a VR!" screamed the child again.

"Who gave you that?" Antonio asked, rejoining his nephew with a big smile.

"Mr. Wesley," the replied.

"Who is that?" asked his brother.

"Aunt Nan's friend," the child answered.

"That's her over there," Nadine heard the voice of Denice say from behind her.

"He left you for her?" asked another woman.

"She has money," Denice responded.

A different voice, later identified as belonging to a Teresa, said, "Did I hear you say Wesley left you?"

"You did. Why?" snapped Denice.

Having heard the entire conversation, Nadine and Drew turned to watch the events unfold. Three of Wesley's conquests—Teresa, Denice, and Wanda—began a heated exchange.

"Because Wesley and I have been seeing each other for over a year," Teresa responded.

Drew and Nadine looked at each other, grinning.

"Look, slut, I don't know what you think you have with Wess, but he's at my house every week," snapped Denice.

"Slut? He's at my house every week too. Every Tuesday, in fact," argued Teresa.

"Hold up! Wait a minute," said Wanda. "He's at your house on Tuesday. My house on Wednesday. What day is he over there laying up with you?

"Every Monday, skank! And sometimes Saturday too. So now what?" responded Denice.

Tracie, Antonio, and other parents gathered and moved the children away not wanting them to witness this about-to-turn-physical altercation.

"How can that be?" whined Sabrina, walking toward the group, having kept a low profile the entire event. "He's with me on Saturdays."

Glancing around the crowd, Nadine and Drew looked just in time to see Wesley drive away.

"Where's Wesley?" asked Tracie.

Nadine and Drew pointed toward the car, driving away. The three of them looked at each other and burst into laughter.

*****

Wesley never expected the woman to confront each other. Standing beside Nadine and Drew, he had heard the start of the exchange and hoped it would fizzle out. When the two of them turned to watch the escalation, he made his way to his car. He knew when to remove himself from a situation.

"Oh my god," said Nadine, grinning. "Those poor women."

"Wesley's the man," joked Drew, stopping at a traffic light. "He has a woman for every day of the week."

"Teresa on Tuesdays, Wanda on Wednesdays, and poor Sabrina on Saturdays," recited Nadine, shaking her head.

"I kind of felt bad for the Sabrina girl," said Drew, reaching for Nadine's hand. "She sounded like she was going to cry."

"I met her last week when Wesley had lunch with me and Vee," she said.

"I remember you mentioning him having lunch with you guys."

"The way she acted, it was if he had been avoiding her," said Nadine. "Vee and I thought it was funny but never to this extreme."

"That's a dangerous game he's playing," said Drew, shaking his head.

"How can you have relationships with that many women?" asked Nadine.

"Those aren't relationships, love," said Drew. "Those are just bootie calls. He has looks and money. None of those women mean a thing to him. He probably already has replacements lined up."

"You think so?" asked Nadine, looking at Drew, grinning.

"Yeah. He wanted you to be one of them." Drew laughed.

"I wasn't interested in him like that," said Nadine. "Whew! I dodged a bullet."

"Your best move was making sure I was at that gathering," said Drew.

"He said something?"

"He asked how we knew each other?"

"Did he?' Nadine asked, surprised.

"Everyone wanted to know. I told him you were mine."

"Did you?"

"I did."

"But we hadn't made it official."

"Didn't matter. In my heart you were mine," he said, giving her hand a kiss.

"That was sweet, love. But you're right, looking back on things," she admitted.

"You knew. You just weren't ready to accept it."

"I knew? Why would you say that?"

"Your response to me when we make love for one thing," Drew explained. "It isn't sex for either of us anymore. It hasn't been for a while."

Nadine thought for a moment. She realized how right he was. She did respond to Drew in and out of bed. It was like they were in sync.

"You're right," she finally agreed. "I guess I hadn't noticed."

As they pulled into the driveway, Nadine pressed the garage door opener, allowing him to park inside. He noticed how quiet she had suddenly become. Once inside, he grabbed her hand to stop her.

"What's bothering you?" he asked.

"I was just thinking about some things is all," she said, attempting to walk away.

"Don't do that," he said.

"What?"

"Don't shut me out. Something's bothering you, and we need to talk about it," he said.

"We'll talk about it, I promise," she said. "You hungry?"

"Not after the huge plate Tracie forced on me," he said, stroking his stomach. "Why don't you put on something relaxing and meet me in the media room?" he suggested.

"Deal," she said, heading for the stairs.

Drew had learned that when something bothered Nadine, he had to get her to talk about it because she internalized things. There were so many blanks in her life that she hid from him. It was close to six months after their little agreement before he finally got her to open up about the heartbreak of the cheating. It had pained him hearing how it had affected her health and mentally.

That night she had cried so badly that all he could do was to hold her. It had taken two bottles of wine and him sharing some of his past hurt to relax her enough to trust that information with him. She transformed from being just a beautiful woman with whom he had a sexual arrangement with to a vulnerable woman. They never discussed that night or the information again.

It was also that night that he made love to her for the first time, and she responded. No real words were needed. Their bodies spoke, strained for, and clung to each other. It was the first time that she allowed herself to moan his name repeatedly in passion. He answered with the words her heart needed and his felt, "I'm here. I'll always be here."

"Miss me?" she asked, interrupting his thoughts.

"Always," he said as she snuggled next to him.

"Tell me," he said. "What's bothering you?"

Tilting her head to look into his eyes, she said, "When and what did you tell your family about me?"

"Oh, that." He laughed.

"Tell me," she said seriously, knowing he'd never lie to her.

"It started about six, maybe seven, months after we began our little arrangement," he said, smiling.

"That long ago?" she asked, shocked.

"Somewhere around that time. And no, I didn't say anything about our arrangement then," he said, seeing the look on her face.

"Then?" she asked still mortified.

"Calm down, love," he urged.

"I told my mom one Sunday that I had met someone, that I liked her a lot and wanted to bring her to meet the family," he said.

"How did she take it when this woman never showed up?" asked Nadine.

"After a while, she asked if I was still seeing the woman and when was I going to bring her over."

"Drew, that more than a year ago!" said Nadine.

"Trust me she kept asking, and I kept saying, when the time is right." He laughed.

"What about your dad? I know you told him more. He hinted that you did," said Nadine with a shake of her head.

"I did," he confessed. "I knew you loved me. You just had this shield up and wouldn't let me get but so close. I was trying everything and getting nowhere. I didn't know what else to do. I was frustrated."

"So you went to Dad?"

"I needed help and advice."

"You tell him everything?"

"I did. I also told him how much I loved you and wanted you. I was honest," he said with a deep sigh. "I told him that I love you, but you won't let me love you or love me back."

"What did he say?" asked Nadine softly.

"Don't laugh," he said, smiling. "He asked if you ever called out my name in passion?"

Nadine's mouth fell open. "Are you kidding me?" she asked.

"Scout's honor." Drew laughed. "I told him you didn't at first, but you do all the time now."

"Oh my god. I can't believe I'm hearing this," said Nadine, covering her face with her hands.

"Dad said that if you're responding to me when I make love to you, that's my proof that you have the same feelings. He said you were free to be you at those moments. Other times, he said, you were just scared. Scared to love. Scared that I was going to break your heart."

Nadine sat silent, looking down, listening.

"He also said that your heart needed time to learn to trust love and to love—again. He said you already loved me. You just hadn't realized it. So I just waited."

"Did all of this take place around the same time?" she asked.

"It did."

"I'm sorry I put you through all of that."

"I'm not," he said. "It made us stronger—together."

"I do love you, Drew," she confessed. "Thank you for not giving up."

"I'm here," he said. "I'll always be here."

Nadine looked at him with pools of tears in her eyes. "You promise?" she asked as the tears fell.

"I promise, love," he answered, kissing her deeply.

She clung to him with a tightness he'd never felt before but completely understood. Neither of them had bothered to seek out other partners. There was satisfaction and the potential for a deeper relationship that each of them knew existed.

Detour

"WESLEY? THIS IS Dan. How are you?"

"Doing good, sir. Doing good," Wesley responded. "How 'bout yourself?"

"Not bad, not bad at all," Dan replied.

"I take it you have some news for me," said Wesley.

"That I do. I spoke with Jim, and we looked over your proposal," he began.

"And what did the two of you decide?" Wesley asked.

"We decided to give your plan a chance," he said.

"That's good," responded Wesley happily.

"I want to let you know, Wesley, that Jim was a bit skeptical. This has never been done before."

"It hasn't. But I plan to show you how efficient and profitable this strategy will be," Wesley stated confidently.

"You do realize that the two sites are on completely opposite sides of the city?" asked Dan.

"I do, and it won't be a problem," said Wesley with confidence.

"The second site is slated to begin in two weeks," Dan informed him.

"I'm well aware and prepared to start immediately, sir."

"That's what I wanted to hear. I'll let you put your plan into action," Dan said, then signed off the Skype connection.

Wesley leaned back in his chair with excited anticipation. This was the break he needed. He'd have to be sure and let Nadine know that her suggestion is taking form. He planned to thank her properly as soon as he could get her alone.

Studying the cameras, Wesley noted the progress he had made so far on the community center. The walls and roof were complete.

The crew was working both inside and out. The structure was very modern and sleek with its angled roofline and numerous windows. Soon, work on the pool would begin. The timing of the approval couldn't have come at a better time for Wesley.

Shortly before Wesley and his crew ended their day, he noticed Nadine had parked her car beside his truck and was standing in front of his office.

"Hi there, lovely," he said as he approached.

"Hi, yourself." She smiled.

God, I loved the way this woman smell, he thought, giving her a hug.

"Haven't seen you since the party," she joked.

"Don't start." He laughed, shaking his head.

"It's really looking good, Wess," she said, looking past him to the building.

"I was admiring it myself earlier."

"How close is it to completion?"

"We still have a long way to go. A lot of detailed work inside, plus the pool. The playground and putting green will be easy."

"Wow, I can't believe how much you've accomplished, and the building itself looks amazing!"

"Thank you. This is what I do." He smiled. "So what brings you by?"

"Vee wanted me to invite you to his nuptials."

"You're joking, right?"

"No. He stopped by my office today and said for me to be sure and invite you. So here I am." She smiled, handing him an invitation.

"Wow, I didn't think he cared for me."

"He acts like an asshole, but he's really sweet."

"Oh wow, never had sweet asshole before," Wesley joked, grinning.

"No. But you've had the loud, jealous, fighting kind," Nadine said, bursting into laughter.

"There you go."

"I'm sorry. But you set yourself up for that one." She laughed.

"I have something I need to tell you," he said seriously.

"What?"

"It's a surprise. A special surprise. Let me take you out to dinner."

"Oh, Wess, I don't think that's a good idea."

"Andrew?"

"Yes, Drew, but also me."

"That serious, huh?"

"It is."

"Okay. How about lunch tomorrow? Just you and me, not Vee."

"Okay. Lunch, it is."

He knew she would mention it to Andrew, and he didn't care. *Just a little time alone is all I want*, he thought.

"I see the pretty lady stopped to talk with you again," Miguel said as Nadine drove off.

"She did."

"You guys must be pretty close."

"Yeah. She has something I definitely want," said Wesley.

Miguel immediately burst into laughter.

*****

"I have to be honest and tell you that I don't like it," said Drew over the phone later that night.

"It's just lunch with a friend."

"A friend that wants to fuck you," snapped Drew.

Nadine sat quiet before saying, "It doesn't matter what he wants. All that matters is that I love you and I'd never jeopardize what we have."

"I know. I'm sorry. I just know what kind of man that he is."

"So do I. That's why I agreed to lunch in the middle of the day. I'll listen to what he has to say, and I'm back to the office."

"I trust you."

"Good. Because I love you, and I'm free to say that."

"I love you back."

"Don't laugh, but sometimes I feel like Vee."

"What do you mean?"

"Like we're getting married or something. It's crazy."

"You feel like that?"

"When I admit to people that I love you, yes. I feel like a giddy bride-to-be or something. It's crazy."

"You don't understand how good that makes me feel. To know that your love for me is that powerful."

"So when are we getting married?" she joked.

"Are you serious?"

"No! I was only teasing. I thought you were going to have a heart attack or something."

"Don't tease. I might take you up on it," he said, gauging her reaction.

"Well, sir, you'll know when the time is right." She chuckled.

"See you tomorrow?"

"I'd better," she answered, smiling, then ended the call.

*****

Nadine was just walking out of her building the next day when Wesley pulled into a parking space and rushed to open the passenger side door.

"Hop in," he instructed.

"We're not walking?"

"Special news deserves a special place."

Reluctantly, Nadine walked toward the opened door. *This is odd*, she thought.

"I can have you back within an hour." *But if it takes longer, you'll come up with an excuse*, he thought.

After a short drive, Wesley pulled into the parking lot of a waterside restaurant. He strolled to the passenger door and opened it for Nadine.

Glancing out over the mesmerizing water once they were seated, Nadine commented, "I love this view."

"It is lovely, isn't it?"

Too lovely for a lunch break, she thought.

After placing their orders, Wesley looked across the table and said, "You are amazing!"

"What did I do?" asked Nadine surprised.

"Remember the suggestion that you gave to me about dual management?"

"Yeah, a couple of months ago."

"Well, I took your advice and received approval yesterday."

"Are you serious?"

"Now that calls for a celebration. I'm so happy for you," she said sincerely.

"That's why I chose this place. Without you, I would never have thought of that idea."

"I remember that night. You helped me too, Wess."

"I guess we helped each other."

"Your encouragement that night, it helped me move pass some of my fears."

"And your help put me on the path to my dream position."

With contagious excitement, Wesley shared his strategy with Nadine during lunch. She listened and offered suggestions.

"So where will you be based?" she asked.

"My home base will still be here, but because the other location is completely on the outskirts across town, some travel and over-nights can't be avoided."

"And you're good with that?"

"Oh, definitely. There have been jobs that kept me and the crew away from home for weeks."

"Okay. Well, Wess, I'm proud of you."

"I guess I should be getting you back," he said finally.

"We'll have a real celebration at my place. So we can have drinks and listen to Vee's wise cracks," she said, smiling.

Wesley reached for her hand as they walked to the car, which caught Nadine completely by surprise.

"If you weren't in love with Drew, we would make a great couple."

"We're friends. We're good friend. That doesn't change."

"I'd be lying if I said I didn't want more," he confessed.

"And I'd be lying if I said I was willing to take the chance."

He reached as if to open the door for her but instead ducked his head and kissed her. He was prepared to be slapped across the face. She didn't slap him. She just looked at him.

"Wess, don't complicate things," she said softly.

"I had to try."

"Don't do that again. We're friends. I love Drew. I don't sleep with my friends." With that said, she sat in the set and waited for him to close the door.

Damn, she's hard, thought Wesley. She didn't kiss him back.

"Forgive me?" he asked once in the driver's seat.

"It never happened," was all she said on the subject.

On the drive back to her office, the two chatted about Vee's wedding, Nadine purchase of upstairs furniture, and Wesley's dodging of the women from the party. They acted as if the kiss never happened—but it had happened.

*****

As Nadine and Drew sat down to dinner, she brought up the subject, knowing Drew was waiting for her to mention the subject.

"Now lunch with Wesley," she began.

"Finally," he sighed.

"A few months back I gave him an idea on how to convince Terner to view him as candidate for director."

"Okay."

"He used my plan and received an approval notification yesterday."

"That's why he wanted to take you to lunch?"

"It was more like a tell-you-the-good-news-thank-you lunch."

"I'm not going to lie to you. He brought up the subject as we were about to head back, and I let him know to forget it."

"You said forget it?"

"Actually, what I said was that I love you, Drew, and I wasn't going to do anything to jeopardize what we have, and that he should be content with just being friends."

A smile crept upon Drew's already handsome face as he sat quietly, nodding his head. Finally, he looked up grinning and asked, "You want to have my baby?"

"Shut up!" Nadine said as the two of them burst into laughter.

Later, as Drew walked into the bedroom after his shower, Nadine was playing a voice message on her phone.

"Look, Nan. I'm sorry. I was out of line at the party. You were right. Who you attend parties with is none of my business. I just want you to know that I still care. Give me a call when you get this message."

"Call deleted," said an electronic voice.

"How many of those have you gotten?"

"Too many."

"Did you know he was planning to inform me that you were cheating with Wesley?"

"What?"

"Wesley told me at the party."

"How did Wess find out?"

"Apparently, when you walked away, he mumbled something to the effect of, he wonders what I was going to say once I found that you attended the party with Wesley." Drew chuckled.

"I'm so glad we discussed it."

"Did you tell Wesley that we had discussed it?"

"I did. I didn't want to give him any wrong impressions either."

"Well, our little friend gladly let him know that I had cleared everything."

"Good for you, Wesley!"

"Yeah, that was a smooth move."

"Not as smooth as you, my love," he said. Grabbing her in his arms, the two fell onto the bed with Nadine squealing and Drew laughing.

*****

For the next few days, Nadine found herself having difficulty concentrating. Her work didn't suffer, but she found it growing increasing more difficult to get through the day. By the time she got home, she was exhausted and fell asleep as soon as she and Drew crawled into bed. He noticed how she either clung to him in her sleep or would become agitated. Several nights he spoke softly soothing her back to sleep.

Something is bothering her, he thought.

*****

"Wasn't that a great message pastor gave today?" Drew's mother, Lucille, asked.

"Sounded like the same message from last Sunday to me," answered his father, Andrew Sr., who was more often than not referred to as Pop-Pop.

"No, Dad, it was the same one from two weeks ago," joked Gayle, his sister.

"Stop talking about Pastor," scolded Lucille. "That man really brings the word."

"Yeah, the same word," they all said in unison, then burst into laughter.

"Nadine, was that the same word from last week?" asked Lucille.

They all grinned at her, waiting for an answer.

"Please, I don't have a comment," she said, smiling, not wanting to take sides.

"Yes, love, was it the same word?" asked Drew, grinning, forcing her to take a side.

"I'm not sure."

"You take notes every week, Nan," Gayle stated, smiling.

"Just check your notes, love," urged Drew, nudging his father, who laughed between puff on his cigar.

"Well, it sounded a little bit the same," mumbled Nadine.

A cute baby girl was trying to crawl into her lap.

"It's the same message!" yelled Drew.

Gayle and his father laughed hysterically.

"Stop all of that making fun of the pastor and come and eat," scolded his mother.

As they all sat around the table, the baby refused to leave Nadine's lap, which she thought was cute. The baby clung to Nadine and cried whenever someone attempted to remove her.

"That's odd," commented Drew. "She doesn't usually act that way."

Gayle and Lucille exchanged glances that was missed by Nadine but not Drew. When the deviled eggs were passed to Nadine, she slid back so fast with a look as if her entire meal was about to come back.

"You okay, honey?" Lucille asked.

"I don't know. I just felt a little queasiness there for a minute."

"Are you sure?" asked Drew, looking concerned.

"You normally get sick at the smell of eggs?" Gayle asked.

"Not normally," answered Nadine. "I don't know. It was weird. But I'm fine."

"Are you sure you're okay?" whispered Drew.

"I'm fine really. That's never happened before."

As the family sat and chatted, Drew noticed the way Nadine and his little niece clung to each other. Nadine seemed content, slowly rocking and cuddling the child. She barely joined in the conversation. Her entire focus was on the small bundle in her arms. When it was time to leave, she gently passed the sleeping child to Gayle, kissing the baby on its head and looking at her with longing eyes.

When she stood, her eyes met Drew's. She smiled and walked past him to the car. Lucille glanced after her as she walked away. When Drew gave his mom a hug, she whispered something in his ear that caused him to turn and look toward Nadine with an expression she couldn't read.

"Can you stay over tonight?" she asked on the drive home.

"Of course. What's wrong?"

"I don't know but for the last few weeks I can't sleep unless you're there. I just want to sleep."

"What is it, Nadine?"

"I can't tell you," she said, bursting into tears.

Pulling into the nearest parking lot, Drew turned off the engine and said, "You're telling me and you're telling me right now."

"Please, I can't," she said, continuing to cry.

"Why?"

"Because I'm so embarrassed."

"We're not moving until you tell me."

After a moment, she said, "I have to get it all out at one time. So please don't stop me."

"Okay," was all he said.

Taking a deep breath, she began, "My birth mother and father had an affair. She didn't want me because he didn't want her. So she left me and a note with his name and phone number at the hospital. He came and adopted me. He was a good father, at first. He thought his wife would learn to love me because she couldn't have children. She hated me.

"When he wasn't around, she constantly yelled how much she hated me and how I looked like my mother. 'Your hair is a mess! Your hair is a mess! Don't leave this house with your hair a mess!' Then my brother was adopted. I hoped she'd focus on loving him and leave me alone. It just gave her another person to scream at when Dad was gone.

"We would cry when he was about to go on business trips. He thought it was because we were going to miss him. We did miss him, but it was hell in that huge house alone with her. She'd force us to be prim and proper in front of guest. Then scream and smash things the moment they left. 'You didn't smile bright enough, Nadine.' 'You didn't sit straight enough, Daniel.' There was always something to yell about.

"Then one day I went into the pool house to hide from her. I heard her and a man having sex. I didn't know that's what it was at the time. Then I walked in on her and my father's attorney having sex in my dad's office while he was out of town. I thought the men were hurting her, so I gladly kept quiet. This went on all the time when Dad was out of town.

"Finally, when I was about to go away to college, I heard her telling my dad that he should let me earn my own way so I'd learn discipline and appreciation. What did she know about appreciation? I got angry. I yelled out every time and man that I had seen her with over the years. She said I was lying, and my dad didn't believe me.

Not until Daniel heard the commotion and came in and told of similar men he'd seen her with over the years.

"That night Daniel and I were each given a few thousand dollars and ordered to leave the house. I was eighteen, and Daniel was sixteen. Daniel blamed me even though he'd told too. Daniel refused to come with me. He left me and went out on his own. I rented a long-term motel room and went to work in a retail store and worked my way through college.

"I saw Daniel on social media, but I didn't contact him. I figured he's seen me there too. So we just pretend we don't know each other," she finished.

"I'm glad you told me," he said with sorrowful eyes.

"I'm strong now. I don't know why this story is making me cry. I've told it to Vee, and I told some of it to Tony. It just seems like lately, everything makes me want to cry."

"You can cry to me anytime. I'll always be here."

"I don't know what's wrong with me. I just haven't been feeling like myself."

"Maybe we should go to the doctor."

"It's not that serious," she smiled, drying her eyes.

Drew started the car and headed home. His mom had whispered something to him, but this was not the right time to bring that up. It would come out in time. He just hoped Nadine could handle it if was true.

That night she slept clinging to him just as she had for the last month. It didn't bother him; he just didn't understand the change.

*****

"Ms. Swift, there's a Mr. Williams here to see you."

"What the hell is he doing here?" Nadine silently asked. "Send him in Cassandra."

"Hi."

"Hello."

"May I sit?"

"I'm really busy, Tony. Yes, sit."

TAINTED

"You wouldn't answer or return my calls, so I took a chance on coming down here to apologize."

"You were way out of line with that comment."

"I was, and I'm sorry. I had no right to say those things to you."

"I'm not a whore. I never was."

"I know that. It was my stupid jealousy talking."

"Jealous of Wesley?"

"Yes! You were at the party. The man has more women than a sheik."

The mention of the party made Nadine laugh.

"That was the most entertaining birthday party, I have to admit, I've ever had the honor of attending," she said, grinning.

"It got worse after you and Drew left," he said with a shake of his head.

"Did it actually get physical?" Nadine whispered, smiling.

"Both physical and emotional. Sabrina left crying. We had to restrain two of the others."

"Denice and Teresa?"

"How'd you guess?" he asked with a roll of his eyes.

"Poor Wesley."

"You're joking, right?" asked Antonio, staring at her.

"I'm sure he never expected that to happen." Nadine chuckled.

"He didn't. Did you see how fast he left the scene?"

"Yeah. Drew and I laughed about that for days."

"I won't do that again. Please forgive me."

"Make sure you don't!"

"Scout's honor," he said, rising to leave.

"You're forgiven. Now get out of here so I can work." She smiled.

*****

Antonio's corporate contracts were on the rise. After leaving Nadine, feeling elated that she had forgiven him, he headed to another office building a few blocks away. Walking into what felt like a sterilized lobby, Antonio felt out of place. The space was massive

147

with marbled floors. The two security men had a 180-degree view of the street.

"Can we help you, sir?" a stern-faced middle-aged man asked.

"Yes. I have an appointment in the Emerton office."

"Your name?"

"Antonio Williams."

The second guard checked the computer screen and nodded to his partner. Handing him a temporary badge with barcode, the man said, "Use the barcode to access the elevator to the fifteenth floor."

"Will the office be to the left or right?" he inquired.

"The entire floor is the office," the man replied.

Exiting the elevator, Antonio glanced around the space. It held the same sterilized feeling. The cold ceramic and glass were replaced by deep shiny mahogany. Large gold letters on the wall behind the receptionist's desk spelled out "Emerton."

A dour-faced older receptionist sat behind the desk, glaring at him as he approached. Her graying hair was coiffed tightly. Antonio noted the way her face and neck were different shades.

"Is there something I can do for you, sir."

"Antonio Williams from Secure Systems. I have and appointment—"

"To install cameras," she finished with a forced smile.

"Yes. My appointment is with—"

"Mr. Briggs," again the woman finished his sentence. "Please have a seat. I'll let him know that you're here."

Antonio sat and began glancing through the portfolio and invoice he had prepared for this meeting when a familiar voice got his attention.

"Belle, can you get me the asset purchase agreement from my meeting yesterday?"

So this is where he works, thought Antonio, staring at the man.

"Right away, Mr. Noah. And, sir, Ms. Swift called."

Turning to leave, the man glanced toward him and stopped.

"Antonio?"

"How are you doing, Andrew?"

Andrew walked over and offered his hand, which Antonio shook.

"You're doing the installation?' Drew asked, smiling.

"That would me."

"Wow, when we voted on which company to give the contract to, I had no idea Secure Systems would be you."

"You voted for Secure Systems?"

"I did. Small business, sole proprietor, besides Terner gave you great reviews."

"If you had known it was me, would you have changed your vote?"

"Not at all. You're doing your thing and obviously well. Why would I change my vote?"

Antonio stared at the man before him. They were similar in some ways, yet different in others. They were both businessmen trying to succeed at making their mark in an industry that was already established. Yet he would have changed his vote because regardless of how honorable Andrew appeared. To Antonio, he was still competition.

"Here you are, Mr. Noah," said the receptionist.

"Thank you, Belle."

"Mr. Williams? I'm Jason Briggs," a man said, extending his hand as he approached. "This way, please."

"Great job on that merger deal, Noah," Briggs said, slapping Andrew on the shoulder as he passed.

"Thank you."

"I'm going to have to tell Nadine to start bugging you for that ring," the man joked.

"I wouldn't hesitate for a minute," Andrew responded.

"Mr. Noah, don't forget your call from Ms. Swift."

"Thank you, Belle," Andrew said, disappearing into his office.

*****

"Hello, beautiful."

"Hey, love."

"What's up?"

"Guess who just stopped by my office apologizing?"

"Guess who just walked into Jason's office to discuss camera installation?"

"No way!"

"Yes, way."

"Did he see you?"

"He saw me before I saw him."

"I'm sure you were a gentleman and spoke."

"Of course. He's the one threatened by me."

"You sound pretty confident in yourself, sir," she joked.

"I shouldn't be?" he challenged.

"You'd better be."

"What do you say to us leaving work and going straight to dinner?"

"I'd say that I'd love to."

"Where are we meeting?"

"I'll pick you up."

"My handsome prince is picking me up!" she said in a playful voice.

"Bye, beautiful," he said, laughing.

Moments later, Belle's voice said, "Mr. Noah, Mr. Williams would like to speak with you before he leaves."

"Send him in, Belle."

Entering, Antonio glanced around the space. *Executive*, he thought.

"Have a seat," said Andrew. "You wanted a word with me?"

"I do."

"What is it?"

When Antonio didn't immediately answer, Andrew said, "It's about Nadine." Closing the portfolio on his desk and leaning back in his chair, he said, "Go ahead. Speak your peace."

"What is it? What is it that she sees in you that she can't see in me? A corner office and a business suit? Or is it the money?"

"Don't you get it? It's none of those things. She already has all of that. Hell, she had that when she was with you."

"Then what is it? Nan loved me before you came along and tainted her mind against me."

"You did the tainting. Don't blame that on me. You guys had been broken up six months by the time I first laid eyes on her."

"You don't stop loving someone the way she loved me in six months!" retaliated Antonio, struggling to keep his voice down.

"You're right. Let me tell you some of the things I know for a fact that it took for her to stop loving you. And it was a hell of a lot longer than six months. Prescribed pills just to sleep at night because the over-the-counter brand no longer worked. A visit to a therapist every two weeks for three months—thank God to Vee for demanding that she go—so she could voice her hurt and stop internalizing it."

Antonio sat silent listening as Andrew's expression grew angry and leaned forward on his desk.

"You sounded upset a minute ago. Well, let me tell you what upset me. Being with a woman and loving her with all my heart for over a year. Yet every time I make love to her, she's so afraid I'm going to break her heart or to love me back. She'd bit her lip rather than moan or call out my name in passion. Wait, you want to know what really hurt, when I'd tell her that I loved her and look into her eyes and could see the love but having her tear up afraid to let me know she loved me, thinking I'd use that against her.

"And to answer your question about what is it? It's what she feels, man! It's the way being with me makes her feel. She feels safe. She knows she can relax because she trusts me. She knows I'll always be here and that she is loved by me, above all, and everything else, except God.

"She came into my life at a time when I needed her, and she needed me. We found each other, and we stayed together. We bonded in a way that fulfills us both. And through it all, she forgave you and is willing to be your friend. But Antonio, she loves me. I trust it, and I believe in it.

"As for me, I thank you for what you did. Not because it hurt her—I hate that—but because you brought us together. And I want you to know that I'm going nowhere. What I can't understand is, knowing what she went through as a child, how could you do that to her? You're unbelievable. And here it is, two and a half years later, and you come back thinking and acting like she's supposed to pretend nothing ever happened."

Without uttering a word, Antonio stood and left the room. There were no words to be said. The guilt that he thought was gone resurfaced with a vengeance. He walked away blindly, handing the badge to security and leaving the building.

He had taken Nadine's love for granted. He had always assumed that he could do anything and she'd be his and would continue to love him.

Forgive and forget, he thought as he strolled to his minivan. That's exactly what he had been expecting. He was sure Andrew had embellished his version of what Nan had gone through. He knew exactly where to the find the unembellished version—Everett.

*****

"And where do you think you are off to?" asked Everett, stopping Nadine before she could enter the elevator.

"I have a date with a handsome man," she said, batting her eyes rapidly.

"Handsome man? The only handsome man I know, bitch, is named Chris," he whispered, smiling.

"Shut up." Nadine laughed.

"Have fun."

"Always."

*****

Later, Nadine exited the elevator on Emerton's floor.

Looking up, Belle smiled brightly. "Ms. Swift."

"Hi, Belle. Is he available?"

"Yes, ma'am. Go right in."

"Is that you, Nadine?"

"Jason. How are you?"

"I'm doing well. You here to drag Andrew home at a respectable time?"

"Yeah, I'm here to get my honey." She grinned.

"You look happy, Nadine."

"I am. He makes me happy." She blushed.

"It's a wonderful thing, isn't it?"

"Indescribable," she said, turning to leave.

"Come on in, Belle," said Andrew with his back turned, stuffing papers into his briefcase.

Nadine entered and quietly took a seat.

"Listen, Belle, I'm leaving early because I'm taking my wife to dinner. You can go on and head home for the day," he said, turning to find Nadine seated in front of him.

"Wife?"

"Come on, babe, don't be mad. I hate calling you my girlfriend," he pleaded.

"But that's what I am, Drew," Nadine replied softly.

"I know. But I don't like it," he snapped.

"You don't like me being your girlfriend?" she asked in a barely audible voice.

"No, Nadine, I hate it!"

Nadine stood slowly, looking as if about to cry.

"I want you to be my wife! The mother of my children! My spouse! My beneficiary! I want you to be my everything! Because dammit woman, you are my everything."

She ran into his arms. They held each other tightly.

"You scared me," she whispered.

"I need more, babe. You have to give me more."

"Where do you want to start?"

"You already have that big house. I'm there more than at the condo. I want to move in."

"Okay. Can we start today?"

"You're okay with that?"

"I can't sleep when you're not there. Plus the house feels better with you in it."

"Now we're getting somewhere."

They left the office holding hands like high schoolers. They'd go home in Drew's car and leave Nadine's in the parking garage overnight.

"Good night, Mr. and Mrs. Noah," the security guard said as they passed.

"Good night," said Andrew, smiling.

Nadine didn't reply and refused to look in the man's direction.

"Get used to it," Andrew whispered, pulling her closer.

*****

Everett paused as he walked across the parking garage to his car.

"What the hell are you doing in here?" he asked when he spotted Antonio standing beside Nadine's car.

"Waiting for me or waiting for Nan? Because Nan already left."

"Her car is still here."

"I didn't say her car left. I said she left. Now move before I call security."

"I'm not here to see her. I'm here to see you."

"Now you see. As soon as I get in my car, you won't," Everett said, shooing him away with his hand, only to have the man stand his ground. "I'm not standing in here talking to you about anything. Now move."

"Please, man. It's about Nan."

"What about Nan? You better make it good because I'm about to call security."

"It's about what Nan went through, what I put her through. The sports bar on the corner. I just want to talk."

"You got thirty minutes, slug, and not a minute more. Now move."

*****

At the bar, the waiter asks, "What can I get for you?"

"I'll take a Bob Marley. No two Bob Marleys. The slug's paying," said Everett in his most feminine voice.

154

"A beer. Draft," said Antonio.

The waiter walked away with a smirk.

"Okay, slug, what is it?"

"I want to hear every detail, leaving nothing out, about what the breakup did to Nan."

"If you're trying to convince me that you care, please save yourself the time."

"I do care."

"How did you think it would affect her?"

"I figured she'd be mad as hell and stop talking to me for a while, then forgive me and the two of us would get back together, put it all behind us."

Everett sat, staring at him disbelief. "You are a bigger slug than I thought."

"Can you stop calling me names and just tell me what happened?"

"Your drinks," said the waiter, placing a bottle in front of Antonio and two mixed drinks in front of Everett.

"Well, dumbass, it wasn't pretty," began Everett, taking a swallow of his drink. "Let me begin at the beginning. First, she spent two weeks at my place, crying her eyeballs out every evening. That's when she started taking four, sometimes five, pm tablets just to fall asleep. After a month or so, they didn't work. I know this because I saw a prescription bottle on the nightstand when I visited. She said the other pills didn't work anymore. This was three months after your hood-rat-at-the-apartment incident."

Finishing off the first drink, he continued, "Around six months, she started working crazy hours because she didn't want to go home. That paid off because she ended up getting a huge promotion. On the outside, it looked like she had it all together, but on lunch breaks she'd go to her car and cry her eyes out. How do I know? I was there beside her. A few eye drops later and she'd come right back inside and work the rest of the day.

"It was around month nine, I think, when she started refusing to go to lunch with me for like two weeks straight. That's when I made an appointment with a therapist and told her if she didn't go, I was going to report her to the director. She was mad as hell and quit speaking to me for a couple of weeks. I called the therapist just to make sure that she was coming.

"After a few months of therapy, it was decided that she was strong enough to be dismissed. She started going on a few dates with some guy. I now realize that guy was Drew. She was guarded for a long time. I have to give it to the guy. She must have put him through hell at the beginning. I wouldn't know about that part. You'll have to ask him about that if you're brave enough."

After taking a deep sigh and finishing off his beer, Antonio looked at Everett and said, "How did they meet?"

"He bought a condo in her old building." Everett smiled, taking a swallow of his drink. Then standing, Everett took the final swallow of his drink and said, "She's happy now, Antonio. Let her be happy." He walked away in a huff after rolling his eyes.

Antonio sat quiet.

"Another beer, sir?"

"Yes."

Andrew hadn't embellished the story at all. He only knew one side of what Nadine was going through. Based on what Andrew hinted at, Antonio was sure she had problems with intimacy as well.

Everett was right. It had been bad for Nan, thought Antonio. It had been worse than he'd imagined.

By the time he headed home, four additional empty bottles sat on the table.

*****

"I can't believe we're officially moving in together," said Nadine, smiling.

"It has been a long time coming."

"So what are you going to do with the condo?"

"I figured I'd do the same thing you did with yours, just lease it out."

"I can give the management company that I used a call if you'd like."

"Absolutely. Are you comfortable handling that for me?"

"Of course!"

"Did the fact that I referred to you as my wife bother you?"

"It surprised me."

"You looked shocked for sure."

"I guess, just hearing you refer to me as 'wife' for the first time to Belle shocked me."

Andrew looked at her for a moment and smiled brightly, then said, "It wasn't the first time."

"What do you mean it wasn't the first time?"

"I've been calling you my wife in the office since you attended the game."

"That was months ago!"

"Well, that's how long I've been referring to you as my wife."

"Why?"

"Because to me, you are my wife. We just haven't made it official," he said, smiling.

She stared at him from across the table. "You really see me that way?"

"I don't just see you that way. That's who you are Nadine. We belong together. Can't you see that?"

"I just never think about official stuff, I guess. I'm happy and I just accept things the way that they are."

"Still trying not to complicate things?"

"It's not that."

"What is it then?"

"You came into my life at a time when I was hurt and badly damaged. I needed you, and you took the lead, and now I feel alive again. You taught me how to trust and to love again. I guess I just focus on the fact that we are happy right now. Because I was so unhappy and unsure of myself."

"I've never told you this, but I needed you then too. When I met you, I was getting over a bad breakup. The woman I was seeing—had been seeing—for a few years cheated on me. She didn't just cheat. She got pregnant and didn't know who the father was. I was willing to accept the child on the chance that it was mine because I cared for her."

"What happened?"

He chuckled slowly, shaking his head, and said, "She let me know that the feeling wasn't mutual, and she had no intention of keeping the baby regardless of who the father was."

They sat quietly eating, consumed in their thought for a few moments.

Nadine was questioning herself on how she would handle a pregnancy situation.

I have no idea how to be a mother, she thought.

Andrew thought of how good fatherhood would feel. His thoughts soon turned to Nadine. She was financially stable and independent.

I wonder if she would trade her career for motherhood? he thought.

"Hey," she said, interrupting his thoughts. "I'm on the pill. I have been for years."

"Nothing's guaranteed, love."

"We'll cross that bridge when we get to it," she said with a confidence she didn't feel.

"We?"

"Yes, we," she said, touching his hand.

Giving her hand a kiss, he smiled, liking the sound of her words.

*****

The remainder of the week went by in a flurry. Andrew worked days, packed his condo in the evenings, and carried the boxes to his home with Nadine. She spent her days juggling her usual workload and arranging for the condo to be cleaned to go on the market the following week. By the weekend, everything Drew owned was in Nadine's garage waiting to be placed in its new home.

"Dad, why don't you and the family visit me and Nadine this weekend? The move was brutal, and she hasn't been feeling a hundred percent."

"Are you sure there's enough room for all of us? I'm sure both of your sisters and the grandkids are coming."

"There's plenty of room. Don't worry."

"I'll spread the news."

"See you Sunday, Dad."

"So they're coming?" confirmed Nadine.

"They'll be here."

"I'm sure I'll feel better by then."

"It's the move. It wore you out," he said, kissing her forehead.

"It comes and goes. A good night's sleep and I'll be good to go."

"Sleep? That sounds like a great idea."

*****

Across town, Wesley packed a suitcase for his first visit to the new location he would be managing. A knock on his door interrupted him. Opening the door, he saw Angie standing before him.

"What are you doing here? More importantly, how did you find out where I live?"

"Hello to you, Wesley."

"That was two questions. You got any answers?"

"I'm here because I wanted to see you. I found out where you live by asking a few questions."

"Look, I don't have drama at my home."

"I'm not here for drama. I'm just here to see you."

"See me? For what purpose?"

"To see you," she said with a sultry look.

Wesley stepped back, allowing her entrance. He knew why she was there, and he intended to oblige her. He had already given his notice to management and applied for a condo downtown. His days at his complex were limited.

*****

Loading his car a few hours later, Wesley felt revived after his visit with Angie. With equipment and luggage, he drove off for a three-day stay across town.

It's time for a fresh start, he thought. *New career, new women, new location, and new position.* He smiled as he entered the expressway.

*****

"Oh my god, Drew, this place is amazing," said Gayle as she entered the foyer.

"It's huge!" screamed the children, running off toward the open patio door.

"No running inside!" screamed Gayle, going after them while carrying a large package of what Andrew knew was prepared food.

"Where's Nadine?" Lucille asked, after giving him a quick kiss on the cheek.

"She's in the media room setting up snacks for the kid."

"Living room, then turn left, Mom."

"How many rooms does this place have, son?" asked his father, forcing additional food into his arms while taking in the view of the foyer.

"Five bedrooms, Dad. Where's Claudine?"

"Baby has an upset stomach, so she'll come next time. Where can I smoke? Can't smoke in the car with the kids."

"Balcony, Dad. Straight ahead."

"Nadine!" exclaimed Lucille, embracing her in a tight hug.

"I'm so glad you guys came!"

"The way my boy's been going on and on about the house his girl bought, we've been dying to have a look."

"So what did you do with your condo?"

"I lease it out."

"That's what Andrew said he was doing with his."

"Please have a seat."

"Oh no! Come and show me where we're putting all this food."

"You brought food?"

"You see how these people eat on Sundays. Wouldn't expect you and Andrew to feed all of us."

"Come on now," the woman urged, heading toward the kitchen.

"I love this place," a child commented to another.

"It's big!" said another.

"Sounds like you'll be getting some sleepover requests," said Andrew's father between puffs on his cigar.

"There are four extra bedrooms upstairs, so sleeping won't be a problem," commented Drew with a chuckle.

"So it's official? The two of you actually living together now."

"Honestly, Dad, I've been living here for a while. I just had half of my belongings at the condo."

"Whose idea was this?"

"It was mutual."

"That's good."

"So what's next for the two of you?"

"We'll see, Dad. We'll see."

"Your mom thinks Nadine maybe pregnant."

Andrew chuckled, then said, "Nadine's been on the pill for years. That's not likely."

"Your sister agreed."

Andrew looked at his dad for a moment. "Why would they say such a thing?"

"Why would they say it? Because they've both had a few kids and know the symptoms."

"She'd tell me if she was," said Andrew thoughtfully.

"Would she know if she was?"

"She'd know," said Andrew, not believing his own words.

Andrew and Nadine divided the children among the kitchen and sunroom while the adults ate in the dining room. Youthful chatter and giggles could be heard loud and unabated.

"What plans do you and Drew have for all of these room, Nadine?" asked Gayle.

"I have no idea what Drew plans to do with the basement area. As for all the bedrooms upstairs, I guess we'll just furnish them in case you guys or Vee and Chris stays over."

"We're all family now, so I'm just going to come right out with it," began Lucille. "Are the two of you just going to live in sin forever or do you plan on getting married?"

"Seriously, Mom? Not on the first visit," Gayle whispered.

Nadine glanced at Drew and began to pour herself another glass of almond milk.

"When the time is right, Mom," he said, watching Nadine drink her third glass of milk.

"Never seen you drink milk during dinner before, baby girl," his father said, also noting the amount of milk she was drinking.

"I guess it's the almonds. It just tastes so good to me." She smiled.

"That whole milk makes me a little nauseous," lied Gayle, waiting for a response from Nadine.

"Yeah, me too lately. So do eggs and raw poultry," Nadine said with a shake of her head as she proceeded to pour another glass of milk.

The three guests all glanced at each other.

"She was sautéing chicken the other night for dinner wearing a face mask," Drew commented, chuckling, unaware of the stares directed at the two of them.

"I can eat it. But uncooked, it smells awful," Nadine said with a little shiver.

"It was delicious though, love," Drew said, leaning over to give Nadine a quick kiss on the side of her head.

"Dang, all of the milk's gone," said Nadine with a little frown, shaking the carton.

"I picked up two more cartons this morning."

"Did you?" Nadine said, grinning at him.

His family exchanged longer glances this time.

"You always liked milk, Nadine?" Lucille asked.

"I do! Just the almond kind," she responds with a blissful expression.

"Honestly, I need to buy a cow that produces almond-flavored milk and tie him outside the sunroom," joked Drew.

The family knew she was displaying symptoms of pregnancy and the two of them had no idea.

"Remember when I used to drink chocolate milk all of the time, Drew?" his sister asked, hoping he'd get the hint.

"Yeah! You'd drink two or three gallons a day." He laughed.

"Then another time it was bananas, remember?" she continued.

"Yeah, you were eating them as fast as we bought them." He chuckled.

"And you developed this crazy aversion to scrambled eggs once too," Lucille added to the conversation, hoping her son would see what they were trying to say.

Pausing, Andrew looked at his sister. "You know, all those times you were—"

"Yeah," she said, giving him a look. "I was 'expecting' it to just go away any day."

He looked at Nadine as she continued to eat, unfazed by the conversation.

"But it passed, right?" Nadine asked Gayle as she continued eating.

"Honestly, it took some months for it to completely pass, Nan."

Andrew began to stroke Nadine's hair softly as he looked at her.

"What's wrong, babe?" she asked, putting her fork down, growing concerned by his expression.

"Babe, how long have you been feeling not yourself?"

"I don't know a few months maybe. I've been tired furnishing the house and all. It's nothing. I'm okay. Don't worry."

"I think we should visit the doctor, love," he said softly.

"Why? I'm fine."

"I don't think you are, babe."

"I just like milk! That's not something you run to the doctor for." She laughed. "Come on."

"Babe, you're craving certain foods. You can't stand the smell of others. Foods that you've prepared for me numerous times. Plus you're sleepy a lot, and you get nauseous at different times of the day."

Nadine started to laugh. "Babe, Gayle just said she's had the same symptoms. It's nothing. I'm fine."

"Can we please visit your primary?" begged Drew, touching her hand.

"I'll make an appointment tomorrow, love. I'm fine. Stop worrying. It's probably the same thing Gayle had," she said, smiling.

"Yeah, I'm kind of thinking the same thing," he said softly.

"Babe, stop worrying. The doctor's probably going to tell us that I have the same thing Gayle had."

"Gayle had a baby." Drew's father laughed.

"I was pregnant during those times, Nan," confessed Gayle softly.

Nadine stared at everyone for a long time.

"No," she whispered with eyes that started to tear up. She turned to Drew. "I can't get pregnant. You know that. I'm on the pill. I've been taking them for years." Her breathing started to increase as she stared at Drew. She looked at her plate, then her stomach. Slowly, she pushed the plate away, then redirected her gaze back to Drew.

"It's okay," he said, grasping her hand reassuringly.

"Drew," she whispered as a tear slid down her face. She swiped it away, not wanting their guest to see her cry.

"I'm here. I'll always be here. You know that," he said softly.

The two hadn't noticed Lucille leave the table for another carton of almond milk.

"Here, dear, have some milk," Lucille said, handing Nadine a fresh glass of milk.

Taking the glass slowly, Nadine drank the entire glass and began to pour another before realizing all eyes were watching her.

"I'm sorry! I just really like milk!" she said and burst into tears, then she drank the entire glass.

They stifled their laughs.

Gayle finally said, "Nan, we're family. If you like milk, drink your milk, love."

After pouring yet another glass, she turned to look at Drew and demanded, "I'm not pregnant. I just like milk—a lot."

"And I'm going to make sure you have all of the milk you want, love." He smiled as she drank another glass.

*****

A few days later, the two of them sat in her primary doctor's office waiting to be called.

"Nadine Swift," the nurse called out.

To Nadine's surprise, Drew rose with her. In the examination room, the nurse took blood, checked her vitals, and gave her a small cup for a urine sample.

When the doctor came in, she smiled at Drew, appearing happy with his presence.

"So tell me what brings you in today, Nadine?"

"I don't know. I just haven't been feeling like myself."

"Can you describe your symptoms?"

"Well, certain foods seem to make me experience nausea. I feel tired, like I need a nap when normally I'm fine. I struggle to make it through the day some days."

"She cries at the drop of a hat," added Drew, ignoring a dagger-like glance from Nadine.

"Are you still on your birth control pills?" asked the doctor.

"Yes."

"And you haven't missed any?"

"No. Well, last month I ran out for a few days, but I went and got the prescription refilled."

"How long were you out of your pills?"

"Maybe a week. I was really busy, but I figured I had enough in my system, and I started back as soon as I got them."

"Are you sure that's the only time?"

"It was the most recent. But like I said, I never miss more than a few days."

"I'm going to need you to stop taking those," the doctor instructed.

"You think that's what's making me feel sick?" asked Nadine concerned, then glancing at Drew. "It's only been a couple of times," she said to Drew nervously.

The nurse entered and handing a form to the doctor. Drew stood, placing a hand on Nadine's shoulder, anticipating the results.

"Thank you," the doctor said, reading the form the nurse handed her.

"Test results?" asked Drew.

"Yes," said the doctor, smiling.

"What does it say?" asked Nadine, reaching for Drew's hand.

"It says that you're perfectly healthy and that you're pregnant." The doctor smiled at the couple.

Drew beamed with excitement. Nadine's eyes widened, and her mouth fell open in shock. She looked at Drew and started to hyperventilate. Immediately, the doctor and Drew helped her lie back, telling her to relax and breathe. Leaning close to her ear, he repeatedly whispered, "I'm here. I'll always be here."

The doctor wrote out a prescription for prenatal vitamin and handed it to Drew.

Nadine touched her stomach and said, "I'm flat. How can I be pregnant?"

"You're only about twelve weeks pregnant. You won't see that right away." The doctor smiled.

"What can I do, Doc?" asked Drew.

"Make sure she eats healthy, exercises, takes her vitamin daily, and gets plenty of rest."

"Will her nausea pass?"

"For some women, it does. Things that the two of you identify that result in feelings of nausea avoid. Come back to see me if it continues or gets worse."

Drew kept his arm around Nadine as they walked to the car, fearing she may lose her balance due to the shock.

"Nadine?"

She looked in his direction but appearing as if in a daze.

"Are you okay?"

"I don't know," she said, turning to look straight ahead. "I think I should just go home and lie down," she said mechanically, staring straight ahead.

*****

Drew watched as Nadine climbed the stairs without saying a word once they arrived at home. He was worried so he called his parents. Then he called Vee.

"I need you guys to get over here right away."

"What's wrong?" asked Everett, sounding concerned.

"Nadine's not doing well. I need you to come now."

"What the hell happened?"

"We just found out that she's pregnant. And she's not taking it well. I'm worried."

"Pregnant? She's on the pill!"

"She missed a few times."

"How far along is she?"

"Twelve weeks. She's acting very robotic."

"She's probably scared to death, never having a real mother."

"I never thought of that."

"You wouldn't. We're on the way," Everett said, hanging up immediately.

*****

"Baby, Vee's here."

"What is he doing here?"

"I called him, love. You need to talk to someone."

"No, Drew," she whined.

"Yes, now come on."

As soon as Nadine walked into the room, Vee embraced her in a hug, holding her the way Nadine needed to be held at that moment.

"So you're about to be a mommy, huh?"

"I don't know what I'm going to be, Vee."

"What does that mean?"

"It means I don't have a clue how to be a mom!"

"Motherhood doesn't come with a manual, Nan."

"Yeah, but most people have role models as a foundation. I don't, Vee!"

That statement brought some clarity to what she was feeling for Drew.

"What kind of foundation do you wish you'd had?"

"One that was caring and loving and protective. One that wanted me. I have no clue what that feels like."

"Tell me one person that's shown you that they care about you, love you, and will protect you."

"Not counting you, of course, only Drew," she said, looking at him. "You guys are the only ones really."

"We're the same, Nan. The only people that have shown me those things are you and Chris."

"Neither of us came from loving families. You were kicked at eighteen because of a wicked stepmother and I was kicked at eighteen for being gay. But we can't let that stop us from living a full life. We haven't so far."

"I guess you're right. But I'm scared, Vee. I'm really scared," she said with a trembling voice. "I'm scared I'm going to mess up!"

"Okay then, it's your body. Do you want to get rid of it?"

"No! Everett!" interjected Drew.

"Quiet, Drew," Everett said sternly.

"Babe," said Chris softly.

"No! Nan needs to speak right now. From the heart. Do you want to get rid of the baby?"

"What?" Nadine said, looking shocked.

"Do you want to have an abortion? It's your body. Do you want to get rid of it?"

Nadine slowly wrapped her arms around her waist as if shielding the baby.

Drew sat holding his breath.

"I can't, Vee," she said softly. "I would never hurt the baby. No, I don't want an abortion."

"Then do you want to give it away for adoption?"

"To somebody else?"

"Yes, to somebody else. To somebody that's not scared. Do you want to give it away?"

"No!"

"Then why do you have your arms wrapped around your waist like that?"

Drew and Chris began to understand what Everett was doing.

"Because you're talking crazy. Talking about hurting him or giving our baby to someone that may not love him and take care of him. Why are you saying all this crazy stuff, Vee?"

"Think about everything you just said. Those are the things that a real mom would say. Nan, you are a mom. A great mom. Just do those three things—love it, protect it, and take care of it the best that you can. And when you're feeling like you need help, hell, give him to Drew! He's as much to blame as you are!"

Nadine started to laugh as she sat, gently stroking her flat tummy.

"So we're keeping the baby, right?" confirmed Everett.

"Yes!" said Nadine, looking at Drew. "Drew, I don't want to give him away. I can't. I want to keep him. Even if I'm not a perfect mom. I want to try. I mean, I love him, Drew."

"I don't want to give him away either, babe. I love him too. We can do this, okay?"

"Okay."

Everett jumps to his feet and begins to perform a cheer, repeating, "Yes, you can!"

"I need a drink," said Drew.

"So do I," said Chris.

Nadine and Everett followed the men into the kitchen. Everett poured a glass of wine while the men opened beers. Chris and Everett stared as Nadine drank an entire glass of almond milk without stopping and poured another.

"You're kidding, right?" asked Everett in shock.

"Please let her drink that milk, or she'll start balling," Drew whispered.

She smiled at them after swallowing the second glass, saying, "I just love milk."

"How long has this been going on?" asked Everett, giving Drew a shocked look.

"Weeks," mumbled Drew, smiling at Nadine.

"How much?"

"About a gallon a day right now. Don't let her hear you or she'll cry," he mumbled, pretending to drink his beer.

"What?" asked Nadine, glancing between Drew and Vee.

"I was telling Drew I love the way you are enjoying that milk," lied Everett.

"I know, Vee. It's so good. I could drink it all day," she said, smiling.

Everett smiled and redirected his gaze to Drew, who mumbled, "She does."

Chris who normally has very little to say looked at Nadine and said, "You guys are the most entertaining group of people I've ever met. This is better than a movie."

"Never a dull moment with us!" Nadine and Everett said in unison, then laughing hysterically.

Drew looked at the woman he called his wife, who was now the mother of his child, and felt blessed. As Nadine chatted with Vee and Chris, he noticed how she unconsciously stroked her flat tummy as if soothing the child inside.

"Babe, come," she whined, motioning for Drew to be near her. Now he understood her clinginess. They were always close. The pregnancy, however, increased her desire for him. Standing behind her, he wrapped his arms around her, gently stroking his growing child. She continued chatting with her hands atop his as she leaned back into the safety of his arms.

Yield

"BUT, SIR, IF my hours are cut, I won't be able to afford my apartment," Kristie said softly, sitting in William's office.

"I'm sorry, Kristie. We simply don't need the staff right now," replied William smugly.

The young woman stood turned to leave, feeling defeated.

"What did he want?" asked a female coworker.

"He cut my hours," whispered Kristie near tears. "I don't know how I'm going to afford to keep my apartment."

"You've only been there for six months," the coworker said sympathetically.

"I don't know what I'm going to do," Kristie said, fighting tears.

*****

A few buildings away, Nadine sat in a meeting of executives, listening to the director discuss the company's plan for internal promotions.

"Of course, this initiative is open to all current employees," he announced. "However, only those that have demonstrated the aptitude, ability, and the necessary skills will be considered. Those of you in this room have this opportunity to think for a moment and refer anyone that has shown the potential that this company needs."

Nadine glanced around the room. She personally knew that more than half the executives in the room had their secretaries and assistants writing their reports and creating their presentations. Yet they all sat as if dumbfounded.

Glancing at his executives and waiting, the director finally said, "It looks like maybe you could all use a little time."

"Sir, I'd like to refer my assistant, Cassandra Harris," said Nadine.

All eyes turned in her direction, wondering why she would voluntarily refer her assistant. They had all noticed their teamwork in meetings. If you give up your assistant, then the work falls to the executive. They looked at each other and smiled at her ill-fated maneuver.

"Cassandra Harris, is that?" repeated the director, writing the woman's name down.

"Yes, sir."

"Swift, you do understand that you'll have to locate and hire another secretary to replace her."

"I understand, sir. I already have someone in mind."

"I'll also expect you to train Ms. Harris since you are the person referring her."

"That won't be a problem, sir," she stated confidently.

"Well, I have another meeting to get to. So I'm also going to leave it to you to inform Ms. Harris of her new role, which will begin on Monday, and to have a replacement by then as well. Are we clear?"

"Perfectly, sir."

As the only slightly noticeably pregnant Nadine walked across the office, she paused in front of Cassandra's desk.

"Cassandra, I need to see you in my office in about ten minutes," she said.

"Yes, ma'am," Cassandra said, appearing nervous.

Taking a seat, Nadine pressed a few numbers on her cell phone.

"Hello?" answered Kristie, still sitting in her car outside the furniture store.

"Hello, Kristie, it's Nadine Swift."

"Hi, Ms. Swift. What can I do for you?"

"Are you still attending school at night?"

"Yes, ma'am. I just started my last semester."

"I have a proposition for you. The only problem is that I'll need an immediate answer."

"What is it?" Kristie asked, praying it was another huge purchase.

"I want to offer you a job," said Nadine.

"A job?"

"A position as an assistant. My assistant, in fact. It's more like a secretary really. Are you interested?"

"Yes, Ms. Swift! Yes!"

"Great. The position starts on Monday, promptly at eight fifty. Dress professionally. You will also need to meet with my current assistant, Cassandra Harris, today or tomorrow, so that on Monday the transition is smooth."

"Oh my god, Ms. Swift! Thank you! Thank you so much! I'll be there. Can I meet her today? I promise I won't let you down."

"That would an advisable move. Just ask for Cassandra Harris at the security desk," said Nadine, ending the call.

With a huge smile, Kristie made her way back into the store to inform William that she was quitting.

*****

"Ms. Swift, you wanted to see me?" asked Cassandra.

"Please sit down."

Cassandra sat thinking she had done something wrong and was about to be reprimanded. She sat squeezing her pen and notepad nervously as Nadine scribbled on her to-do list before speaking.

"Tell me honestly, Cassandra, what do you think of the work that executives do?"

"All of the executives, ma'am, or just you?"

"Both," answered Nadine. She thought, *What a unique response.*

"Please don't hold this against me, ma'am, but I think most of the executives have their secretaries and assistants doing their work for them. My opinion is that the other executive's work is also their secretary's work."

"And me? I won't hold it against you."

"Ma'am, I think your work is very precise and deliberate. You're dedicated to always presenting your best in meetings. Your secretary is used to finalize whatever you create. By finalize, I mean to bind and copy. Our work is not the same. I see your work. But I've never done your work for you."

"That's interesting because I want to teach you how to do my work, Cassandra. That's why I asked to speak with you."

"Yes, ma'am," said Cassandra, thinking she was about to experience her coworker's torment firsthand.

"I've recommended you for a promotion to junior executive starting on Monday. I'll be training and assigning cases to you, which you will present in meetings.

"Junior executive?" repeated Cassandra with teary eyes, realizing she was being promoted not reprimanded.

"First thing, you never cry in the office under any circumstances. Secondly, like me, you are going to hear a lot of nasty things from your coworkers. Why? Because you, so far, were the only one recommended. Third, never miss a deadline. Fourth, triple check your own work. Finally, dress like a full executive even though you're a junior. Understood?"

"Yes, ma'am," Cassandra replied, struggling to hold her tears in check.

Standing, Nadine placed a small vial of eye drops on her desk in front of Casandra and walked to the blinds. Cassandra didn't immediately realize it, but her training was about to begin.

"I'm going to close my blinds and leave the office for a few moments. You can cry then. Take advantage of my little survival tool on the desk. Be sure to pick you up a bottle this evening. And, Cassandra, please know that I'm very proud of you."

*****

"Hi, I'm Kristie Elliot. Ms. Swift said I'm to meet with you to find out about my new position."

"I'm Cassandra, Ms. Swift's, well, I was Ms. Swift's assistant. Starting Monday that'll be your position." Cassandra smiled.

"Where will you go?"

"Ms. Swift got me promoted to junior executive!" whispered Cassandra.

"That's awesome!" whispered Kristie, wondering why they were talking in hushed voices.

As they walked through the office, other assistants and secretaries raised their heads curious about the guest.

"Here, I brought you a notepad. Never go into her office without something to write on. Date everything that she tells you to do. Use the same pad until it runs out. That way, you have something to refer to. She's nice, but she'll replace you if you forget to do things. Be here before she arrives. Make coffee every morning and do not allow her almond milk to run out."

"Is that what she uses in her coffee?"

"No, she pregnant and craves almond milk."

"If you forget the almond milk, you may get fired. Her husband called and told me she craves almond milk nonstop and that I am to never let it run out."

"Is it stocked now?" asked Kristie nervously.

"Instructions on delivery is taped to your desk. Check the supply throughout the day. She won't mind you coming into her office for that. Just be sure to knock first."

"This is the file room," said Cassandra, turning on the lights to illuminate a huge room filled with file cabinets and shelves. "To the left everything is filed based on dates. To the right filing is alphabetically. On the shelves are company files. She'll ask for a file based on date, name, or company."

"Why did we have to whisper when we got off the elevator?"

"No one knows about the promotion yet. Trust me, you'll hear the mean comments. Don't let the office jealousy get to you."

"I'm only a secretary. Why would anyone be jealous of that?"

"You're not just a secretary. You're an assistant to a top executive. We have a class of newly graduated recruits, and you've been hired over them."

"I see."

"Also, they've started having assistants attend meetings. Make sure all of Ms. Swift's reports are copied and bound before the meeting."

"Before the meeting," repeated Kristie, taking notes.

"Honestly, I'd do them as soon as she gives them to you."

"Keep up with her calendar. Remind her of meetings. When she's out of the office, call her for everything that requires her decision. Text her about every call she receives. If you're not sure, call her. Otherwise, you may get fired."

"Wow," said Kristie, looking bewildered as they walked across the office again toward Cassandra's desk.

"Stop looking scared," warned Cassandra in a hushed voice.

Glancing around, Kristie notice everyone wore business suits. There were no trendy hairstyles and not a hint of urban wear. All the women were dressed with a classy professional elegance.

Kristie immediately altered her expression the best that she could.

"This will be your desk. Everything that you saw in the file room is accessible on your computer. Have a seat."

Kristie saw a mini fridge tucked discretely behind Cassandra's desk. She glanced down and noticed a to-do list taped to the desk and stroked it with a finger.

"Follow that on Monday, and you'll have a great first day."

"I can do this," said Kristie confidently.

"It sounds like a lot but trust me. Be glad you work for Ms. Swift. It would be a lot worse with some of the others," whispered Cassandra.

"I don't want to disappoint her."

"You won't. Now for the bad news."

Kristie's eyes widened. "There's more?"

"Not only will you be assisting Ms. Swift, you'll be supporting me as well."

"So everything I do for her, I'll be doing it for you as well?"

"Yes, except for the almond milk, of course." Cassandra smiled.

"Be here at eight fifty, dress professionally, and ignore all office gossip, and follow the to-do list. Correct?"

"Correct."

"Do I check in at the security desk again?"

"No. Ms. Swift had them create a badge for you. Just flash the badge and keep walking."

"That's easy enough."

"Now I'll take you to human resources so you can fill out all your paperwork. Before I forget, she instructed me to give this to you before you leave," said Cassandra, handing an envelope to Kristie with a questioning expression.

"Would it be okay if I come in and shadow you tomorrow?"

"That would be great!"

After leaving human resources, Kristie opened the envelop once inside her car. It was a note and a gift card.

It read, "*Congratulations on your new position. By now you've had an opportunity to tour the office. You deserve to be here just as much as anyone else. Please use this gift card to assist you in looking the part. Regards, Nadine Swift.*"

*****

Walking up to the counter of the lady's department in a retail store, Kristie handed the card to the cashier.

"Can you tell me what my limit on this card is?"

"Five hundred dollars, ma'am."

Hugging the card, Kristie smiled and began to select pieces that she could mix and match for as many days as possible starting the following day. Although she wasn't a fan of blazers, she knew they were essentials, expected, and, she discovered, costly. With three blazers, three matching skirts. and a couple pairs of slacks, her gift card was maxed out. She'd borrow a couple of blouses from Kristina to complete her look. She left the store thankful and proud.

"Eight fifty," she repeated as she walked to her car elated. She couldn't wait to get to share her news with Kristina.

*****

When Kristie arrived at her apartment, her sister was standing outside chatting with Tracie, their neighbor. Jumping from her car, she ran into her sister's arms.

"Oh, Trina!" she exclaimed.

Thinking something wrong, Katrina held her.

177

"What's the matter?" she asked as Kristina danced in her arms. "What is it?"

Controlling herself long enough to allow her sister to see that she was laughing with excitement and not crying.

"First, my hours got cut by William," she said.

"Oh no! Honey, I'm so sorry."

"Then I went back in and quit."

"Kris, you didn't!"

"Yes, I did because while I was sitting in my car feeling sorry for myself, Ms. Swift called only a few moments later and hired me as her assistant! I start on Monday!"

"Are you serious?" Katrina asked as they both began to jump up and down.

"That's absolutely wonderful, Kris," said Tracie, smiling.

"That's not all," began Kristie excitedly. "She gave me a five-hundred-dollar gift card for professional work clothes!"

"Ms. Swift did that?"

"Yes!"

"I told you. Nadine's wonderful once you get to know her," said Tracie.

"She's amazing is what she is!" exclaimed Kristie. "Wait until you see what I bought. Oh, and I may need to borrow a couple of blouses to go with my outfits." Kristie rushed back to her car.

"I'll have to thank her for all she's doing for Kris," said Katrina to Tracie.

"Just wait until she has her baby, Trina, or send her some almond milk. Her assistant says that's what she is craving," said Kristina, rushing upstairs.

"Wait!" said Tracie, shocked. "Did you say she's having a baby?"

"Yeah, that's one of my duties. Her husband called and gave specific instructions not to let her almond milk run out. I'm assuming she gets super cranky if she runs out of her milk. You guys should know about being pregnant and cravings. I don't have any kids," she said. "Come on, Trina!"

Why? Why would you visit at this very moment? thought Tracie, seeing Antonio exiting his van just as Kristie yelled for her sister to come and see her new clothes.

"New clothes cause this kind of reaction?" he asked, smiling, as Katrina dashed toward the yells of her younger sister.

"I think you should come inside," said Tracie, dreading what she was about to tell him.

"Mom."

"Not now," she snapped, pointing toward the bedroom.

"But, Mom."

"I said not now," she repeated with a stern look, which sent the child scurrying back into his bedroom.

"Tony, are you okay?"

No response. He sat staring at the floor.

Tracie got up and lit a cigarette for him and placed it between his fingers. He inhaled deeply from the cigarette but no response.

"It'll be okay. I promise, it will," she said.

"I've lost her, Trace. I've actually lost her."

"No one knows what the future holds, Tony."

"I've lost her. He told me I had, but I just couldn't believe it."

"I know right now there doesn't seem to be much solace, but you guys are still friends."

"It's not the same, Trace."

"I know," she said, unable to think of anything more comforting.

"I always thought that, at the very least, I had a chance," Antonio said. "What did I do wrong? I didn't rush her. I tried to give her space. What did I do wrong?"

"Tony."

"No! You're a woman. Tell me what I did wrong?" he demanded, misdirecting his anger.

"You waited too long! You crushed her, and then you waited too damn long to try and fix things," she snapped back. "He cleaned up the mess you made of her heart, love. While he soothed it and patiently waited for it to heal, he fell in love with her, and she with him. I'm sorry."

"It's over, isn't it?"

"Yes, love, it is. Be her friend. Wish her well. But it's time for you to move on."

As the ashes from his unsmoked cigarette fell to the floor, so did the tears from his eyes. Antonio wept with a pain that Nadine and Andrew had experienced firsthand. He also cried because he knew that if it had not been for his actions, Nadine would be his wife, carrying his child. He cried because he finally realized that scenario would never be.

Tracie cried, seeing the pain her brother was suffering and understood Everett's frantic calls more than two years ago. She cried, because like Everett, there were no words capable of healing a heart that is broken by someone that you love. And like Antonio, she cried because she knew that all of this was a result of his decision to have an affair and then wait two years before trying to correct the situation.

*****

On the outskirts across town, Wesley settled into his satellite office. His view of the of the Dolce Vita Community showed a job near completion. The building and playground were complete, and construction on the pool had begun. He decided now was the time to locate two additional sites for the next phase of his plan. He hadn't been feeling his best lately, but he pushed through as always.

The managing of both sites hadn't been difficult at all. He couldn't wait to get back to town the weekend and share the news with Nadine and Everett. He'd been so busy lately, he hadn't even spoken to her. Other than Miguel and his family, he hadn't talked to anyone in the city.

Outside of the job, he had been successful in setting up a new network of women—all with their designated day for him to visit. This time he was careful, being sure they were in completely different neighborhoods. The party fiasco was not something he wanted to relive.

"Hello, lovely lady."

"Hey, Wess! Someone's been hiding," said Nadine, happy to hear from her friend.

"I'll be back in town this weekend. I was hoping to see you."

"Of course! Let's make it a party. I'll invite Vee and Chris."

"That sounds good. So what's new with you?"

"I do have some news to share." She laughed.

"Good news or bad news?"

"It's good news. It really is."

"If you got married while I was away, that's not good news to my ears," he joked.

"I didn't get married, but the news is still good."

"So tell me now," he urged.

"No, you have to be here."

"I can't wait. Is seven o'clock Saturday, okay?"

"Yes. That's perfect."

"See you then," he said, ending the call.

He didn't even bother to ask if Drew was going to be there, already knowing the answer. He'd just wait to see what this great news of hers was. As he contemplated the long drive ahead of him, he thought of how tired he'd been feeling lately. That thought prompted him to call his primary for an appointment the following week.

*****

"Babe?"

"Yes, love," answered Nadine.

"Honey, I know you are convinced the baby is a boy and he already has a name. Don't you think that just in case, we should decide on a girl's name?"

"Okay. What girl names do you like?"

"Me? I was thinking maybe you could come up with a girl's name."

"I named AJ. You name our daughter. What do you like?"

"Babe, I'm not good at that stuff."

"Sure, you are. Just think of what you're going to call her if she cries, or when she doesn't want to practice her alphabet, or when she wants to go on a date with a boy." Nadine grinned.

"From birth to her teens, huh?"

"Think of something that starts with the letter *A*."

"Help me," he said.

"Alexis. You can call her Lexi. How about Andrea? You can call her Drea."

He sat repeating the names softly. "I think I like Andrea," he said.

"Andrea Teresa Noah. Andrew Trevor Noah. Drew and Drea. Drew and AJ," said Nadine, smiling.

"I like it. A little bit you, Teresa, and a little bit of me," he said.

"Exactly."

"Want to know a name I'd really like?"

"What name is that, love?" she asked, smiling.

"Nadine Teresa Noah."

"Not that I'm opposed to it, but why is marriage such an issue? We don't need a piece of paper and a ceremony to know that we are committed to and love each other. We're a team. We have a family— me, you, and our baby," she reasoned.

"Listen to me, love. Everything you just said is true. But the law looks at things differently. According to the law, AJ, is your child. I just fathered him. You are the legal guardian. You make all the decision when it comes to him. Legally, I have no say so at all. He is your baby. I just planted a seed and have no true rights."

Wrapping her arms around her waist protectively, she stared at Andrew. "I don't think I like that."

"Neither do I. But that's the way things are. Just think about that, okay?"

She nodded as the doorbell rang out, and Drew went to see who their unannounced visitor was. Nadine sat pondering his words. She hadn't considered the legalities of their situation. Drew was there. She trusted him to guide the family.

What would happen to AJ if something happened me? she thought.

"Hey, Mommy!" called out Gayle with open arms.

"Hey," she responded, smiling.

"Somebody's in deep thought. Baby okay?"

"He's great!"

"Marcus and I were in the area and decided to drop in since we are rarely on this side of town."

"We're glad you did. Where is Marcus?"

"Oh, girl, Drew dragged him off to see his new pool table."

"He's excited."

"So what were you in here all deep on thought over?"

"Drew said something that kind of bothered me."

"What did he say?"

"He said he has no legal rights when it comes to AJ."

"Oh, honey, it's true. You guys aren't married. I know you guys are happy and all that. You probably feel like it's not necessary. For love, it's not. But when it comes to the law, property and children are viewed completely differently. You know about property, you're a businesswoman. It's different with children. You can't will your children to someone. He would have to go through the legal system for them to grant him certain rights. That's just the way that it is."

"I was adopted and none of my friends have children. Honestly, I never really thought about being a mom before, it just kind of happened."

"I hope I didn't make you sad."

"No! I'm glad you explained it to me. Drew will just have to decide what we are going to do."

"Nadine! My brother would marry you right this minute! You must decide what to do." Gayle laughed. "This is all you, girl."

*****

Drew scrolled through social media reading the "About" section of every Daniel Swift he could locate. Nadine hadn't given him much to go on except he would be two years younger than she was. After narrowing it down to three of the correct race and age, he decided to send message to each.

Hello, my name is Andrew Noah, and you don't know me. I'm trying to locate the brother of a Nadine Swift. She is two years older than you, and you were both adopted. If she is your sister, I wanted to inform you that you'll be an uncle in a few months. I know she'd love to hear from you. We're not trying to cause trouble. I love her, and I want her to be happy. I look forward to hearing from you.

Andrew

The only thing left to do was to wait for a response.

*****

"Good morning, Kristie," said Cassandra. "You are right on time."

"I've already made the coffee and placed three containers of almond milk in Ms. Swift's refrigerator and three in yours. I hope that's okay."

"That one belongs to her too. Her husband had it delivered months ago."

"I don't remember seeing that desk yesterday."

"It wasn't. That is my new desk. Junior execs don't get offices, we get cubicles with our names attached." Cassandra smiled.

"I see."

"Ms. Swift wanted me to inform you that you will be paid for the entire day."

"I thought I would be training today," said Kristie, confused.

"Oh, you are." Cassandra laughed. "On-the-job training. That's why you're getting paid."

"Wait is there a specific greeting that the company wants me to use?"

"Yes. Use '*Jared and Jakowski. This is Ms. Swift's office*' for outside calls. For internal calls just say, 'Ms. Swift's office.'"

"Got it."

"You'll have to transfer all calls to her. Her husband will call on her private line. If she doesn't answer, it automatically come to you. If he calls—"

"I know, text her immediately."

"We'll both be attending a meeting with her today. You'll be doing my old job. I'll only direct you so pay attention to her and no one else."

"Quick test beforehand, the meetings can run up to two hours long. Besides the stack of bound reports that I left on your desk, what else should you have?"

"Two hours? Her milk," answered Kristie.

"Correct. She'll enter with one container. You are responsible for having three additional containers already filled. When she runs out of one, and she will, simply replace it with a filled on without interrupting the flow of the presentation."

"All of the cups are in the desk drawer. And you must clean them every evening before leaving."

Cassandra noted with satisfaction that Kristie jotted down everything.

"Also, there is a foldable cart beside the file cabinet. Use that to carry the reports and anything else you need for the meeting. Sit behind her and follow her lead."

Kristie took a deep breath. "Okay, I think I'm ready," she said and walked the short distance to her desk and began reviewing her notes and comparing them with her to-do list. She began to add to the list when a familiar voice caught her attention.

"Good morning, Kristie."

"Good morning, Ms. Swift."

"Kristie, can you have three cartons of almond milk delivered to my office?"

"I placed three cartons in your refrigerator this morning, ma'am."

"Very good." Nadine smiled, staring at the girl. Her smile quickly gave way to a professional demeanor. "Get me the financial statements for the last quarter, Kristie. Check your email. They're there. Read your email first thing every morning from now on. Cassandra, familiarize yourself with the Keller file. Be ready to give me a full report in two hours," said Nadine, disappearing into her office.

With the closing of Nadine's office door, the day had begun.

*****

After having a lunch with Nadine and Everett, Andrew returned to find a response from all his messages. Two thanked him for his inquiry but did not have a sister named Nadine Swift and wished him luck. He clicked the third message expecting to read the same thing but was surprised by the response.

> *Hello, Andrew. I have a sister named Nadine, and she is two years older than I am. Just to make sure this isn't some crazy scam. Tell me something that only my sister and I know.*
>
> *Daniel*

Andrew was elated with the response. He quickly typed a reply, pressed Send, and headed off to a meeting.

> *You were kicked out of the house at sixteen, and she was eighteen, for disclosing the indiscretions of your adopted mother. You were angry at Nadine. You felt she should have kept her mouth shut. If this is evidence enough, give me a call at the number listed. And by the way, Nadine still loves you.*
>
> *Andrew*

"Mr. Noah, you have a call from a Daniel Swift," said Belle.

"Transfer it to my private line please, Belle."

"Andrew Noah."

"This is Daniel. Daniel Swift. Naddie is my sister."

"Hello, Daniel. Nadine is my wife."

"So why is her name still Swift?"

"Minor technicality that will be corrected very soon."

"So what made you look me up? Naddie never has."

"She has. She was afraid you'd reject her. Why haven't you looked her up?"

"I have many times. She's the only family I have. I figured she wouldn't want to hear from me after the things I said to her," Daniel confessed.

"They hurt her. But you're her only family, and she still loves her little brother."

Daniel was quiet. "Looks like she's pretty successful by the look of her social media posts."

"She's worked hard. She still does."

Daniel was quiet. "Our adopted mother used call her lazy all the time growing up. I guess Naddie finally proved her wrong."

"She's a wonderful woman, Daniel. She's caring, generous, and she loves with all of her heart. You should be proud of your sister."

"I am. She just doesn't know it."

"So where are you? Where do you live?"

"I'm north. Not far. Maybe an hour from where you guys live. Naddie posted her current city."

"So do you have a family of your own?"

"You mean a wife and kids?"

"Well, yes."

"No wife and no kids. I have a woman that I care about, but we don't need a piece of paper and a big ceremony. The heart is enough for us. That's what's real."

"If you don't mind me asking, what do you do for a living, Daniel?"

"Look, you contacted me. I don't want your money."

"I'm just trying to get to know you, Daniel. You are going to be my brother-in-law."

Daniel was quiet. "I always liked to draw. I'm an architect. My fiancé, she's trying to start a decorating business on the side. She's a teacher. Teaches special needs kids."

"Nadine's going to be so excited when I tell her."

Daniel was quiet for so long Andrew was about to think he had hung up.

"Look, Andrew. I sorry for snapping at you a little while ago. I'm glad you reached out, and I'm real glad to hear Naddie is doing good. I mean that."

"I'm glad I reached out too, man."

"How pregnant is my sister?"

"She'll be going into the seventh month soon," said Andrew with excitement. "She's pregnant, beautiful, and drinks almond milk nonstop!"

"Almond milk, huh?" Daniel chuckled.

"Just between us guys, if she runs out of that almond milk, she cries like a baby."

"I heard those cravings can be brutal."

"I learned early on to keep a never-ending supply on hand." Andrew laughed.

"Good to hear. Real good to hear."

"I'm going to send you our address. We're having a small gathering this weekend. I'd love it if the two of you would come. It would be a great surprise for Nadine."

"Yeah, well, we'll see."

"I hope you decide to come. I look forward to meeting you," Andrew said, ending the call.

He chuckled and shook his head. Nadine and Daniel grew to be more alike than they realized. He knew Daniel would come. He would want to make sure the man that had gotten his sister pregnant was taking good care of her.

*****

Tracie and Katrina met Kristie for lunch in the restaurant adjacent to the office building.

"So how's training going?" asked Katrina, smiling.

"It's a lot. But it's not actually training."

"What do you mean?" the women asked in confused unison.

"When I arrived, I was told that I was getting paid for the day and that training was on the job."

"You're actually working?" asked Tracie.

"Full duties."

"Is there someone you can go to for help if you need it?" asked Katrina.

"Cassandra is there, but Ms. Swift assigned her duties as junior exec today too."

"Not much transition time," said Katrina, concerned.

"Don't worry. Nadine is going to give her a taste of everything that will be expected of her today and make sure she is able to perform the task. So ask plenty of questions today. Because if it comes up next week, she's going to expect you to have a general idea how to do what she asks. My first assignment was to get her a financial report. She told me that it was in my email and that I am to check my emails every morning."

"See, what I want. Where to find it," said Tracie.

"I'm sure no executive would hire you, then expect you to know everything," said Katrina.

"Ms. Swift is training Cassandra. Her first assignment was to familiarize herself with a file and present a full report in two hours!"

"Wow," the two women sang.

"Cassandra told me to be thankful I had Ms. Swift because some of the other executives were difficult to work for."

'How much time do you have?"

"I have an hour for lunch, but I want to get back early because the three of us have a meeting to attend in the afternoon. I want to make sure I'm all set."

"Good for you," Tracie said.

"Otherwise, I would've grabbed something to eat at my desk."

"Overall, what's your opinion of the job?"

"I like it. It's a world I'm completely not familiar with. So many hidden rules of behavior. I've printed several reports, added to Ms. Swift's calendar, answered several calls, and learned how to bind reports for meetings. When I get back, I'll be assisting Ms. Swift in what I've been told could be a long meeting. Cassandra will be there, but she'll be observing and taking notes on how to do a presentation herself."

"Wow, this is exciting, Kris," said Katrina, smiling.

"I'll let you know how I do in the meeting, but that's all I can discuss. I signed a nondisclosure forbidding me from discussing anything about clients or the company, other than public information."

"So what does this company do? If you can say?" asked Katrina.

"Stocks, finances, and money says it all."

"I don't think Nan and I have ever discussed what she does for a living," said Tracie, smiling. "I just knew she always dressed and carried herself like she was a bigwig female executive."

"You guys stay and finish. I have to go. I want to be sure and have her almond milk ready for the meeting."

"Wait! Almond milk in a meeting?" asked Katrina, confused.

"Remember, she's pregnant and has cravings. Her husband called me this morning personally to remind me to have at least three containers of her milk ready before she gets in the meeting. He's really crazy about her. And he's cute too. Gotta go!"

"Can you imagine?" said Katrina, looking at Tracie as she spoke. "The guy is so in love with her, he knows when she has a meeting and calls to make sure her cravings are satisfied even at work. He has to love her."

"I've met him. He does love her, very much," admitted Tracie softly.

"What's wrong? Don't tell me you're jealous?" asked Katrina, surprised.

"No, not at all."

"Then why the long face?"

"Tony and Nan used to date several years back. That's how she and I became friends."

"I can see them together," said Katrina after some thought. "What happened?"

"Tony cheated, Nan left him, and the rest is history. Don't mention it to Kristie. Nadine does not mix business with her personal life. If Kristie slips and says something, it may cost her that job she seems to love so much."

"Kris would be crushed. I'm not saying a word."

*****

Walking into the massive conference room, Kristie felt overwhelmed.

"Breathe," whispered Cassandra. "I was the same way."

Kristina and Cassandra sat in seats against the wall along with other assistants and secretaries. Nadine and the other executives sat around the huge conference table. Kristie watched how the other assistants performed their duties, not really attending to the presentations much. The person she watched was Nadine. The woman sat listening and taking notes but rarely looking up. A few times she asked questions about information that was presented. The executive would immediately recheck his information and instruct his assistant to make corrections.

Nadine turned and whispered to Kristie, "We're next," then sipped her milk.

*****

"This is my new assistant, Ms. Elliot," introduced Nadine to the group.

Kristie smiled and nodded to the group, displaying a confidence she didn't feel as she noticed a couple of the assistants glance at each other, then proceed to stare at her.

"As you know, this is Ms. Harris. What many of you don't know is that Ms. Harris has been promoted to junior executive and will be attending and participating in these meeting from now on in a totally different capacity."

As Nadine spoke, she displayed a visual presentation, then took a sip of her milk. Cassandra smiled and nodded but never took her eyes from Ms. Swift. Katrina, however, saw the jealous expressions and the stunned dropping of a couple of jaws. The executives appeared unimpressed and busied themselves making corrections on their reports.

Nadine spoke with the same confidence she displayed before her pregnancy. She took sips of her milk during pauses, never interrupting the flow of her presentation. What Kristie noticed was the fact that her presentation corrected or clarified where others failed.

Suddenly, she attempted to sip her milk, only to give the cup a slight shake, then sits it back onto the table and continued speaking. Kristie immediately replaced the empty container with another to which Nadine immediately reached for.

"I've prepared reports for each of you to review," Nadine said, looking toward Kristie, who immediately stood and began passing out the reports.

"What a mess!" said a male executive, having spilled coffee on his report.

"Kristie, make sure Thomas, Thomas Green, gets an electronic copy of this report," Nadine instructed.

"I have an extra copy right here, Ms. Swift," she said, then waited for Nadine's approval to proceed.

Nadine nodded, smiled, and continued with her presentation.

After the meeting, Cassandra praised her for doing an excellent job. She was proud. They both were.

"I'm glad you two are having such a nice time," said Nadine, interrupting the young women's moment of celebration.

"Cassandra, there's a junior executives meeting after lunch on Monday."

"Yes, ma'am."

"Be ready to present on the Keller case. I'll be observing."

"Yes, ma'am," said Cassandra, obviously holding her breath.

"And, Kristie?"

"Yes, Ms. Swift?"

"You're assisting her," Nadine said and walked away.

They looked at each other both with terrified expressions. They hurried to their desks knowing there would be little time to work on the presentation on Monday.

"I'll finish up my to-do list," said Kristie.

"I'll email you my report to copy and bind, then create my visual," said Cassandra.

Within the two remaining hours before the weekend, Kristie was able to copy and bind all of Cassandra's reports, making a few extras just in case. She washed the milk containers, updated Nadine's calendar, and filed several reports. She then went to remove the milk from Ms. Swift's office fridge, only to discover she was opening the last container.

"No need to restock until Monday, Kristie," Nadine said.

"Yes, ma'am."

"Kristie?"

"Yes, Ms. Swift?"

"You did a great job today."

"Thank you, Ms. Swift." She smiled.

Kristie printed off three reports that came through her email and placed them in folders with labels ready to present to Nadine when asked. Her to-do list was complete. She glanced over at Cassandra, who was consumed with creating her visual for Monday.

"Kristie, I need a copy of one of those reports."

"Right away," she said, walking over and handing the bound report to Cassandra.

"Can I do anything to help?"

"I'll finish the visual at home if necessary. I must review the report for errors."

"What are you going to do if you locate errors? We have less than an hour left in the workday."

"I'm going to review for errors and copy and rebind if necessary."

"That can take hours!" said Kristie sadly.

"There were many evenings, I'd leave and Ms. Swift would still be here. Sometimes freshly bound reports would be on my desk the next day. When I attended my first meeting with her, all the executives were yelling for their assistants to make corrections. I almost cried when realized I hadn't checked a single error. Ms. Swift noticed and said, 'Stop worrying. I checked, more than once. We're fine.' She demanded that I do my job as an assistant with excellence. But she did the same thing as an executive. I appreciate the offer, and it's tempting, but she wants me to learn that it's not going to be easy. I have to earn this, just like she did."

Kristie walked back to her desk deep in thought. Nadine didn't just get to the top and forget about others. She promoted her assistant when the other executives chose to ignore the potential of theirs.

She saw a struggling college student and gave her a job over recently hired graduate that were already with the company.

She glanced around the office. Most of the executive were chatting, preparing to leave for the weekend. Some assistants were as busy as Cassandra on a Friday afternoon. She realized that one day, she would be sitting in Cassandra's desk. It was then she looked up and saw a handsome man exit the elevator.

"How did her meeting go, Kristie?" he asked with a smile.

"It went well, sir," she said, smiling.

"Cassandra, how's the new position?" he asked.

"I'm doing my best to make my mentor proud, sir," she replied, smiling.

"You'll do fine," he said, going straight into Ms. Swift's office.

"Hi, beautiful," was the last thing heard before the door closed.

I like working here, Kristie thought, smiling, as she began to create her to-do list for Monday.

*****

Wesley pulled into what was his designated parking space at his newly leased condo. Unlocking the door, he went inside for a first look.

Nice, he thought. *Already furnished.*

The view of the city's skyline was magnificent. All he needed was to unpack. A quick check and he discovered he also needed linen, groceries, and kitchenware.

"Simple enough fix," he decided.

He deposited his luggage in the bedroom and set out to make the necessary purchases.

He paused before exiting the condo, bracing himself on the doorframe.

That's new, he thought. Having never experienced dizziness before, Wesley attributed it to not eating the entire day. His visit to his doctor was scheduled for Monday. He would be glad when it was over, and he'd have an answer to why he had been feeling differently lately.

*****

Nadine and Andrew exited the elevator in the parking garage.

"Why don't we look at some baby furniture tomorrow?" he suggested.

"I like that idea, but we have to go early because guests are coming tomorrow night."

"I already had Belle order the food. It will be delivered by six."

"You called a caterer?"

"I'm not having my pregnant wife cook for a house full of guests."

"That was so sweet of you, love."

"I know. Now give me a kiss for being such a caring husband."

"You can have two kisses, love."

"You hear that, AJ? Your mother's trying to bribe your father with kisses," Andrew said, talking to her tummy.

"And it's working, AJ," Nadine replied, stroking her visible mound.

As the couple were about to enter a furniture store for kids, a voice stopped their progress.

"Looks like a happy couple to me."

Turning, they are face-to-face with none other than Antonio.

He glanced at the store logo and asked, "Furniture shopping?"

Drew immediately placed his arm around Nadine's shoulder and answered, "We are. How are you, Antonio?"

"I'm good," he responded, repeatedly nodding his head as he stared at Nadine.

"How are you, Nan?"

"I'm doing good, Tony. Thank you for asking," she replied, then took a sip from her cup.

"So what kind of furniture are you about to purchase?"

Nadine spoke before Andrew could answer. "We're looking at baby furniture, Tony."

"Baby furniture, huh?"

"Yes, baby furniture," she replied.

"Baby furniture," Antonio repeated, continuing to look at Nadine as she sipped from her cup once more.

"Nadine and I are having a baby, Antonio," announced Andrew.

"You're pregnant, Nan?"

"Yes, Tony, I'm pregnant," she said, unconsciously stroking her tummy, which drew Antonio's gaze.

"How pregnant are you?"

"She's almost seven months. Now if you'll excuse us," said Andrew, leading Nadine away from the interrogation.

"Congratulation, Nan," he said before they could completely pass.

"Thank you," said Andrew.

"I guess that cat's out of the bag," Nadine whispered.

"He already knew. He was just confirming."

"He didn't seem surprised. His behavior was odd, don't you think?"

Turning her to face him, Andrew asked, "Do you trust me to take care of you and AJ?"

"Of course, I do. Why would you need to ask me that?"

"Because I'm about to ask you to do something and I'm asking you to do it because I think it's best."

"What is it?"

"I want you to stay away from that man. Right now he's jealous and he's hurt. A jealous man should not be underestimated."

"You think he might hurt me?" she asked softly.

"His goal will be to hurt me and get back at me. But to hurt me, the way he could be successful is to hurt you—or AJ."

"Our baby?"

"Nan, stay away from that man. Do you understand me?"

"I will."

"Nadine!"

"I promise. I'll do what you say."

He hugged her close. "I only want to keep you and AJ safe, love," he said, kissing the top of her head.

"I know, love. I know."

*****

An hour later the happy parents-to-be left the store, having completely furnished their nursery, and headed to a diner for dinner.

"Are you two ready to order or do you need a little more time?" the waitress asked.

"Do you have almond milk?" asked Nadine with the huge, bright smile Andrew loved to see when she mentioned her milk.

"Yes, ma'am. Would that be a large or small?"

"Can you bring a pitcher of milk?" Andrew asked.

"You mean like a mug?" the woman asked, confused.

"If that's the largest container you have, then yes," said Andrew. "My wife is pregnant, and she must have her milk."

The woman smiled and said, "I understand. I have two. What will you be eating, ma'am."

"The blackened flounder, scalloped potatoes, and salad with vinaigrette."

"Very healthy. And for you, sir?"

"The steak special, loaded potato, and vinaigrette dressing as well. And a beer. No almond milk for me."

The woman returned and sat a beer in front of Andrew and a glass of almond milk in front of Nadine, which she immediately began to drink. A glass pitcher filled with almond milk was placed in the center of the table by a male waiter who glanced at Nadine and smiled. Nadine's eyes lit up at the sight of the pitcher filled with milk.

"Drew," Nadine said, looking across the table as he cut his steak.

"What is it, love?"

"I think we should get married," she said.

"What?" he said, staring at her.

"I said, I think we should get married."

Placing his silverware down, he stared at her. "What made you come to this conclusion?"

"Don't you want to marry me?"

"Of course, I do. But I want to know what changed your mind. You didn't seem too convinced the last time we talked about it."

"The things you said changed my mind. We love each other, and it may be enough for us. Or for me, but we have to do what's best for AJ and our other children, you know."

"I agree. Other children?"

"Just a figure of speech, love." Nadine laughed at his expression. "Don't you want more children?"

"Let's just get through almond-milk episode number one first," he said, smiling with a shake of his head.

After their plates were cleared away, Nadine enjoyed the last of the almond milk.

"I'm going to have them fix you a milk to-go. I'll be right back."

Nadine turned in time to see him whispering something to their waitress, who flashed a huge grin, nodding yes to something he'd said. After reaching into his pocket, he handed the woman what Nadine assumed was a tip for making the milk to-go.

"Is she going to bring it over? I'm almost done with this one."

"It'll be here in just a second, love."

"How much did you tip her for fixing a milk to-go?"

"What?"

"I saw you hand her something."

"Just a little token, love," he said dismissively.

Just then a huge take-out cup was sat on the table followed by a slice of cheesecake. The plate was decorated with writing.

Nadine glanced at the woman, saying, "That was so sweet of you." Turning the plate, she read the writing, "*Will you marry me?*" The dot in the question mark was a diamond ring. Her mouth dropped open in surprise as she stared at Andrew, who smiled across the table at her.

"What do you say, Mommie?" he asked, smiling.

"I say, 'Yes, Dad.'"

Andrew grabbed the ring and placed it on her finger. Nadine glanced at the ring and started to cry her usual pregnant cry. Andrew wrapped her in his arms and whispered to her, which soothed her immediately. The waitress stood by wiping tears.

"That's the most beautiful thing I've ever seen," she said as the entire diner cheered.

"Here, love," said Andrew. "Drink your milk."

After a few sips, Nadine looked into Andrew's eyes and said, "I love you, Andrew Trevor Noah."

"And I love you, Nadine Teresa Swift, my lover of almond milk," he said, grinning.

They would leave the little diner officially engaged. What Nadine wasn't aware of was that sitting in a corner booth with her husband was Shawn. She had recognized Nadine the moment she and Andrew entered. Her husband knew nothing of the incident from her past where she faked a pregnancy. She didn't really know this Nadine Swift, but was happy that, like her, the woman had found true love.

Leave the past in the past, she thought as she cheered and clapped with the crowd.

It was at that moment that their eyes met. Nadine's head tilted slightly in recognition as she stared at the woman.

Oh my God! It's her, she thought.

Shawn's face took on a panicked expression. She quickly glanced at her husband and back at Nadine, touching her face to reveal her wedding ring. Her eyes pleaded with Nadine not to approach.

Andrew's eyes followed Nadine's. "Do you know her?"

"Yes."

"Are you going over?" asked Andrew.

"No. Let's go home, love," she said, smiling up at him.

Before leaving, she looked at Shawn, who mouthed the words, "Thank you." Nadine turned and walked out of the diner.

Once in the car, Andrew asked, "Who was that woman?"

"That was the woman that Antonio had an affair with," she answered.

"Really? She looked terrified."

"She was."

"Why? Did you beat her down or something back then?"

"She was scared because she's pregnant and married now. She has a lot to lose. She was scared that I was going to come over and ruin her life like she did to mine."

"Did she ruin your life, Nadine?"

"For a while she did. But then you came along and showed me a better, more beautiful way. I have a new life now. And I like this one better." She smiled, then began drinking deeply from her cup of milk.

"I'd better get you home before that cup is empty," he said, smiling as he pressed the ignition button.

*****

Across town, Tracie, Kristina, and Katrina were sitting eating pizza and watching a movie while the boys played video games in the bedroom. During commercial breaks, the two questioned Kris about her first day on the job.

She shared with excitement everything from how the other assistants and secretaries reacted to Nadine's news to the way she performed her presentation while drinking her beloved almond milk. The three laughed and at times pitied as Kristina attempted to mimic the antics of some of the executives and their treatment of their assistants.

It was a knock at the door that interrupted a moment of laughter. "Tony!"

"Hey, Trace. Oh, you have company," he said, seeing the sisters.

"No, we were about to leave anyways," announced Katrina.

"We were not!" whispered Kristina.

"Send the boys home in about an hour, Trace," said Katrina, ushering her sister from the apartment.

"Sure thing," said Tracie, humored by Kristina's reaction.

"What's up, bro?"

"I saw Nan today."

"Where?"

"Her and her baby's daddy were about to go in a kid's furniture store downtown," he snapped.

Tracie sighed. "How did it go?"

"I'm asking her questions, and he's doing all of the answering."

"Tony, come on. He's probably just trying to protect his family."

"I would never hurt Nan," he snapped.

"Well, she is pregnant with his child."

"I don't care anything about that baby."

"Tony! You don't mean that!"

"I do mean it."

"Tony, you're letting this jealousy control you. That baby is a part of Nan too. If that baby is hurt, Nan's going to be hurt. Can't you see that?"

He sat, not speaking. His knee thumped up and down nervously.

Tracy could tell all manner of unhealthy things were racing through his mind.

"Hey! Snap out of it!" she yelled.

"What?"

"You're driving yourself crazy with this obsession with Nadine and her pregnancy."

"I'm not an advocate of illegal substances, but you need to go smoke a joint or something. This is crazy!"

"I don't use illegal drugs, and you know it!" he snapped.

"Then go see a fucking shrink! She did. Because you're scaring me with this crazy talk."

"How do you know she saw a shrink?"

"Her friend Everett told me. He said he had to force her to go because he was scared she was going to hurt herself. You need help, Tony, just like she did."

"I'll be fine."

"There are a lot of people that look up to you. Nadine still values you as a friend. Don't ruin every aspect of your life because of jealousy. Please just think about it."

"Okay! I'll think about it. I gotta go."

"Boys! Come on, I'm going to walk you home," she called out.

"We're not babies," the eldest said.

"No, but I'm still walking you home."

*****

An hour north of the city, Daniel and his companion, Genesis, sat staring at Nadine's social media posts.

"Oh, Danny, she's beautiful," Genesis said.

"Yeah, Naddie always was pretty."

"I'll bet she gets compliments all of the time."

"If she's still the same, she won't react."

"Why?"

"It's a long story."

"She looks successful."

"Yeah, her boyfriend, fiancé, husband, I'm not sure what the hell he is, said she's successful. He is too based on what I could find out," said Daniel.

"That must be him," Genesis said. "What did you say his name was?"

"Andrew. Andrew Noah."

"She must call him Drew," said Genesis pointing to a caption. "Did he sound nice?"

"I don't know. People can say and sound anyway they want over the phone. Calling me brother-in-law and talking about he hopes we come down tomorrow."

"He invited us? You didn't mention that."

"Well, I hadn't decided if I wanted to go or not," he said softly.

"What about if I wanted to go?" she asked, looking at him sadly.

"I'm sorry. I should've said something. It just caught me off guard. I'm sorry, honey, really."

"Do you love me, Daniel?"

"What? Of course, I do."

"Are we a team?"

"You know we're a team. I just have this stuff from my childhood that messes with me sometimes. I'm sorry."

"We must get past it, Danny, or we're not going to make it."

"We'll get past it. I'll get past it. I promise. We'll drive down and meet my sister tomorrow."

"Yes!" she exclaimed.

"Gen, we haven't seen each other since I was sixteen and she was eighteen. It may not be a happy reunion," he said softly.

"We'll cross that bridge when we get there. Either way, we do it together," she said.

Daniel sat looking at the pictures of his sister. A sister that was abandoned as a baby. A sister that tried to protect her younger brother. A sister that took the verbal abuse of a wicked, verbally abusive adopted mother stoically. A sister that held her tears until only the two of them were alone before she would allow them to fall. As a child he could never pronounce her name correctly, so she answered to Naddie. He wondered if she'd remember.

*****

"Babe, do you think we have enough food?" asked Nadine as she arranged to table.

"There's plenty of food and everything, including your milk," he said, giving her a kiss.

"I may need more milk from the kitchen."

Just then the doorbell sounded, and Nadine moved to go and answer it.

"No, I'll answer the door and you stay down here and greet the guests as they arrive," he instructed.

"Yes, Daddy," she said in a childlike voice, leaning back, rubbing her growing tummy. She refused to admit that her back could use a break.

"Hey, guys. She's in the basement," Drew said to Vee and Chris.

"We're taking the elevator," yelled Everett.

"Good. Hopefully, it'll encourage Nadine to do the same."

Before he could close the door, Gayle and her husband, Marcus, drove up followed by Wesley. He waited at the door and directed them to the elevator as well. Glancing at his watch, his spirit dropped as he realized Daniel had decided not to come. Closing the door, he joined Nadine and the rest of their guests.

"Are you pregnant?" asked Wesley shocked.

"Drew beat you to it, didn't he, Mr. Dick Magnet?" joked Vee with exaggerated sexual gestures.

Everyone burst into laughter.

"He never gives me a break," said Wesley, laughing. "I've missed you too, Vee."

"I tell the truth, honey. Nan, did you tell them the story about the waitress?"

"No," said Nadine. "Wait until you hear about the birthday party that Wesley and I went to."

"I've never witnessed anything in my life like that." Andrew laughed.

"Where's the male support here?" Wesley asked Andrew.

The doorbell sounded.

"You want me to get it this time, love?"

"No, baby. Sit. I've got it," said Andrew, having completely forgotten he'd invited someone else.

*****

"Can I help you?" Andrew asked a young man standing before him holding a grocery bag.

The man glanced at the woman beside him. "I'm looking for a Mr. Andrew Noah."

"He invited us to a gathering at seven. We got caught in traffic and are a little late," the pretty woman beside him said, smiling.

"Daniel?" Andrew whispered. "Daniel Swift?"

"Yes. I'm Daniel, and this is my fiancé, Genesis."

A huge grin spread across Andrew's face. He grabbed the young man in a huge bear hug. The woman watched the spectacle, grinning, with teary eyes.

"Man, I'm so glad you came. Thank you. Thank you for coming. Please. Please come in."

"Nice place," commented Daniel, glancing around the foyer.

"Oh my God! It's beautiful," said Genesis.

The two glanced at each other when doors to an elevator opened and Andrew invited them to enter first.

"Nadine is going to be so surprised," Andrew said, smiling.

"I hope so," mumbled Daniel, worried.

Everyone was busy talking and didn't bother looking when the elevator doors opened. Andrew exited first followed by Genesis, with Daniel being the last to enter the room. Daniel stepped forward and quickly located Nadine, who had her back turned.

"Naddie," he said.

He was about to repeat himself when she began to slowly turn in the direction of the voice. The moment she identified the source of the voice, she dropped her cup of milk and began crying.

"Danny," she said through tears, hurrying to her brother. He handed the bag to Andrew, quickly rushing to embrace his sister. Brother and sister held each other and cried. They cried for the joy of seeing each other after so many years. They cried for the painful childhood they had endured. They cried because no one understood what they endured as children but the two of them.

"How did you find me?" Nadine asked, wiping tears.

"Your husband orchestrated it all," said Danny.

"Are you happy, love?" asked Andrew.

"Drew, this is the best gift ever!" she said. She looked at Danny with pride. "I've missed you so much."

"I missed you too, Naddie. Oh, this is my fiancé, Genesis. I call her Gen."

Nadine embraced her and welcomed the young woman. Everett cleaned up the spilled milk. Gayle handed Nadine a fresh cup.

"Here, before the excitement wears off," Gayle joked, handing Nadine a cup.

"I have to have my milk," she said apologetically as she drank the entire glass. "Drew."

"Here," said Gayle again, handing over a cup filled with milk.

"We brought more almond milk as a gift," said Gen.

Nadine's eyes lit up. "Really?"

"Yeah, Andrew said you really like almond milk," said Daniel.

"I hope it's the right kind," said Gen.

"It's the right kind," announced Andrew, revealing a container.

"I really love milk," she said, smiling.

"And she turns into a blubbering crybaby if she runs out," announced Everett, rolling his eyes.

"I do not, Vee."

"Yes, you do!" everyone except Wesley and Andrew said in unison.

"Don't believe them, Danny. They're all lying," Nadine said with a smirk, then looked at Andrew. "Right, Drew?"

"Baby, I love you. But without that milk, you're a blubbering crybaby," he answered, then kissed her on the forehead.

"What do they know? Come on in. Eat, drink, and let's be merry," Nadine said, locking arms with Daniel and Genesis.

"Everyone! This is my baby brother and my sister-in-law," Nadine announced, smiling.

Everyone cheered.

"Keep your wife away from Wesley. Every woman that comes near him gets addicted to the dick," said Vee with animation.

"What?" asked Daniel, confused.

"Vee loves to embarrass Wesley about his many conquests. Ignore him," said Nadine.

"Yes. Please ignore him," said Wesley. "Chris, please put a leash on him."

"Oh, honey, he did that last night. And I loved every minute of it!" said Everett with a wink.

Danny and Gen grinned at each other, loving Everett's feminine antics. Gayle and Marcus laughed hysterically, thoroughly enjoying their first encounter with Nadine's best friend.

"I don't understand why everyone is trying to shut me up," said Everett. "If it wasn't for me, Nan and Mr. Bulges all over his body would be sitting in rocking chairs playing checkers on the patio. Danny, I saved your sister, honey. And your brother too, Gayle."

"Bulges all over his body," repeated Gen.

"Oh, Danny," said Everett. "Wesley's already affecting her. She's blind if she can't see that Drew is bursting out of that too little shirt that he has on!"

Nadine spit milk as the entire room laughed to the point of tears, including Andrew.

"What's the matter with you people? Are you all as blind as Gen?"

Their laughter made Everett laugh at himself.

"I know, I crack myself up too sometimes," he said, enjoying their reaction.

*****

As guests began to leave, only Daniel and Gen were left.

"Why don't you two spend the night rather than drive an hour home?" asked Andrew.

"That's a great idea, Danny," said Nadine, looking hopeful.

"Sure, Naddie, we'll stay the night." Her brother smiled.

"Great! Genesis let me show you the nursery," Nadine said.

"Take the elevator," instructed Andrew as the women walked away.

"You're a good man, Andrew," said Danny. "I like the way you take care of her."

"I love her."

"It shows."

"Trust me, if I dared break a nail on her hand, I'd have to content with Vee," he joked.

"That guy's something else." Daniel laughed. "How did you do it?"

"Do what?"

"How did you get her to trust you and open up to you like this?"

"I made a promise, and I work every day to make sure that I keep it. I'm honest with her, and she's learned to trust me and also be honest with me, no matter what it is."

Danny sat thinking of the words *honesty* and *trust*.

"We no longer hide things from each other," added Andrew.

"What did you promise her?"

"I promised her that I would always be here."

"That's it?"

"Not just physically here, man. Mentally and emotionally here too."

Again, Danny sat quietly contemplating the words.

"Tell her," Andrew instructed.

"What do you mean?"

"Tell her about your childhood, about your fears, about all of the things that you've been hiding from her."

"I don't know if I can, man," said Danny softly.

"Am I perfect? Not by a long shot. I lived for a long time thinking it was my inadequacies that led my ex to cheat on me and kill what could have been my child. That bothered me on a level most people can't understand. I know I have this alpha male trait that makes me want to protect what I believe is mine. Nadine is perfect for me because although she's an alpha female outside, she's soft inside and compliments me. I'm free to be me with her. She doesn't need me, but she makes me feel as if she does because she loves me. We're perfect for each other."

"What should I do if it doesn't go well?" asked Daniel nervously.

"How long have you two been together?"

"A few years."

"If she's been around that long, she loves you, knowing that you're hiding something from her. She's not going anywhere. She just wants to be your partner. Remember, real partners don't keep secrets. They look out for each other no matter what."

"We're back!" announced the women.

"Are you tired, love?"

"Yes," said Nadine, moving into Andrew's arms.

"Danny, I love you. I'm glad to see you, but I'm tired."

"Go to bed," said Genesis. "I know where the guest room is."

"Thanks, Gen," said Andrew, leading Nadine to the elevator and off to bed.

"Are you okay, love?" asked Genesis, seeing the serious look on Daniel's face.

"I will be. Let's go to bed. We have a lot to talk about tomorrow," he said.

Stop

I HATE DOCTOR offices, thought Wesley, glancing around the sterile room. "But I like the nurses," he mumbled, flashing a dimpled smile at the receptionist sitting in front of him.

"Wesley Johnson," called out young Hispanic nurse that quickly looked him over when he stood.

She would be a nice addition to the weekly rotation, thought Wesley, liking the sway of her hips as she walked.

"This way sir," the nurse said, glancing back with a smile, leading the way to an examination room.

"I'll be drawing some blood, taking your vitals, and the doctor will be in shortly." *He smells good*, the nurse thought, inhaling deeply.

Wesley checked the jobsite cameras on his phone as he sat waiting for the doctor. A few moments later, the gentleman entered.

"Mr. Johnson, how are you today?" asked the doctor, moving to the sink to wash his hands.

"Not as good as I'd like to be, Doc."

"Tell me what's going on."

"Well, I haven't been feeling like myself lately."

"How is that?"

"I'm thirsty all the time, seems like I need to carry a restroom with me wherever I go. I've started to experience some dizziness lately. And my energy level is in the toilet."

"Doctor," the nurse said, handing over a folder and flashing a look in Wesley's direction.

"Thank you, Nurse."

The doctor sat quietly reading the results.

"Can't be that bad is it, Doc?"

"It's not that bad, Mr. Johnson, but it's definitely going to require a lifestyle change."

"What do you mean?" asked Wesley, concerned.

"Well, first your glucose level is extremely high."

"First? What does that mean?"

"It means you're a diabetic, Wesley."

"A diabetic?"

"Yes, that means you are going to have to take medicine daily to control it."

"What, a pill?"

"Pills and injections. If your glucose level gets any higher than what it is right now, you'll need to be hospitalized. Extremely high glucose can result in a stroke, Wesley," said the doctor sternly.

"Daily injections," repeated Wesley softly.

"Three to four times daily depending on your levels to be exact—and with pills," said the doctor.

"I can't be that sick, Doc."

"You are, Wesley, and you must implement some discipline into your life if you want to remain healthy."

"You said 'first,' Doc. What's the second thing?"

"Your blood pressure is high also. I'm prescribing pills to manage the level of your pressure."

Wesley's head was spinning. He had never been sick a day in his life other than a cold. Hearing that he would have to take daily injections for the rest of his life was more than he could comprehend.

The nurse came in with a vial and a small paper cup with a pill on a metal tray.

"Because your levels are so high, I'm going to give you your first injection now. This pill is to lower your blood pressure," the doctor said.

He handed him the small paper cup, then a cup of water.

"You're going to feel some pressure," said the doctor as he injected insulin into Wesley's arm.

After the procedure, the doctor said, "Get this prescription filled immediately and follow the directions. You'll also need to check your glucose several times a day."

Wesley glanced at the strip of paper.

"Here is a pamphlet on diabetes and a diet plan," said the nurse.

"I have to follow a diet plan too?" he asked, looking at the doctor.

"Diet and exercise go hand in hand to control diabetes," said the doctor. Not liking the expression on Wesley's face, the doctor continued, "Diabetes is a serious thing, Wesley. I know it feels like you're not in control of your life. Take back the control by making the needed adjustments."

"Do I have any other choice?" asked Wesley, sounding defeated.

"There's always a choice. Change your lifestyle and live with the diabetes or ignore the instructions and die because of it. I'd like to see you live, Wesley."

"I will, Doc."

*****

Leaving the pharmacy, Wesley sat in his car, reading the directions of his new lifeline. Remembering to take injections throughout the day was going to be a difficult, if not embarrassing, adjustment.

He envisioned himself having just finished rocking some woman's world to the moon when he says, "Before we start cuddling, baby, I have to go and take my injection."

Wesley knew he hadn't cuddled with a woman in years. For him, it was bone and gone.

Pressing the ignition button, he said, "Fuck!"

As he drove, he noticed that he had begun to feel better. He was sure it was the high blood pressure pills and not the insulin that was causing the change. He'd read the instructions on how to use the glucose meter when he got home that evening. At the jobsite, he stored his insulin in the refrigerator and went about his day as if nothing bothered him.

*****

Downtown, Nadine sat observing Cassandra as she presented at her first junior executives meeting. The woman presented with confidence. She was prepared and her report was void of mistakes. Kristie moved on cue to pass out reports to the other juniors. Nadine was pleased with the fact that Cassandra's reports were bound and her presentation complete. It was obvious that, unlike her cohort, she had spent the weekend making sure she was prepared for Monday rather than attempting to wait until that morning to finish.

"How did I do, Ms. Swift?"

"You did good. Next time minimize the details to the juniors and save the meat for the executives."

"I'll be presenting in the executives' meetings?"

"All of you will," said Nadine.

"So do I just recreate what I did today?"

"No. Add something unique but vital to each section of your presentation. The juniors have already seen this presentation. They are going to copy what you just showed them. The executives haven't seen it. If your presentation is the same as the others, you're just one in the crowd. You're better than the crowd. Make yours stand out. How will the company benefit? How will the clients benefit?" said Nadine, walking away.

Cassandra sat at her desk, reading over her case file. She had put everything into today's presentation.

"What else can I add?' she asked herself aloud.

Kristie heard the comment but pretended she hadn't. She felt bad for Cassandra but was completely powerless to help. Technically, Cassandra was her supervisor, but the two were also becoming friends.

"Kristie, get me the activity for blue chips stock report for this week and the chart analysis from my presentation on Friday."

"Right away, Ms. Swift."

Noticing Cassandra's defeated expression, Nadine said, "Cassandra?"

"Yes, Ms. Swift?"

"Focus on repetitive waves."

"Repetitive waves, ma'am?"

"The Elliot Waves Theory. Work that into your presentation. What filters should the company and the client focus on?" said Nadine, disappearing into her office.

After a moment of thought, Cassandra said, "Kristie, I need the market cycles and finance report and the investment outlook report."

"Right away, Ms. Harris," replied Kristie as she quickly emailed Everett in finance and searched the company's mainframe.

As the blue chips report printed for Nadine, she emailed Cassandra the finance and outlook report. After placing all four in folders, she placed two on Cassandra's desk and delivered two to Nadine.

"Maybe I should familiarize myself with these reports," said Kristie, only to be interrupted by a series of phone calls for Nadine, which she either immediately logged into the calendar or took a message requesting a call back.

*****

Wesley glanced at his phone and quickly typed a response. A female was inviting him to dinner at her place.

"Right after work," he wrote, smiling. *No diabetes is going to slow Wesley Johnson down*, he thought. He was Wess, the ladies' best, and fully intended to live up to the mantra.

*****

He dressed being careful as always to match his clothes and shoes.

"I'll check my levels when I get back," he decided, feeling better than he had in the last month.

The woman was a great cook, and he fully intended to show his gratitude in the bedroom. He always put a little more effort into the first encounters. Experience had taught him that her request for money would be expected from then on. Once the women began to request money from him, he made sure they earned it by fulfilling every fantasy and nonfantasy he could dream up. It amazed him the extent to which some women would go if they thought it would lead to marriage.

"I have a lot of female friends," he said to the Brenda.

The woman was quiet. "Can you explain that?" Brenda asked.

"They're just friends though. Not relationships," he lied.

"Oh, okay," she said. "I have male friends also."

Yeah, but are you sleeping with them? Wesley silently asked, not caring one way or the other.

*****

It was late when he returned to his condo, tired and sexually satisfied. Tossing his keys on the counter, he strolled to his bedroom, undressing as he went. Forgetting his new lifestyle change, he went to bed, never checking his glucose level or taking his pill or injection.

The following morning, he dialed the correct dosage of his insulin pen and injected himself.

That was no fun, he thought.

It didn't hurt. It was the annoyance of just having to do something he wasn't accustomed to. Slinging the pen onto the refrigerator shelf, he turned to leave, then remembered his pressure pill. Placing the pill in his mouth, he swallowed it without liquid with an agitated expression.

This shit is going to get on my nerves, he thought, leaving the condo in a huff.

Just as he pressed the ignition on his truck, his phone rang.

"Hey, Wess, what are you up to?" asked Nadine happily.

"On my way to the site. Somebody sounds happy this morning," he commented.

"That's because it's officially month number eight for me!"

"One more and it's time for a serious countdown."

"I know, I'm so excited!"

"You all set for the big day?"

"I think so. We furnished a nursery but decided to start with a cradle in our room."

"I can understand that as big as your house is. You'll have to walk a mile every two hours in the middle of the night," he joked.

"I know. I don't want AJ to have to wait that long before we get to him."

"Understandable for a first-time mom."

"You all stocked up on supplies?"

"I think so. I'm going to check with Drew's mom just to make sure."

"Good idea. Just don't ask Vee. He'll have the kids looking and talking like Liberace."

"Shut up!" Nadine laughed.

"I have to go. We'll do lunch one day soon, okay?"

"Sure thing, Wess."

Because he had eaten at Brenda's house the night before, Wesley didn't have lunch. There was a fried chicken restaurant close to the jobsite. He'd pick up something there when the time came.

"How's it going, boss?" Miguel asked.

"Same thing. Different day," answered Wesley.

*****

The day was uneventful for Wesley. It was work a usual for him: supervise this, redirect that, correct this, approve that. Miguel rejected his offer of fast food.

"My wife gets up early every morning, boss, to make sure I have a lunch," said Miguel. "I would never take her for granted by not eating what she prepares for me."

Wesley laughed, finding the man's logic humorous.

"I'm not trying to change your mind. I just don't understand." He chuckled. "You mean to tell me, you can't skip eating what she prepared for one day?"

"No, boss. It's not that I can't, I choose not to," Miguel responded in his heavily accented voice. "She's my wife, not my slave. Her getting up extra early shows that she loves me. Me not eating the food says I don't appreciate her effort."

"You're a dedicated man, Miguel." Wesley chuckled.

"One day you'll understand, boss."

As he got into his truck, he noticed his entire crew, all of which were married, sat eating lunches prepared by their wives.

"It must be a Hispanic thing," he mused and drove off.

*****

Later, feasting on fried chicken, French fries, and a roll, at his desk, Wesley overheard Miguel in a phone conversation with his wife.

"No, Maria," Miguel whispered. "You take care of the house. I will take care of that. It doesn't matter. I will make it look beautiful just the way you like. *Te amo*."

With a sigh, Miguel ended his call.

"Everything okay?" asked Wesley.

"Oh yes, boss. My Maria likes the yard to be all pretty. She was just telling me some things she wanted done to the yard."

"Keeping you busy, huh?"

"She does, but some things are just too much for a woman. She is trying to keep our home nice. I have to get out there, boss, and do what needs to be done."

"Is it something that she can't do?" asked Wesley.

"No, she can do it! She's a strong woman."

"So what's the problem? You work long hours here. You should go home and just kick back."

"If I do that boss, I won't have my woman long. My Maria works, and she is a tiny woman. I can't expect her to work, take care of the inside and the outside of the house just because I work hard. She works hard too."

"You are too soft, Miguel." Wesley chuckled.

"I don't want her doing a man's work, boss. You have not found the right woman yet. When you do, you will understand."

"If I'm working, she should be able to handle everything else," said Wesley.

"Stay single, boss. You will never keep your wife like that." Miguel laughed.

Wesley sat watching Miguel walk away.

No woman is ever going to rule over me like that, he thought.

He was an independent man, and the way he lived right now was the way it was going to be. He didn't care if a woman got up at the crack of dawn and prepared him a lunch. That was her job if she was with him. And if he decided to eat something different from what she packed, he would. And he wouldn't give a rat's ass how she felt about it.

He thought of Andrew and Nadine. There was no doubt she was a beautiful woman. It sickened him the way Andrew fawned over her like a puppy, running around making sure she had special milk for her cravings and massaging her back. Hell, she was pregnant. Back pain was a part of the process. That was the very reason why he never left home without a supply of condoms.

*****

After work, he headed to a different woman's house, Carla. She was a little on the chubby side, but he didn't care. She was a female. She had prepared a meal of ham; mashed potatoes; green bean casserole; and buttery sweet, candied yams.

Wesley ate to the point of feeling stuffed. He liked having someone cook for him, but he wasn't committing to her or any other woman.

He mustered up the strength to provide the woman with a satisfying sexual experience knowing that was expected.

"You know, Wess, you could spend the night," said Carla, caressing his shoulders.

"I have to start work early in the morning," he lied.

"I'll wake you up. We could cuddle," she urged, trying to change his mind.

"I'm going to be busy the rest of this week on this project. I'll stop by again next week," he said, growing agitated by her insistence, and his head was starting to throb.

*****

Arriving home late again, Wesley was about to drift off to sleep when he remembered his pill. Strolling into the bathroom, he popped open the bottle and flipped a pill into his mouth, washing it down with a handful of water.

I'm feeling fine. No need to get all medicinal, he thought, deciding to take the injection in the morning.

With that thought behind him, he went to his bed feeling tired, which he assumed was from the heavy meal and the sex. He fell immediately to sleep.

*****

Giving Chris a quick kiss goodbye, Everett hopped from the car in front of his building only to be stopped by The Slug.

"What is it now?" he asked, looking irritated.

"I wanted to ask you a question," Antonio said, looking frazzled.

"Please, 1-800-Clean-Me-Up, I don't have time. My lunch break is almost over," Everett said about to walk away.

"It won't take long," said Antonio desperately.

"Yes, Nan is pregnant. Yes, she is engaged. No, you are not invited to the ceremony, says me. What else could it be?"

"I need a referral," Antonio blurted out.

"A referral to what?"

"A referral to the therapist friend of yours."

"Oh, please," said Everett, turning to leave.

"I'm serious, Everett. I need help," he said, sounding as desperate as he looked.

"What's the problem?"

"I just need to talk to someone."

"Are you thinking of hurting yourself?" he asked, smiling.

"No, I'm thinking of hurting Nan."

That got Everett's attention.

"Are you fucking kidding me?"

"No, I'm not fucking kidding!" he whispered. "I need the number, and I need it now!"

Everett pulled out his phone and dialed a number.

"Hey, this is Vee. Listen, I have a desperate situation standing in front of me as we speak. Tell me you have an opening, like yesterday. Yes, it is that urgent. Great."

"Next building, fifth floor. Ask for Doctor Lowe. He'll see you now," Everett said, then walked away, dialing Andrew's number.

*****

Weeks went by with Wesley never checking his glucose level. In fact, the meter was in its original container unopened. He either skipped his injections all together or took them when he just happened to look in the refrigerator. His high blood pressure pills were taken when he felt the need to.

"What's the matter, Wesley? I've never known you to have difficulty in this area," questioned Brenda, irritated.

"I've been working hard lately. I guess I'm just a little tired," he said, confused by his body's refusal to cooperate.

"Lately? This has been going on for the last few weeks!" she snapped.

"I told you I'm just tired," he said.

Brenda stood and began getting dressed.

She said, "Listen, I'm not an old woman. And I certainly don't have time to be cooking for a man that can't perform. Give me a call when you fix whatever it is that's going on with you."

This had never happened before. Wesley was confused and deeply concerned. The entire scene replayed with Ashley and Gwen. It wasn't until Carla made her declaration that he realized something was truly wrong.

"I've had one good encounter with you! It's been six weeks of me cooking you these great meals, and I can't even get oral sex as repayment. I heard you were Wess, the ladies' best! Hell, you can even get it up! You're more like Wess, a dried-up mess! Let yourself out, asshole," she all but yelled.

*****

219

That weekend Nadine and Andrew exchanged vows. It was a private videoed ceremony. Aside from the officiant, the bride, and the groom, there were only eleven guests. Having entered the last month of her pregnancy, her protruding stomach was clearly visible under her simple yet elegant off-the-shoulder gown. Danny proudly gave the bride away while Everett served as matron of honor. To his surprise, Andrew asked Wesley to serve as best man, which he readily accepted.

The couple danced to Rod Stewarts's "Have I Told You Lately." Danny was so proud of his sister for all that she had endured. He was happy she and Andrew had found each other. As the guests watched them dance, everyone knew that the love they shared was real, true, and solid. Genesis cried at the beauty of the moment. Danny listened to the words and reached for Gen's hand. She knew that although the song was for the bride and groom, Danny was letting her know that the words were meant for the two of them.

In place of a father-daughter dance, Danny and Nadine danced to "One Call Away." Nadine cried at the joy of having her brother back into her life. Danny had chosen the song. He wanted to let his sister know that the years they had spent estranged had not diminished his love for Naddie, his big sister.

Wesley was impressed with how beautiful ceremony turned out. When Nadine had said small, he had envisioned a civil ceremony. The only thing small about this event was the guest list. The location was a beautiful waterfront room that had been transformed with huge white magnolias and sapphire-blue ribbons. Everyone wore white accented by sapphire blue. The men wore blue ties and cummerbunds. Nadine's carried a bouquet of white roses with tiny blue flowers. The only thing missing, in Wesley's opinion, was more single women. The champagne flowed, and the food served. The couple announced that their official honeymoon would take place after the birth of the baby.

By the end of the event, Wesley was sporting a throbbing headache. He went home and lay in bed, not knowing what to make of his new symptoms. His overactive bladder had started up again several weeks earlier, so he had begun to put a little effort into taking his injections at least once a day. Still, he was feeling somewhat out of sorts again.

"Siri, remind me to make a doctor's appointment tomorrow at 11:00 a.m."

He really didn't want to hear the old man nag at him about the injections, but he didn't have much of a choice.

Wesley woke unable to move one of his arms. The pain was close to unbearable. He dressed and left for work determined to make it through the day. His determination did not work.

*****

At the same time in the suburbs, a cry from Nadine woke Andrew with a start.

"What's the matter?"

"My stomach is hurting really badly!" she moaned, holding her protruding belly.

"Is it the baby? Should we get to the hospital?" he asked, panicking.

"No, it went away," she replied, trying to breathe, then lay back into his arms.

A few moments later, another pain. Only this time she yelled out and rolled from his arms, struggling to catch her breath.

Andrew jumped from bed and began putting on his sweats and stuffing his feet into a pair of sneakers, asking, "Can you put your robe on?"

"Yes," she said as the pain subsided.

As soon as she stood, another pain buckled her knees. Scooping her into his arms, he made his way to the elevator and then to the garage with her experiencing another pain before he could deposit her into the front seat of the car.

As he drove, he called Vee, informing him that Nadine was in labor, and they were on their way to the hospital. After Vee, he called his parents and Cassandra.

*****

"Mr. Johnson, I'm highly disappointed with the way you've handled your condition," said the doctor who had agreed to see Wesley
when he arrived in severe pain.

"Doc, I'm in pain," Wesley asked, moaning.

"We're about to transport you to the hospital right now."

"How bad, Doc?"

"It's very bad, Mr. Johnson."

"How bad is it, Doc?" moaned Wesley.

"We won't know until we get you to the hospital and run some
additional tests."

"The ambulance is here, Doctor," said the young Hispanic
nurse with a concerned expression.

*****

In the labor and delivery waiting room sat Andrew's entire
family including the children, Everett and Chris, and Daniel and
Genesis, who arrived thirty minutes after receiving Andrew's call. It
was apparent that the man had exceeded the speed limit the entire
way. Eventually, Tracie arrived with her three boys. Andrew paced
the floor.

"Son, she'll be all right," his father said.

"No, I need to be in there with her."

"You did your part. You got her here. Now let her do her part,"
his dad said.

I have to be there, thought Andrew. *I promised her.*

He continued pacing and worrying. Whenever a nurse walked
by, he'd stop pacing expecting to hear some news only to start again.

"It's been too long," he said anxiously.

"It's different for every woman, Andrew. I'm sure she's fine,"
said Tracie, trying to ease his nerves.

"It's been over an hour! The pains were close and hard before we
arrived! Something's wrong. I need to be in there with her," he said.

"I don't like this," whispered Everett to Chris. "The pains were
hard." His eyes were watery. "I could hear her over the phone when
he called."

"Oh my god!" yelled Andrew.

His behavior was upsetting everyone.

"Is Auntie Nan going to be, okay?" Tracie's oldest son asked.

"Yes, honey, don't worry. Auntie Nan is a strong woman," she said, hugging the child.

Daniel abruptly left the room and headed for the nurse's station.

"I don't give a damn! Get your ass back there and find out what's going on with my sister! Do your fucking job, you lazy cunt, and get us some news!"

"Sir, if you don't calm down, I'm going to have to call security," the nurse responded.

"Baby, come on. Nan is fine," urged Genesis, wiping a worried stream of tears from her face.

Daniel walked away, barely holding his anger in check. Suddenly, he yells out, "Security! Security! Maybe they can get us some damn news!"

Genesis wrapped him in her arms to calm him down.

"We have to be strong for Nadine and AJ, Danny," she said soothingly, leading him back to his seat.

A somewhat panic-stricken nurse appeared in the doorway, glancing around the room.

"Andrew Noah?"

"I'm here!"

"Come with me, sir," she said, ushering him off in a hurry.

All the adults stood to their feet. Something was wrong.

"Something's happened to Auntie Nan!" Tracie's eldest child cried out.

With that, all the children began to cry with mothers doing their best to reassure them.

"No!" whispered Danny, covering his face with his hands. "This can't be happening."

"We don't know what it is," said Everett, taking Andrew's place in the center of the room. He then began to pace, worried.

*****

"I can't do this by myself! I need Drew!" screamed Nadine over and over as the pain wracked her body.

"Nadine, all you have to do is push," her doctor said in a soft voice.

"I can't do it by myself!" she continued to scream. "I'm scared! I can't do it without Drew!"

With her and the baby's condition deteriorating, the doctor sent for Andrew. Nadine was in so much pain she didn't realize he was beside her. They had ignored her cries for long she had almost given up.

Immediately grasping her hand, Andrew began whispering into her ear.

Delirious from the prolonged pain, she ignored the words and continued to repeat, "I need Drew. I can't do this alone."

"I'm here, love. I'm right here."

It wasn't until he physically turned her face so that she could see him did she acknowledge his presence.

"I'm here. I'll always be here."

"Drew," she whispered.

"What do you need her to do, Doc?"

"I just need her to give me a couple of long, hard pushes on cue."

"Are you ready, baby?"

"I'll try," she answered weakly.

"Push!" said the doctor.

"Push, baby, push!" yelled Andrew.

Within ten minutes, baby Andrew Trevor Noah III was announcing his arrival with a strong set of lungs.

"Please! Please let our family know! They've been going crazy with worry," said Andrew, kissing Nadine all over her face.

Soon after being allowed to cut the navel cord, he was holding his son for the very first time.

Nadine kissed her son's forehead and whispered, "Mommy loves you, AJ," before falling to sleep from exhaustion.

*****

A few floors above them, Wesley was being rushed to surgery. His diabetes had gotten so out of control an infection was attacking the muscles on one side of his body. His prognosis was grim. His family sat in a similar waiting room praying for his survival.

"The infection is very bad, ma'am," said the doctor to a teary-eyed elderly woman.

"What are his chances?" she asked.

"Right now I honestly can't say. We'll just have to wait and see how he responds."

"He's my only son, Doctor," the woman said with tears streaming down her face.

"I understand, ma'am. I'll come back when the surgery is over," the doctor said, patting her on the shoulder, then turning to leave.

"He's my only son," the woman whispered, staring after the doctor.

About the Author

REGENIA BOWENS IS a veteran educator that authored the books *The Lyrics of Life: Executive Decisions* and *Conversations: Woman to Woman*. She also previously hosted a contemporary radio broadcast also entitled *Conversations: Woman to Woman*.

CPSIA information can be obtained
at www.ICGtesting.com
Printed in the USA
BVHW031329260423
663002BV00007B/378

9 798887 633435

TAINTED

Strikingly beautiful, seemingly untouchable, Nadine Swift has reached the pinnacle of her career. The puzzle of her life is nearly complete, with the exception of true love and commitment. She is faced with two pursuers—the handsome Andrew Noah, who agrees to an arrangement with Nadine that traps his heart; and the confident, arrogantly handsome, irresistible Wesley Johnson, who has a reputation with the ladies and sees Nadine as a challenge. Both men accept the ultimate challenge of taming Nadine's tainted heart.

$19.95

ISBN 979-8-88763-343-5

51995

9 798887 633435

Newman Springs
PUBLISHING